the Jailbird's Jackpot

PJ COLANDO

The Jailbird's Jackpot First Edition

Editor: Laura Taylor

Cover illustration: Damonza

Book interior formatted by Damonza

www.pjcolando.com

Paperback ISBN: 978-1-7349339-0-1

the Jailbird's Jackpot

PJ COLANDO

Fourth novel in the "Faith, Family, Frenzy!" series
Stashes
Hashes & Bashes
The Winner's Circle

OTHER BOOKS BY PJC:

There's Always an Upside

I AM... a Character

I AM... a Quarantine Survivor

Dedicated to Amy Breeden a sassy-yet-classy young lady who knows how to steer a book

Prologue

I am free, released from the Pen early due to my uncommonly good behavior. Good behavior as an artifact of laser-like focus on a goal: to take Travis Castro down.

Does Castro sound like 'castrate' to you, too?

Chapter One

A TICKET TO A MISSION

THE DUST WHORLED, but Amy held fast to the ticket, allowing ultrafine particles to stuff her nose. The coughing spell that followed was potentially worth half a billion bucks.

Odd, Amy thought, as an image of Jackie Breeden rose like a genie before the road dust re-settled without eliciting a sneeze or a tickle in her throat. Did Jackie's gentle manner, so firmly affixed in memory, hold the cough at bay?

Asthma was the only affinity Amy shared with her ex-mother-in-law, unless one considered her hapless son, Brandon, a thirty-something *ne'er do well.* He'd been handsome, ambitionless, and semi-literate—a waste of Amy's quality time—so she'd dumped him after nine months of marriage.

A ladybug landed on Amy's palm and walked in tight figure-eights before flying off. A bit of Swedish folklore caused Amy to shudder. If a ladybug landed on your hand, you'd soon marry.

Not Travis. Banish the thought.

Amy felt strange that ex-mother-in-law, Jackie, the enduring template of the steadfast Christian farmwife, intruded in the first moments after release from the gray bar hotel. Jackie was spunkier than most, and mildly subversive.

Here I stand at the crossroads of my happily-ever-after, and I ponder "What would Jackie do?" Of course, I'll do the opposite. I'm golden, not good. I shall exact revenge on a madman, who skipped the premises and set me up for the fall.

Travis Castro is a dead man.

Amy tucked the lottery ticket into her bra so she could run her fingers through her hair. She hoped to shake the dust while air-conditioning her scalp. Though she'd spent all of her allotted time walking the prison exercise yard, she didn't recall the sun being this intense. Especially so soon after dawn.

Amy stood rooted, willing her eyes to blink back the moisture. Tears were not allowed in a self-reliant's sphere. She stomped her foot. The dust spiraled tornado-like again, overwhelming her lungs.

Amy bent to place her hands atop her thighs, to steady herself for the onslaught. Though the deep, croup-like coughing lasted many seconds, no one in the crowd looked askance when she righted herself. Everyone milled about. Amy already knew she signaled her loner status well.

She felt relieved that no one stepped forward

to pound her back, an action that never halted an asthma attack.

With no tissues to wipe her nose or blot the perspiration from her hairline, she bent her elbow, unbuttoned the cuff, and dabbed her upper lip. Then she inched the cloth as far around her neck as she could reach.

Grumpy and discombobulated, Amy now felt dumped. She'd been led outside the concrete-and-iron cage, the gigantic doors locked and bolted behind her. All of her belongings in a backpack, including a cellphone, underwear, and three shirts. Oh, a comb, an inhaler, makeup—and a wallet that was leaner by a buck. The lottery ticket vending machine at the bus station practically shouted her name as she loitered among the other newly released prisoners.

She chuckled when other former inmates fell in line behind her to emulate her purchase. She guffawed when the torture over number selection, some ex-cons accessing their phones to find family birthdates while others called out to their posse for numbers to pick. Her final, triumphant laugh, before returning to subterfuge once more, as the others failed to suppress their addictive impulses and clutched fistfuls of tickets. Scattered conversations gathered around the topic of everything one could lavish money on, each eager to spendthrift.

Amy ignored the other inmates who greeted friends and family. She ignored their cheers, whoops, and hugs. She stuffed feelings of isolation, walled deep in her soul, the feelings that began when she was ten and her mom turned schizzy on her and her brother Andy. Back in California, where seasons didn't matter, and where she longed to live.

Amy shrugged off dialing the Breeden dairy farm, within forty-fifty miles of Jackson, the location of the Michigan State Pen. She might be greeted as the prodigal daughter-in-law, but she had bigger game in mind. She aimed to track Travis Castro, the dealer who'd stolen her crop and allowed her capture when the law swept in. He was handsome, ambitious, and semi-considerate. Dangerous, furtive, and conscience-less. What an ass. What a lure.

Amy gritted her teeth. Maybe she could muster the courage to call her gal pal, Veronica, to whom she'd slipped some ganga seeds during a single prison visit. The girl might be good for a ride to Traverse City, which was miles upstate, where Amy'd heard Travis owned a popular bar. But she couldn't face the potential humiliation if V had pounced on Brandon. There were few eligible males in that small rural town she and Veronica had once shared.

She decided. She'd forego meals, maybe reach Traverse City as a hitchhiker by noon. She had cash, gained by tutoring other inmates who sought the GED, but Amy was interested in speed, not spend. She didn't pause to look in a mirror, to refresh her make-up. She'd seen her determined jaw and high forehead before.

Amy hoisted her backpack and nudged the lottery ticket deeper in her bra. She put her back to the revelers and started walking. She'd put out her thumb when she was well away from the herd.

Too late to worry about bridges burned. Amy was resolute. She'd create her own rebelution, as she had all of her life.

CHAPTER TWO

REVENGE INTENDED

AMY'S ENTRANCE IN Traverse City, site of Travis' bar, was not as quiet as she'd intended. The trucker accepted no payment beyond his leer. His truck's brakes screeched, the exhaust belched and fouled the air, and she felt like Sousa's Band had announced her arrival.

Amy stepped out and swiveled around to reconnoiter the resort city. A sign shouted TRAVIS' TRAVEL IN, gigantic red letters on an impressively brown building, drawing her to its butt ugly bosom.

She sailed across the street, an angel of vengeance, a stalker of right. She'd arrived to redeem her life in over-bright daylight. The sun baked. She wished for a hat to complete her disguise as a vigilante cowboy.

The scenario reminded her of Spaghetti Westerns, the movies her mom had watched while slumped on the ratty apartment couch, going through one of her *spells.*

Amy recalled the movies' nickname because, in that time, spaghetti was the only meal she knew how to make.

Amy grimaced at the memory. Soon a fistful of dollars would be in her possession, not merely the ten-dollar bill.

For now, Amy was *millennial broke* like she'd been five years back. When Brandon lost his job and their home, her hopes and future circled the drain.

Amy thrust her hips ahead, squared her shoulders, and stepped forward into the first chapter of her new life.

She twisted the bar's door handle. The door swung open on rusty hinges. It probably needed oil as much as its inhabitants. Was the entire world outside of prison unhinged and odd? If so, Amy figured she might fit in.

She entered, entitled and bold, a romping, stomping chicka who'd scraped and elbowed her way through life, actions which fostered a star turn in a roller derby league years back. A moonlight role for a bank V.P.

Those stints as *Bad Ass Amy* brought a secret self to the fore. Her spine rose to the occasion. She stood near six feet tall. Inches higher in boots. When she stomped to loosen the road dust, the noise on the wood threshold stopped the bar inhabitants in mid-sip. *Arresting.* As Amy acclimated to the altered light of the bar interior, the Eagles' hit, *Hotel California,* corkscrewed her inner ears.

Neon beer signs jam-packed the walls. Each beer distributor jockeyed for position. Perhaps the buzzed bar owner had hung his preferences. More likely, his patrons.

It wasn't like Amy to judge, so she hedged. Someone merely had a poor sense of proportion. Maybe the array extended the bartender's pours, put ideas in his barflies' heads. She knew Travis Castro to be more egocentric and profit-motivated than she.

That wasn't a judgment. It was fact.

A tentative look at the floor assured Amy there wasn't a spot she wanted to step onto. Going forward would be tough. The soles of her boots were an unreliable barrier to germs. A deep breath brought not the resolve she sought, but scents of beer and male sweat. She fought her gut's impulse to heave.

Now she judged. An all-male lair, no feminine parity in sight. TV sports blare mingled with raunchy Country tunes. Sixteen tables, five booths, a patch of grungy linoleum used as a scrappy dance floor on the side. A stripper pole, its brass marked by fingerprints that would make the local crime scene investigator salivate, stood like an Oscar for anyone who chose to perform.

Eighteen eyes, their slit-eyes estranged from sunlight, stared. To avoid eye contact, Amy pondered the synchronous rise of beer foam as nine arms bent to the chore. Slurp-slug-swallow. After the foam melted back, the crowd seemed ready for what was next, in a silence studded with caution and distrust.

A voice hollered, "Shut the damn door!" The large

Pabst wall clock, tick-tick-ticked noon. Amy'd left the Michigan Pen at 7:00 AM. She hoped she was ready for societal re-entry and her pursuit of revenge.

The proprietor didn't run—or dig a gun or ball bat from under the bar. Amy rooted for a bat, which would align with the baseball cap he wore askew, Eminen-style. Grim-faced, he busied himself with the endless task of washing glasses, flavoring it with body tension Amy recognized.

Amy despised doing laundry, yet she willed herself not to empathize.

It was Trav, same husky-chested hunk, dressed head-to-toe in charismatic black. A smile licked at his firmly sealed lips. His smile quickly downgraded to a Grinch slit. Apparently, he'd recognized Amy.

She strolled into the silence, released her hands from her jean pockets, and gripped the bar, wearing imaginary gloves. She wanted Travis to remember. She wanted him to get the gist.

She tried for a classy and assertive lift of the chin, but the mirror behind the bar revealed her failure. Too long in the clink to recoup the pose without practice, but a default to *sassy* wasn't bad.

Wordlessly, Travis clanked two empty glasses to the bar top. "One finger for me," he said as he poured. The sound of the liquid snaked down Amy' spine, liberating its tension before she tasted a drop. She'd just ridden three-and-a-half hours in a semi, boring a hole in the driver's head to keep his hands on the wheel.

Trav tilted his head, allowing a glimpse of the malevolent look the ball cap hid. The misgivings were mutual. "The middle finger for you, Amy." He bit each word off, like a raven ripping at a piece of stale bread.

Amy was flat-ass mesmerized. The chip on her shoulder slipped. She nearly capsized at the knees. Game on. He'd won.

For now.

She missed his kiss, *his lay of the land*. Her resolve collapsed, yet she stood. Her need for revenge over-arched fond recall.

Travis gulped the whiskey and grinned. Stuck the glass in the wash bin and languidly sloshed it. Lifted it to scrutinize her through its formerly spirited lens.

It mattered not that Amy was clean. It mattered not that she was free. It mattered not that she'd paid *their* debt to society.

Travis twirled to set the glass back into line on the slim bar shelf, soldiers at the ready. She ignored the booze he'd poured her. She wasn't about to get *turnt* on her first day out.

Amy tucked the lone lottery ticket deeper in her plain cotton bra, enjoying the salacious look of every lone wolf in the bar *except* Travis. He swiveled slowly, a smooth dancer's move on his boot heels. She noted the boots' wear, the down-on-his-luck lack of shine. Perhaps he hadn't prospered after all.

Amy stone-faced while he nudged his ballcap, the better to check her fully. She watched while his index finger pulled an imaginary trigger in her direction.

But Amy wasn't leaving. She'd waited a long, long

time to see this scoundrel. She'd traveled a long, long way to this bar. To take *him* out.

Amy felt fortunate to have found the address in her iPhone Contacts, so *yesterday* in its features, but at least the prison personnel hadn't lost the phone. They'd courteously returned it, fully charged. "Can you hear me now?"

Retrieval of her earthly possessions should have heartened her. Instead, it made her glum. She'd grown up texting, so her fingertips tingled. Monologues were overrated; she needed to riff.

I need a hug.

Re-connection wasn't possible with Amy's schizoid mom, last sighted cruising the streets of downtown Long Beach, CA. Topless, hair frazzled beyond a good wash. Amy wondered if her mom's voice would still crackle.

Not brother Andy, either. Yet. Seeds didn't fall from the tree or the weed. She longed for Andy, with whom she'd always be heart-string-attached.

Amy admitted that she even longed for Brandon, her n'er do well ex.

Yes, the state of Michigan returned her phone and pre-prison duds, as well as those purchased online from the paltry wages she'd earned by working as a prison librarian. GED tutoring on the side chipped in a few bucks, too. She'd stashed the lot in the backpack purchased online, with its matching skinny pink wallet. She had enough money for a bus ticket to any destination within the state—her parole parameters were clear—and a cheap extended stay motel and meals.

Amy had only spent a buck on a lottery ticket at the bus station and then thumbed her way to Travis. Her cash would last a little longer. Not much of a plan beyond revenge, for which she was hungrier than food. The prison exit staff warned that few felons found jobs, so there was heavy recidivism. Amy vowed not allow that to occur. 2000 days was enough.

Now, in Travis' presence, Amy wished for a better script. Gingerly, she glued a hip to the bar to signify that she wasn't leaving.

Not intimidated by the scoundrel who allowed her to take the rap for a home delivery pot business. She'd loved that business model, riding a motorcycle down winding country roads during the day in addition to tucking dime bags of dope in pizza boxes for delivery at night.

Something had gone awry, and it wasn't *exactly* Amy. She attempted to take over Travis' turf, drain his pot-laced domain. All she wanted was a little dignity. A chance to thrive, entrepreneur style. She could out-ambition him any day, but Travis double-crossed her.

Amy felt the heat rise in her face as she remembered his play. She'd f*cked up.

She focused on the TVs blaring in several corners of the room. The morning news shared its daily dose of bad with a sliver of good. The newscaster was as pretty as Amy used to be, so she watched, mesmerized by a career path she could have elected rather than marrying a small-town *square,* hoping to achieve respectability.

With Brandon, she'd failed up.

Chapter Three

REVENGE SWEETENED

"10. 11. 31. 41. 44. 14. 24." The numbers hung on the above-the-bar screen for several seconds, long enough for Amy to dig her lottery ticket from deep inside her bra, a bit withered by sweat.

She smoothed the paper ticket and looked at the string of numbers, lined like kids at recess, waiting to be picked for the team. She glanced back up at the TV, then back at her ticket. Christ on a bicycle, she'd punched a lucky set of numbers!

Was the room spinning?

Holy Mother of God and all the saints! Incredulous, she stared at the digits! Did the universe love her that much? $536 million dollars' worth! Amy had instant status and cred. Now she stood tall without even trying.

Amy clamped shut her gaping jaw as the reality registered. She felt her face flame from within. Her lottery numbers were her personal combination to Fort Knox. She was golden. She was rich, incomprehensibly rich, zanily, crazily rolling in dough.

Revenge will be sweeter than wine and all mine, all mine, all mine! her mind chanted in-between the clanging of bells. Amy palmed the ticket and gripped the edge of the bar.

Travis slid a few feet down the bar to take a couple of customers' orders, a blessing in the moment because she feared he might hear her pounding heart, which felt as if it no longer fit inside her chest. Amy's brain popped with images of all the things she could buy.

The assortment pack of Tootsie Roll Pops she'd watched the popular girls swing by their sides at recess, so near, yet so far, from her mouth. All the school lunches a teen could ever eat, all the chips and salsa and margaritas, all of the Subaru Outbacks in the world.

Thousands of pairs of shoes. Amy recalled the heat of the cracked concrete sidewalk on her bare feet in her teens. Hot shoes and sandals and boots and boots and boots! Yes, a bounty of boots!

Piles of clothing, in every hue appropriate to enhance blue eyes and blonde hair. No more bare bones.

Amy moved quick, gliding her hand, cupped around the slim paper ticket, down her pant leg. She stuffed the lottery ticket well into the tongue of her ankle-high boot, then reached around the bar's end and swiped a Coke from the open cooler, not minding the icey sting of the water that drenched her hand.

She was used to it. She'd stolen thousands of cokes the same way, beginning with the bodega at the beach. The Long Beach in CA.

Amy clutched the coke low while she unzipped the backpack she'd hung on the hook just under the bar's lip. She slowly edged the chilled Coke inside, not bothering to re-zip the bag. She flung the backpack onto one shoulder.

Amy edged out the door, ahead of a bill and a tip. She did not apologize or offer an excuse. No one called her back. Hell, only Trav knew her name. She was clear.

Amy ran and ran and ran to a future she could only imagine. She ran until she was out of breath.

She looked around furtively, hoping there'd be no witnesses to a brief happy dance. Amy boogied and wiggled her butt! She raised her fists to the sky in triumph!

Only been out of prison a day, and I've already won.

But Amy still lusted for revenge. Trav's deed stuck in her craw. She popped the Coke and took a long, long draught. Dang, she was thirsty! Thirsty for life, thirsty for freedom, thirsty for revenge, protracted and deep, for dear Travis.

Amy fist-bumped the sky again! Woot! Whoopee! YES-S-S!

Travis, the squint-eyed bastard, the pirate of her crop, the stealer of her trust… He'd enticed, snared, and duped her. His chiseled chin, his emerging paunch… Amy hoped he gagged on his guilt.

She glanced around, assuring herself that no one

had followed her from the bar. That no one had witnessed her shouts, her exclamations, her fist pumps.

Amy suddenly crashed. What good was treasure when you didn't have friends and family with whom to share? An entourage to gloat with would be great, would deepen the experience, and would assure her the lottery win was real.

Instead, Amy stood alone in her golden goose moment. In the lengthened days of summer, there wasn't even a sunset to help her celebrate the awe of God's power, the miracle He'd given her.

She'd not breathed evenly since she realized that her lottery ticket matched the winning numbers. Now her exhale was so sudden, the waistband snap on her jeans popped against her skin. She didn't pause to re-snap it. She had other business to attend to.

Amy strode back to the bar building and hunkered to pee, like a dog marking her turf. She continued to hide amidst the unkempt lilac bushes, fading blossoms shattering as she nested to relax and contemplate.

Amy drained the coke, toasting herself and Lady Luck. She scoped the landscape, sighted a couple of stray dogs… and a bus station.

She sauntered to the bus station, thanking Trav for having the business sense to locate his bar nearby. Eerie, wasn't it? Amy wondered if he'd set her up—*again*. She needed to head to Lansing, the state capital's lottery office to claim her prize, as per a quick read of the Boffo Lotto website on her cell phone.

Amy chose to forgo a meal again. Soon, she'd dine in style.

F*ckin A. Now she can afford the dental work prison personnel hadn't completed. Fifteen years of living on the streets, followed by lean college scholarship years and a plummeting-to-earth early career, had ravaged her teeth and gums. She'd soon possess a Hollywood smile.

And she no longer needed to *Listerine* her language—f*ckin' A. She was empowered Amy, as in *Infamy*. She was golden-to-go.

CHAPTER FOUR

GOLDEN PAROLE

A FEW HOURS later, Amy's cellphone rang while she walked along Hall Street, navigating via Siri's directions from Travis' bar to the Greyhound Transit Center. She startled as the phone rang. Her pulse red-lined—this phone hadn't rung in five years.

She nearly stumbled in her unfamiliar stacked-heel boots. Momentarily disoriented, she snagged her phone from her backpack and placed it into her line of sight. 'Unknown' was the call source. *My phone had relationships unknown to me?*

While this interruption by an unknown number intrigued, Amy couldn't relent. To hear a human voice other than Siri might be heaven on earth. She couldn't dump Siri, who represented her sole source of feminine companionship at present.

Amy ignored the call, allowing the message to go to voicemail.

Juan Carlos Hernandez texted almost immediately. Now she recognized the name. "Let me remind you of the terms of your early release. You must remain in contact. And you may not leave the state."

Crap, Juan Carlos. I knew that, but now I feel body-slammed. My phone has GPS and dude is tracking me, quick as the devil and as sure as sin.

Either that or there were cameras everywhere, making Amy's life no more private than it was in prison. What a forfeit for participating in someone else's felony. She wondered vaguely how common folk felt about the burgeoning lack of privacy in the home of the free and the brave. Every 7-11 robbery made the nightly news with brief-and-blurry camera footage, the culprit caught rapidly, slammed in the pokey within days.

Amy's feet hurt. She'd been pounding the pavement, literally, not a great plan in new and not perfectly-for-her-feet boots. She might not be wearing a blister on her ankle, but she dared not unzip the boots to peek. Her winning lottery ticket might blow away. The wind off the lake was strong, carrying scents of dead carp and sea gull crap.

Amy decided to call Juan Carlos. "Hi, Juan? May I call you this or must I address you as Mr. Hernandez? Maybe Mr. Parole Officer or Dad."

"Whatever you prefer, Ms. Breeden. Just remember that you're on a leash."

Amy could envision his black mustache, trimmed tight and shining like patent leather shoes, focusing attention to his face. *Read my lips,* his mustache commanded. *I'm only going to state this once.*

She'd met him once and noted no uniform, though a brass badge was prominent on his brown leather belt. No belly fat lapped over to hide his authority over parolees. His pants, though not those of a uniform, displayed creases so sharp one could shave a chin with them.

Hernandez' manner was quiet, yet stern. He possessed an attitude almost as gallant as a knight. That Amy sensed. Though his cheekbones were chiseled like G.I. Joe, his jaw constantly clenched and unclenched. Clearly a man of action and relentless motion. A guy who saved his bullets for just the right time, hopefully never for her, real or verbal.

"Well, how's your day going, Mr. Hernandez?" Amy knew to establish rapport with genial inquiries in opening conversation. Rapport was as crucial when she'd been a highly paid small-town bank VP as when she'd tutored inmates eager to earn a GED.

"Fine. How's yours?" Here her parole officer paused, to deflect the question back to her. A non-response response, so lawyerly in technique.

But Amy didn't know how it was going yet and didn't want to disclose that she had a winning lottery ticket on her person. Where had she stashed it most recently? In her bra or backpack or boot?

"Like being on the outside?" Hernandez jollied.

"Yes, very much," Amy replied. She felt the wide grin that stretched her cheeks nearly to her ears. She swallowed to regain control. "I was wondering, just hypothetically, if it'd be possible for a felon to win the lottery?"

"Well, I must say, that's a left field question. But I can quote the law for you. Felons are not allowed to play a lottery if they are still incarcerated. However, after their release they may legally play and win. Does that help?"

Amy clutched her phone. She spread her arms wide, looking upward to glory. She spun and spun and spun, like the only childhood toy she recalled. She twirled until she was out of breath and almost wheezy, intermittently hearing her parole officer's voice speaking, sputtering, then shouting, "Did you hang up on me?"

The happy dance nearly flipped Amy off the sidewalk. Fortunately, one of her heels scuffed a crack and disallowed her dizziness to pitch her over the curb.

When Amy righted herself, the line was dead. So, she hit re-dial to get him back, wondering why he hadn't redialed her.

Finally, finally Amy had someone *safe* with whom to share the news. Maybe she'd call him "Dad" after all. He was assuredly old enough to be the dad Amy'd never met. Who cared if he was *ethnic*? He was solid.

But, should I tell? Amy wondered. Trust was tough, but she might have no choice. Brother Andy was out of bounds, and she wasn't ready for the potential heist of the cash by her mom. Nor was she prepared to confront the *snoopery* of the farm folk she knew downstate.

"Thanks for the info, Dad, straight up and straight forward. Let's hypothesize that the 'they' is 'me'."

Amy could see Dad Hernandez lean back and guffaw. It was a department store Santa laugh, when you just knew you weren't getting your wish. Amy had tried that only once, with her only grade school friend, Ann, who came from a good home where wishes came true.

Amy could see Hernandez slide his mirrored sunglasses off, maybe rub the indented bridge of his nose. She Mona Lisa smiled when she heard him say, "Don't that beat all. So, are you Lansing bound, Ms. Amy?"

Amy said, "Sure," instead of "F*cking A." She pulled her water bottle from her backpack and swished a sip, to *Listerine* before she swallowed.

She swore her next drink would be an entire fifth of champagne, stolen from Travis' bar.

Chapter Five

BUS HOUND

THE LOBBY OF the Greyhound Transit Center had been a delightful blue-gray when it was built, perhaps in the '50s. Mid-century bland, functional and inviting to potential bus riders, the smell of Lysol smothered by peachy air freshener. The combination was *not* pleasant.

Welcome, the floor, walls and high windows declared. Pay the fare, ride a bus, please help us remain in business. Michigan, after all, was once the nation's chief auto-making state, but now its entire economy had been humbled.

The casinos, owned and operated by the Grand Traverse Band of Ottawa and Chippewa Indian tribes, had given buses a new mission. The upper third swath of the state was populated by people prone to betting their meager incomes with great hope, yet reams of bad luck. Riding a bus provided cheap transport for pie-in-the-sky dreams.

The subdued blue-grey was likely branded by Greyhound, but the color was too near the gray Amy had endured for five stubbornly-lonely years. The high slivers of windows revealed a sky that near-matched the walls.

She peered through the glass doors. The gigantic and unadorned wall clock inside the building declared high noon. She'd been awake for hours and was tired beyond words. Though potentially wealthy, she'd felt incomplete ever since departing Travis' bar. Her feet hurt—and rightfully so - because she'd stomped every step since then. It was tough to feel frustrated and elated at the same time, but her body persisted in championing both emotions.

Amy sighed and ventured deeper into the room. The scent of Lysol and peach was repugnant, so she pinched her nostrils to avoid a chemically-induced asthma attack. One of the chief plagues of prison—the noxious odors of cleanliness—had followed her out. It was a damned shame.

She crossed the stippled grey floor of the vast space to the ticket window. Despite the noise of her boots, Amy didn't get the counter gal's attention until she slammed her hand on the 'ring for service' bell. The clerk responded with a jolt which nearly toppled her hyper-hived hair. The woman had apparently gauged precisely how much hairspray the climate required and then topped off the top of her beehive.

The bland-faced clerk didn't lift her head until

Amy slammed a wad of small bills on the counter. Beehive grimaced and returned to the cash drawer, chin not lifted to greet Amy or make eye contact. She was clearly counting the drawer's contents, in haste to clock out. 'Justine', as her name tag declared, was *outta here.*

Justine grabbed the cash, dragged it across the counter and punched some keys. She didn't glance up when she thrust a bus ticket toward Amy, with change from the fifty dollars.

Amy asked if the ticket and its change were correct. "How'd you know where I was going?" Her tone demanded eye contact and acknowledgement. She wasn't refused to remain anonymous in Justine's *bored-with-this-job* sphere.

Justine pulled herself out of the cash drawer and slammed it shut. "Uh-hmmm" was all she uttered—as a freakin' two-syllable word. Amy's college English degree was affronted. Her lottery-winning self was pissed. She put her arms on the counter and leaned in to Justine and her *I-hate-this-job* attitude.

"Everybody who enters this station is going to the casinos, Lady." Justine pronounced Lady in two syllables as if the word translated to filth. She turned and stalked off. Amy glanced up at the clock. 12:25. Justine was done, done, done for the day. Maybe her fat ass needed a lunch break.

Amy borrowed a congrats card from the slim pickings on the circular display rack in the bus station. She spun the rickety rack as if it were a hyper-fast merry-go-round on which she could ride..

I stole the card, just like I'd stolen the pen from the ticket window ledge.

Amy signed her card—with a flourish because her name was short—and pretend-mailed it to herself, shuffling it through pockets in her backpack. No one was witness to her proud face or her ebullience—except the circular display—so she gave it another twirl. Better it than her.

When the contraption nearly fell, Amy took the act as a sign to calm down. She tossed her backpack in one of the linked armchairs that waited like soldiers for the commandant. She sat. Using the blank envelope of her congratulatory card and the backpack as a lap desk, she began to make lists with her newly purloined pen.

First on the list: *don't succumb to petty larceny. Do not steal any more things. You're already a felon, and thievery is beneath the station of a half-billionaire.*

Every point thereafter was the same: keep the main thing the main thing and get revenge on Travis.

Amy worried about her not-so-new habit of monologue. There was no one to disagree, which was not necessarily the best way to make decisions. Even in the vacuum of space, Hal had conversed with David in the movie *2001*.

Matt Damon had conversed with plants in *The Martian,* though it was spooky to watch. Perhaps it was the prison common room as theater venue that made the movie spooky—as well as the fact that prisoners who were allowed plants in their cells spoke to them at will.

She texted her brother, Andy, just for something to do—and to not feel alone in the world. Kept it simple: I'M OUT. HOW R U?

His answer knocked Amy flat—that he responded at all knocked Amy flat. She gaped at her phone in wonder. It had worked twice now… to remind her that she was not alone in this world, whether she liked it or not. Time would tell.

The bus arrived. Outtahere!

She was gliding on golden gears—plenty of time to concoct a patient campaign of aggression worthy of Travis' bad deed. And, plenty of cash to fund a worthy demise.

Chapter Six

TAKING STOCK

THE BUS RIDE blurred in memory. It was the musky odor released by the window drapes that Amy recalled first if/when she thought of that lengthy trip to claim her lottery prize. For some reason she'd pulled the sturdy drapes immediately, an impulse for privacy left over from the lack of it during her prison tenure, she guessed.

Amy chided herself for the needless action, because she sat near the driver and the bus sported walls of ginormous windows. She'd quickly jerked the drapes back and snapped them in place as soon as the mighty beast's motor turned over, shivered and then the bus glided forth. Thankfully no cloud of dust erupted in the drapes' back-and-forth. Amy hadn't suffered an asthma attack in years and her inhaler wasn't handy.

She was tired upon tired, but afraid to sleep. Not amongst several down-on-their luck gents, squirreled as far from each other and as close to the windows as possible. The three guys' hair hung in equally stringy hanks, reminding her she hadn't showered in twenty-four hours. Her body's skin and her scalp itched. Amy craved cleanliness.

Amy caught herself nodding off. She immediately pinched each wrist. *No, I'll not sleep amongst this skid row group, not with a winning lottery ticket stuck in my boot.*

At least the prized ticket—a limp paper print-out with columns and numbers, some of which were **bold**—rested on top of her foot, not thrust in an arch or the sweaty bottom. Amy fervently hoped the numbers didn't blur in the humid atmosphere of her boot, but she dared not lift it to take a look. These were Sasquatch characters on board, people who looked able to kill her without remorse. The bus driver, his attention focused on the road, looked frozen in place. Amy sensed he'd be no help.

Amy hoped that her enthused-and-winning feelings didn't radiate. Blonde hair and six-foot height already made her highly apparent in her quarter-century experience. She felt like she'd been six-foot since she was 10, but there was no doorway in which her growth spurts were recorded, so who knew?

Or cared.

Amy fought loneliness with daydreams. Dreams and schemes and plots of revenge on Travis. Hell, she'd TP his house, a rite she'd heard ruled Halloween in the Midwest after high school football wins.

A paper trail of my win-win-win.

She ached, body and soul, for revenge. Thoughts of tossing TP high enough to drape boughs fostered imagined physical aches as camouflage. She'd never been a supreme athlete, like Brandon, her ex-ex. Christ on a bicycle! Why did thoughts of that jerk continue to invade her mind. She desired no revenge on him. Focus, Grr-rl.

Amy fought sleep by disallowing herself to pee. The effort fused her mind on *red alert.* She could smell the single restroom's presence in the back of the bus from her seat behind the bus driver. It reeked more than the alleys of Long Beach where she scurried and scrounged in her teens, searching for items to salvage and sell at the Saturday flea market.

She had been a good provider for her baby brother and herself. Mom seldom ate, which Amy tried to worry about for a while, then let the worries go, like everything else about her schizophrenic mom. Zipped to the sky to let God worry, like the nuns taught.

Her fellow bus passengers reminded Amy of characters she'd encountered during that dark time. She most often walked alone—in the school halls as well as elsewhere, seeking out Andy between classes as each other's touchstone. Amy's safe haven was the public library, so it was fine symmetry when she was assigned to work in the prison library. Dewey decimals were well-known and safe.

Amy passed the ride time by applying for credit cards. It was surprising how little information was required to get a Master Card. It would be processed, printed, and stamped with her name within twenty-four hours, except— Amy paused when asked to enter an address.

Waylaid by this detail, she quit and watched a movie, *The Bridges of Madison County*. Tears floated her unwashed face. Amy hoped her spirits would recharge like the phone plugged in at the bottom of her seat.

Amy may have dozed because she startled awake when the bus stopped. With a protracted squeal of brakes that made her imagine the maintenance barn was this bus' next stop.

She pulled her cell from the plug and held it in one hand, backpack in the other, as she checked the seat, which was covered as garishly as the casino carpets in Traverse City.

Ok, I admit I peeked inside a casino as I searched the city for Travis' bar. With doors wide open, how could I not?

But Amy hadn't wasted time—or money—on entering. She focused on revenge, a goal that was quickly superseded. Perhaps she'd make it a goal to return to Traverse City, flash some cash in Travis' face before flashing some in the casinos. An image of Trav's fallen face shimmered and hung in the air for several seconds. As Jackie, Amy's former mother-in-law, used to say, "All things come to those who wait."

Gosh, that woman is haunting me as much as her spoiled son! I had to nevermind her and return to matters at hand.

Amy clicked on her phone's Maps app to search for the nearest clothing store. Time to regroup before visiting the Michigan Lottery Office. She finger-combed her hair, feeling the grit from yesterday's dust. If only there were a decent shower nearby.

Then the faint rumble of thunder shook the air and Amy looked skyward. The familiar cotton puffs of cumulus clouds clustered the horizon. Please, no. Not that kind of shower. Amy felt the summer humidity's build. Best to keep an eye out for the gray tinge that impending rain brought to those ginormous clouds. She needed to find shelter and soon. Even a cheap motel's shower, with mildew and the taint of other people's toes, would be better than to be caught outdoors.

The Map App whirled and spun out info for nearby clothing stores with their dots highlighted within a map of several square blocks. Would you believe the Lansing Community College Costume Shop was seven blocks from the Greyhound Bus Station? Golden! New purpose lifted Amy's knees high as she strode to the store.

The air inside the shop was musty, but someone had artfully displayed the clothing for maximum appeal. That someone was not in sight, but Amy spotted a rounder with her size clothing. The clink of hangers irritated as she rifled the rack.

The hunt for slacks with legs long enough frustrated her. A problem since age fourteen. The basketball coach attempted to bribe her with hard-to-get, extra-long jeans if she'd try out for the team, but she wanted to impress her English teacher. That woman helped Amy finesse her creative writing into a college scholarship. In English, not basketball.

Fifty minutes later Amy sported a broad smile caressed by peachy lipstick, with another dab smudged onto her cheek bones, applied with the aid of a mirror in the tiny dressing room where she tried on clothes.

A slovenly Goth-faced clerk materialized at the counter. Amy paid, proud of herself because she hadn't shoplifted. She paused briefly at the shop's threshold to check her Baggie of money. She'd spent another $40—equivalent of the bus fare—on a pantsuit, blouse, and jeans.

Now to find a place to shower, brush teeth, apply deodorant, and truly brush her hair. Amy felt compelled to look like the winner that she would be. Lady Luck continued to grease her path to become a half-billionaire. The Michigan Lottery Office address was 101 E. Hillsdale Street, literally .2 miles and 4 minutes-walk from the bus station.

And, Amy knew the way.

She soon discovered an ancient Woolworth Store, open despite the hard economic times that felled other stores in the nationwide chain. The gold letters on the store's sign were unburnished and the burgundy background had faded, but open was open and fine by Amy's standards.

A floorboard creaked when Amy crossed the threshold. The lone clerk, who stood at the register, turned toward the doorway and smiled, expectant and ready to help.

"I'm new in town. Looking for a few incidentals."

"Welcome to Lansing. Name's Wilma." A gentle grin spread across the woman's well-wrinkled face. Amy almost melted when the pert, withered beauty extended her hand. She walked to the counter to shake it. Amy considered the handshake her third welcome to the outside—the first the lottery win, the second her parole officer.

"Welcome to my Woolworths, proudly the only store that prevails. My husband's grandfather was wise enough to have bought land as soon as lots were available, so our family owned what are now blocks and blocks and blocks of city development. I'm spending the inheritance to keep this store open. Gives me purpose. Not gonna let the millennial in my family fritter the cash when I'm gone, either. I'm taking it with me to the grave."

Amy didn't know what to say, so she remained silent. Her generation had just been maligned by her little-old-lady-of-welcome, so she tried to maintain a pleasant demeanor to mirror the feisty lady. The one that belied her tough stance.

As if she sensed Amy's edginess, Wilma pointed to aisles just beyond the register. "You'll find sundries, including panties, deodorant, toothpaste, and brushes over there."

Amy sensed her eyes widen and disbelief filled her chest cavity.

The stalwart store owner continued in a honeyed

tone, "We get a lot of bus passengers in here. That's what makes the store a goldmine. The cross section of humanity I can assist with essentials at low prices. My form of welfare, if you will."

Amy blinked back tears and nearly wilted in her new clothes and boots. The crusty-looking old woman had a tender heart.

Further, Wilma allowed use of the store's restroom and allowed Amy to depart with bottled water and more snacks, proffered with a wink, but no cash register ring. As Amy's fingers brushed her benefactor's, she felt a spark. Soon she was spilling her guts, her plight, her plan to this granny-faced woman.

Amy walked as if on air to the lottery office.

Chapter Seven

LOTTERY CONFIRMATION

AMY MARCHED UP to the counter, emboldened by what portended to be a universal welcome in this town, minus the bus station experience smothered in unwelcome.

The feeling of welcome ran cold at the counter. The woman behind it didn't deign to lift her head from the computer keyboard she pounded. "Do you have an appointment?"

Uttered like an officious maître de at a fine dining establishment, the cold remark crippled potential rapport. Amy looked over each of her shoulders and into the back of the space. Dark-painted sidecar paneling and matching floors made the room look as hollow as the spindly clerk's tone.

Amy shuddered as she approached the woman whose hands literally hung in fists by her thighs. She seemed willing to provoke a fight, smug in her gateway status. Amy longed for privacy glass, like that of the Visitors Room at the prison. She confirmed that her backpack was secured behind her and reset her posture to relaxed.

She wanted the officiously official and off-putting woman, whose badge proclaimed Ezekiel as her name, to back off her rigidity and provide the assistance she required. With no friends, Amy needed all the help she could get.

Amy smiled, but only mildly, due to her awareness that her teeth needed work. Further, she attempted to project a meek and demure demeanor, not an easy feat for an over tall young woman people often regarded as over-bearing at first sight.

"My name is Amy Breeden. I think I won the Boffo Lotto." Amy spoke equivocally, with a timid timber that she hoped played into Ezekiel's self-importance. Amy needed Ezekiel to be *so happy* for her later. Then she wouldn't have to happy dance alone.

"Do you have the ticket on you?" Dang, the woman gave nothing away. Her body was a fortress against feelings, unsubtly self-important in every way. Amy could not, would not retreat.

Why is this woman armored against me? Amy fended off an impulse to check her armpits. Did she give off a prison vibe? She leaned in and pressed against the high counter to steady her resolve.

Though the move grounded her, the metal edge pushed into her abdomen and it felt too much like the move Amy used to avoid men—most recently guards and other penal personnel—who hoped to cop a feel or beg a favor in the most direct way. It was so easy to swivel and dig an elbow into an unwanted gut, a move not needed now.

Amy inhaled, re-grouped, and eased back. She wasn't able to unravel the knots in her mind, so she abandoned maneuvers and tried for *abject and humble.*

"Yes." She nodded. "I have the winning ticket with me." She recalled the dumb feelings when she'd forgotten the daily catechism Q & A, as well as scowled at by the nuns, who rapped on knuckles with a ruler if one spoke out.

"We do accept walk-in winners who arrive to claim their prize without an appointment. However, your unannounced visit may result in a longer time to process your claim." Ms. Ezekiel brought one fist to her hip. Amy tried not to flinch—or state the obvious, that she and Ezekiel were alone in this slot of an office.

The lottery office was empty, yet Ezekiel balked. "Let's begin with your name, your government-issued photo ID, and a Social number, so I can enter you in our system. I'll also need your local address."

Crap. The mild expletive, on which Jackie insisted rather than saying "Shit", resounded inside Amy's head. She quickly fetched her cell from her backpack, clicked it on, and memorized the Breeden farm address. She cocked her head to one side and her hip to the other, as if the move would assist her thought processes. The tic had not gone unnoticed all through school, at the bank, and in the prison library, but Amy didn't intend to abandon what worked. Ideas sprouted, like an earthquake had opened a locked fault line, to reveal the best plan.

As she began to right her head, Amy decided to serve up Veronica's address, hoping she still lived in the gingerbread farmhouse with its high cypress tree fence and its surround of wood porch. She recalled that the porch would benefit from a couple of cans of paint. Hmmn. Amy began to believe she could pull this off, and she inhabited her new stiletto-heeled height.

Holy Shit! What would happen when she proffered her parolee ID card, which stated in boldface type that **Michigan** issued the card, with her unflattering prison headshot prominent, as well as her parolee ID number, and her name in small print. Amy's driver's license had lapsed, and Ezekiel was the officious type who would take note.

She'll be on the phone so fast, I'll get whiplash.

Amy retrieved her parolee card, her lapsed driver's license, and her Social Security card. She sandwiched the parolee card between the other two and slid the cards across the counter, smiling mildly like a card player who knew she had the winning hand.

As Ezekiel stepped forward to pick up the stack, Amy's ace in the hole popped into her head. She flicked her ragged pixie-cut as punctuation. Her newly-adopted dad would vouch for her if there were questions, which there were.

Amy tapped his name in her few phone contacts and listened tensely while the phone rang. *Please, please be available.*

Hernandez answered on the second ring. "Good to hear from you, yet why so soon, Ms. B?"

"I'm in the State Lottery Office. I need you to speak with Ms. Ezekiel to verify that I can win."

"Did you really win the lottery, my child?" Amy's parole officer had an instant and infectious laugh. Her tension dampened. Hernandez would be a great anchor for her new life experiences. Before she could interject "yes", he continued. "Amy, if I vouch for you, will you share with me? Daddy needs a new car. To chase you because I can already tell you're setting a fast pace."

Amy gagged. She didn't know Mr. Hernandez well enough to know if he was teasing about the trade. But he'd called her *my child.* She gulped, willing her heart's rate to lower and to cease it's thumping in her chest.

"Whatever you require, Sir."

Amy handed the phone to Ezekiel, who continued her direct. "Sir, please give me your name." Man, that state employee didn't give an inch.

Amy longed to listen to his side of the conversation, but she settled for watching Ezekiel's face. Her parole officer apparently knew how to work a badge, too, because the lottery clerk returned Amy's cell within seconds.

Distrusting a process she couldn't hear or see, Amy felt skittish. Was the phone hot? She grasped her phone in her palm, careful not to disconnect. She peered across the counter at Ezekiel, who smiled. All was golden. Copacetic, as Steve Breeden would say.

Ezekiel broadened her smile. "Let's proceed with your ticket, shall we?"

We. Life was getting more comfortable all the time. And soon *I'd* have a substantial stake to amp the comfort a half-billion notches. Up, up, up!

Chapter Eight

EZEKIEL TURNS

AMY LEANED OVER to extract the ticket from her boot, mindful to not tweak her hamstring muscles, which had endured back-to-back bus trips. Although she'd changed clothes at the Costume Shop, Amy didn't tempt Lady Luck by moving the ticket to a hidey-hole in her backpack. Anyone could snatch a backpack—or worse, she might set the unfamiliar weight anywhere and walk away, unable to trace her path in an entirely unknown town.

Amy trembled, mildly freaked that the lottery win had already threaded superstition into her psyche. Heightened by the sensory overload of prison release. She was free, but not free, and puzzled by possible consequences. She'd need to be vigilant to protect herself as the changes began.

Amy's instant insight was that she was not yet

better off than when she had been as a kid, running the streets of Long Beach to survive.

Her fingertips electrified at the contact with the flimsy paper; her thumb most of all, because of its recent lead roll. She'd never hitched a ride in her life until that grizzled trucker swooped her upstate. The Midas touch of a lottery win hung in the air like a powerful aphrodisiac.

Amy didn't speak as she handed the ticket to the clerk, eyes imploring her to keep it safe as the woman plunged into the mechanics of receiving the millions. Amy fretted and her heart raced. The numbers might be wrong.

Ezekiel's expression didn't change as she looked at the ticket and then slid her hand across the counter to squeeze Amy's sweaty palm. Her eyes told Amy she was right. She had won.

Amy kicked off her boots and jumped around the office, free to wildly, boldly Pogo stick. Then, she emulated every cheerleader move in memory. Years of watching Brandon play football at Michigan State had given her a few. Protecting her stake then, and soon to be protective of her present stake.

She invited Ezekiel to abandon decorum, to join her in making the room into a bounce house, but the clerk remained blasé. She'd been through the process before, but for a $536 million payout? This was boffo, bodacious, and unreal. A cause celebre!

When Amy returned to the counter to steady herself, Ezekiel spoke. "There is another winner, so you've won half, and of course, after the government extracts the taxes up front, you'll receive half of that." She arched an eyebrow and paused to allow Amy to digest the bottom-line.

Amy said nothing because, well, what could she say? If she'd learned anything in prison, it was that, despite an independent spirit, she was not in control. Amy was a brilliant student, equally talented with an English degree and math skills she'd acquired working as a small bank VP, so she understood that she wasn't a half-billionaire.

"YAY!" One final jump. " How do I get the cash? In small, unmarked bills?" she winked-and-quipped.

Ezekiel got in sync with the humor. "If you were to receive the money now, you'd need more than a single backpack."

They shared a laugh, and then the lottery office lady returned to her computer screen to read the procedural details. Her deadpan manner helped to slow Amy's heart rate and allow her to think.

> Jackpot prizes with an annuity option can be paid in one of two ways: as an annuity or in one lump-sum/cash-option payment for the present cash value of the jackpot share. When a winner selects annuity, the jackpot is paid out for a predetermined number of years* (see below for more details). As part of the Tax and Trade Release Extension Act of 1998, lotteries may offer the winner of annuitized prizes an election to receive their prize in a single discounted cash payment in lieu of receiving

> a series of payments spread over several years. To qualify, the winner must make the election within sixty (60) days after the winner claims the prize (i.e. the date the ticket is validated and/or the date the winner comes to Lottery Central).
>
> *Predetermined Annuity Length:
>
> **Mega Millions** - The annuitized jackpot amount shall be paid out through a graduated annuity over 30 years (5% escalation per payment).

"All right, all right!" Amy cried. "Nice to know." She gulped and brought her hands to either side of her head, as if to hold it in place. Super glue might be needed for the rest of her life. She'd lose it for certain in her wild abandon of spending the dough.

The colloquialism of 'dough' reminded Amy of her former baking days with Jackie, her ex-mother-n-law. *Should I gift her some cash to repay her for abandoning her flakey-shaky son—a sort of reverse alimony, if you will—or give her some 'dough to go' to adventure beyond the farm bounds?*

That giddy digression signaled her overwhelmed condition. She needed a spiritual timeout. She needed a week-long yoga retreat, a spa day, a stop in to prostrate herself in a Catholic church—there had to be a saint dedicated to wealth.

Thoughts of tithes brought Amy quickly to a decision. She figured that the one lump-sum-cash-option might not be the best for her, so she abandoned that plan. After all, the win was instant, and she could barely handle that Tilt-a-Whirl moment. Amy suspected she'd be *spendy,* hastening to burn through the cash, and become another poster child for lottery-gone-bust.

Amy didn't question the yearly or quarterly or whatever amount she'd receive if she chose a graduated annuity over thirty years. She would live that long. That was not the problem. Amy was certain it was enough for a young woman who had no prospects, and nothing figured out for her future beyond some unspecified revenge.

It was probably like the allowance her Catholic School peers prattled on about at recess, within earshot of herself and her hunkered brother. The words echoed to bully Amy and, perhaps, egged on her penchant for riches when she became an adult.

Each thirty-year portion would be over the top enough, but yet there was a teensy stumble added to others she needed to surmount: Amy lacked a bank account.

Behind that formidable mountain were problems set up like a Rube-Goldberged machine. Any wrong move would topple the entire contraption. Each decision was intricately woven within a series of decisions and she had no wise counsel, no Yoda to seek. No priest, no pastor, no confidant.

No capable parent or reliable pal. Maybe Hernandez, but Amy wasn't ready to reveal all of the details because, well, he might demand a Rolls. The most solid people she knew wouldn't welcome her to their bosom, not when she'd trampled their beloved only son.

Although Amy longed to be in California, high-fiving her brother, she was constrained. Further, she admitted that Andy had made some remarkably bad decisions, just as she had. Two things were true: logic was relative and neither relative was logical much.

Amy was confined within Michigan state boundaries, but at least the perimeter exceeded a prison cell. Still, her California-bred body vibrated and ocean-spoke. Her ears heard pounding waves, as if she held conch shells near them.

Amy wondered how long the ocean could sustain whispers to calm and relax her spirit? She was transplanted *forever* because she was an ex-con, disallowed from leaving Michigan, a state in which she'd yet to find peace. Michigan would never resemble California. Could money buy happiness here?

Where could she establish a bank account? It seemed unlikely that Harold Prince would welcome her return to his bank in Lodenberg, and Amy felt too embarrassed to knock on his bank's massive door anyway. Think, think, think. Her mind raced as she paced the state lottery office… and then Amy full-stopped. She had an immediate urge to satisfy first. "May I have my ticket?"

Ms. Ezekiel's face contorted. Her posture became fully rigid and Ezekiel spoke as if to a bad child who'd eaten all of her Easter candy and now refused to eat Mama's prepared meal.

"Most certainly not. I've already locked it in our safe."

Amy'd recanted as soon as the question passed her lips, but with no ticket, how could she be assured the lottery deal was real? She needed eternal evidence, so she swiftly switched to another tactic. "Do you mind giving me a copy?"

Ezekiel nodded and promptly pulled a ticket copy from her outbox, as if she'd anticipated Amy's request.

Amy grabbed the evidence and slipped it into her backpack. Sacrosanct material. She paused but didn't turn to leave because the fact was, she had no place to go. "Mind if I spend some time right here, while I process this entire series of events?"

Ezekiel swept up her arms and waved them expansively. "You're quite welcome to sit anywhere. The office closes at 5:00." Then, she winked. "There's no rental fee."

And, just like that, Ezekiel switched her acceptance off and returned to typing on the keyboard mounted into the counter. A state employee *lifer* looking as if at work on an old-fashioned register like the one at the Woolworths down the street. Lots of brass embellishments as armaments against glee-struck lottery winners and interruptions to her work.

The sudden revert to curtness deepened Amy's terror. She looked around and noticed a line of upright wooden chairs that looked, improbably, just like the chairs edged with the library tables in prison. There must have been a sale on utilitarian furniture in the 50s, perhaps a factory closing in the Carolinas from which solid American furniture had been made for centuries. All lost in the recession that lost Amy her house.

Actually, long before her losses. The country had been acrumble for years.

She couldn't resist a smart-ass remark. Ezekiel's stiff and overly-formal demeanor commanded retort. Amy turned toward the counter. "What, no fainting couch?"

Amy didn't linger for the clerk's reply, knowing that Ezekiel already expended what little humor she possessed. Theirs was not going to be an enduring relationship, though Amy did need the woman on her side, just in case. She sat and folded in on herself, daring herself not to stare.

But, of course, that was unnecessary. To Ezekiel, Amy was already gone.

She sank into the wooden chair, which was contoured surprisingly well. It offered a measure of comfort, which Amy deepened by hugging her precious backpack, her only ally in the world.

Yes-s-s, the wood was hard, a perfect metaphor for where Amy was situated: between a rock and a hard place. Stuck. In Michigan. Not knowing where she could/should go or whom she might trust. Amy wasn't even certain she trusted herself with a mountain of money.

A whirlpool that overlaid the already overwhelming sensations since she walked out of prison set off a storm in Amy's mind. She nearly cried. She focused on breathing, harkening back to her fifteen year yoga habit.

In this manner, she refilled her personal well. Amy heaved herself off her berth and returned to the counter.

"Bye, Ms. Ezekiel, you've been very kind. I'm afraid I'm a bit over-wrought right now. Thank you for the copy of my winning ticket. I will return when I have some ducks in a row."

Ms. Ezekiel gave Amy an odd look and cleared her throat. "I'm sorry, Ms. Breeden, but before you leave this office, I must know your address and phone number."

Amy looked at the wall clock. It looked like the one at the bus station, though it seemed to tick more loudly with each secondhand sweep. A clear reminder she had sixty days to make monumental decisions.

Where could she bunk as she cycled through a series of decisions? While Amy had a phone number, Ms. Ezekiel demanded complete details now.

Amy texted Veronica. She'd rather read the news that she'd married Brandon rather than hear her celebratory crow.

CHAPTER NINE

NEW ADDRESS

NOW AMY FELT truly afraid. Fifty minutes had passed, and Veronica hadn't reply-texted. She'd distanced herself by time and morality from the Breedens, largely from guilt.

Bridges burned would not be re-built.

A cell chime jerked Amy back to reality. She squeed aloud when she read Veronica's text. Eureka! Amy quickly texted back: TX NEED ADDRESS.

Amy recognized the address as the same delicately-adorned-yet-decrepit farmhouse, sequestered behind a row of ratty-looking Italian Cypress trees, far out in the country. Far from town and many miles from the Breeden farm.She nearly skipped to the counter, then recited the address for Ms. Ezekiel as if it were the Gettysburg Address. Amy gave her own cell phone number, simultaneously swiping Ezekiel's business cards from the holder in the corner of the counter.

Amy also added the lottery office info to her contacts.

Just as Amy scooped up her backpack to head back to the bus station—or to polish her hitchhiking thumb—Veronica return-texted.

WHERE R U? CLOSE BY? IF YOU CAN WAIT A BIT, I'LL COME PICK U UP. JUST FINISHING ICING A CAKE.

Golden! Through tear-filled eyes Amy texted Veronica back and gave her the address of the bus station. She wasn't about to reveal her lottery secret to Veronica until she knew the full lay of the land.

Amy clicked her heels and re-settled into her boots. Her feet begged for relief, but would have to wait.

She hefted her backpack and slipped her cell, lottery office cards, and lottery packet inside. Amy zipped the zipper, buckled the buckle, and draped the backpack strap over one shoulder. Ready and steady for her rebelution.

"By the way," Ms. Ezekiel called out. Amy turned on her heel at the door.

"Congratulations on your win. Your world has begun a huge shift. Would you like one of our brochures on how to handle your winnings? There's a step-by-step accounting of WHAT and HOW TO. You'll be pleased to know that, if you set up an LLC account, you may have the LLC claim the money and your win will remain private. Be pleased that you won in Michigan and not another state that allows a publicity circus."

Amy's shoulders, which she hadn't even noticed

were tense, relaxed and the backpack fell to the floor. Amy scooped it up, smiled, and stepped up to the counter, reaching across it to extend her hand. "You've been more than gracious. May I please know your first name?"

Amy nearly dropped to the floor, sending her backpack into freefall again, when Ezekiel replied, "Amy." To camouflage the gut punch she'd experienced, she grabbed several brochures and stuffed them into the backpack and hefted it onto her shoulders again. *What a crazy coincidence*!

Amy wanted fiercely to give the other Amy a hug, but refrained, recalling how the woman's demeanor flipped via invisible switch. Amy input Ezekiel's name and lottery office address in her Contacts and fled, afraid to look back. She held her breath as she walk-ran past Woolworths, relishing that she now had a family of five: Dad Hernandez, Mom Wilma, Sister Veronica, Brother Andy, and herself.

Amy hurried to the bus station to await Veronica's Uber service. She plopped on the bench outside the closed doors. It mattered not if the thunder roiled and it rained. It wouldn't be raining on Amy's parade, because her parade would soon be raining cash.

Amy was golden. Travis would be trash. Her list of pranks was endless, and she knew it would grow and grow and grow.

CHAPTER TEN

PICK-ME-UP

VERONICA HAD NEW wheels, but Amy would have recognized her vehicle anywhere by the indie band stickers covering the front and back bumpers. Like tats for a car, she thought.

It was clear that Veronica still favored rap. Still bad-ass, the rap gr-r-rls weren't wasting their militancy on white men. Instead, they called out men of color for their treatment of women. Amy knew she had an ally against Trav.

Because of her feeling of impending affinity, Amy resolved to not plug her ears during the hour's drive—and to allow the music to gird her spirit.

"Hey, girlfriend!" Veronica shouted as she jumped out and grabbed Amy into a bosom-to-bosom hug. Veronica's eyes asked, "What? No prison ink?" Though her mouth remained shut. "No bags?" Her eyebrows wiggled.

Even with her mouth closed, Veronica's cinnamon breath enveloped Amy, welcoming her as much as Veronica's exuberant attitude and immediate hug.

Amy swung her 'luggage', the backpack, onto the passenger side floor and tucked her long body into the Kia Soul. She explored the seat buttons with her fingertips and inched the seat back to accommodate her frame.

Meanwhile, Veronica backed wildly away from the bus station and careened down the street. Soon the gal pals were out of the Lansing city bounds and accelerating toward Amy's temporary bunk. Lil Kim and Beyonce, and other artists Amy didn't know, hip-hopped and rapped and boogied during the entire ride. It was as if solidarity reigned under girl power's rule.

That was *good* by Amy. She sensed Veronica had as many questions to ask as she wanted to ask Veronica. She salivated amidst the lingering scent of wedding cake icing, sorry there were no lingering swathes of icing to lick on the open cardboard box visible in the back. She hadn't eaten much more than a bag of peanuts and a single candy bar since her prison release.

To stave off her hunger, she began to daydream of all the culinary treats her riches could buy in the future, sparing no expense. Pepperoni with any and every topping except anchovies. Not gonna take that bait.

But I was itching to attempt frog legs. Amy mused the entire forty miles, fighting to not smack her lips.

Rather than stave off her hunger, her daydreams stoked it. Not golden today.

Veronica slid her SOUL into her gravel driveway. She parked and both women exited at the same time. When Amy hung back, Veronica arched an eyebrow. "Your special stilettos are safe if you pick where you step."

Amy followed her example. stepping as if each played hopscotch with rocks already thrown. "I'm not used to leading a team," V. called over her shoulder.

"It'll take some getting used to being your sidekick, if that's how it's gonna be. I've missed you, Amy. No one around here knows how to have fun."

Amy winced, but Veronica was direct. "You can tell me about prison, you know. I can empathize like nobody's business. Emphasis on nobody's business."

She could think of no words that might be appropriate. Besides, she wasn't ready to talk. Though V. had been the only person to visit her in prison, Amy knew her trust senses were warped.

The tenuous friendship zig-zagged through piles of clothing in a room that combined to form family room, kitchen, and living room. Amy scanned the clumps for Brandon's ubiquitous Spartan shirts. Her shoulders relaxed when she spied none. This adapting to trust and relationship and everything would take time.

More relaxation came when Veronica turned to say, "By the way, I'm not going to throw shade on your incarceration. You did me a solid when you gave me the kush." When Amy up her face, Veronica instantly provided a translation, "*Throw shade* means to disparage someone."

Veronica was, and continued to be, a benevolent, steadfast pal. She hadn't scooped up Amy's abandoned man. There might be a story there, but she preferred to not ask. As long as Veronica didn't seek details for her life behind bars—five years was a long, long time—Amy could and would leave well enough alone. She didn't feel safe, here or anywhere.

And she had a lot to process on the teeter-totter that was her *after* life, the brink of her rebelution. Amy smiled inside. *I haven't thought of the playground teeter-totter since my youth. It was what Andy and I sought during recess. What an apt image for my circumstances, not knowing what was up or down.*

Amy surveyed her new digs. She noted three doors off a small hallway, one open to reveal itself as a slovenly bathroom. Another aan equally unkempt bedroom. The third door was closed.

When Veronica opened it, cold air met them. "I keep the vents closed to save on electricity," she said in apology.

Amy shrugged and entered the room, grateful for the chill that buried the vaguely stale scent.

But she didn't get far into the room, because it was only a few feet larger than a double bed with a brown bedspread that looked welded in place. Amy hoped that she wasn't committing to a bad mattress on her first night in a real bedroom. As it was, it appeared that the mattress overlapped the frame.

Amy shrugged, said, "Nice" and ventured a single

shoulder hug at Veronica. Veronica was a professional baker, so she knew there would be food. She needed to learn trust. Things would become copacetic if she just hung out, knowing her stomach would rumble loud enough to alert mannerly Veronica. She wouldn't need to say a word.

Amy affirmed her resolve to keep her mouth shut, because no rent had been discussed. She wanted to keep talk of money out of their relationship as long as she could.

"I'm as famished as you probably are, but I don't have much on hand," Veronica said. Amy knew her face must've fallen, because Veronica's body language tightened, and she hurried on. "But I'll bet you don't want to go out, since we're near your former 'hood."

Amy nodded in reply.

"Let's Netflix and chill. I'll make the popcorn," Veronica said. She was already in her pullman kitchen, signaling a decision made.

Popcorn as hors-d'oeuvres, meal, and dessert suited Amy just fine. In fact, she was an addict. Popcorn was one of the few items, along with spaghetti, she could cook. She secret-smiled as she recalled the magic rise and swirl of Jiffy Pop. She could always confuse little Andy with that *trick.*

Before long she heard a cupboard open and close, followed by the beep-beep of the microwave. She dropped her backpack onto the bed, gingerly tested the mattress, and headed to the bathroom to refresh.

"Use any of the toiletries and cosmetics you need. I have every Avon product," Veronica called from the kitchen, but Amy merely splashed water on her face, washing her hands and armpits lavishly with soap. She didn't bother fetching her backpack with its minimal clothing and products. This party was come as you were, as far as Amy was concerned. She had a girlfriend bond to establish. An address for her Master Card applications, and much, much more.

Her hunger surged now that she had a bunker. And Veronica hadn't even asked her how long she'd need the bunker. Yes-s-s! She could smell the popcorn, smothered with butter, and simple friendship.

Veronica plopped two bags on the coffee table and reached for the remote. Her fingers soon scrapped the bottom of her popcorn bag when Veronica said, "What do you want to watch and what beverage may I offer you? Let's get turnt!"

Amy almost choked. Her eyes watered as she inhaled the rest of the popcorn as a stall, keeping her face down in the bag. Veronica grabbed two cans of Coke from the refrig. She popped the tops and thrust one of the cans into Amy's hand.

Amy took a sip and languidly swallowed before she murmured, "I'm not that way."

Veronica glanced at Amy. "What do you mean? I figured you were ready to wig-out party now that you're out. You know, go crazy with some celebration. I always have Silly String in my cupboard, to celebrate after I complete one of the more ambitious wedding cakes. I thought we'd have a Silly String fight to break the ice, since we haven't seen each other in years."

Amy just stared at Veronica's explosion of jackets and shoulder bag purses over-burdening her coat rack. Amy would never be cold again or need more money bags with Veronica's stashes in sight.

Veronica mellowed on, filling in for Amy's silence. "But I'll humor you and start slow with Coke rather than beer or anything more mellow, if you catch my drift."

Amy gulped, but didn't lift her head. "In prison, *turnt* meant to get laid. Forcibly. I had to fend off many women, men, and guards. I fought hard to remain myself, and not become anybody's bitch. I like you, but don't want to trade sex for rent."

Veronica giggled and held out her popcorn. When Amy didn't return her reach, she said, "Please take it from me, because I'm going to need both hands to hold my sides while I laugh at that one." Then Veronica dumped the popcorn bag in Amy's lap to roll on the floor. Big dust bunnies began to float about, and Amy almost wheezed. She joined Veronica in laughter, tentatively, to cover the mini-asthma attack.

When Veronica righted herself, she scooted back onto the couch and grabbed the remote. She click-clicked, gliding through Netflix choices. "I'm looking for a show that will help you learn the latest slang. Your re-entry to society needs some greasing." Veronica winked broadly at Amy. "Pardon my allusion."

Now Amy plopped to the floor. The ice had been broken between her and V., but in a decidedly different way than either of them could have expected. She grabbed a couple of pillows and began to lose herself in some movie about bridesmaids, a movie that mildly aggravated her because she'd had none at her court house nuptials, which her in-laws almost refused to attend. The ensemble of millennial stars' raunchy humor vaguely ruffled her feathers.

Amy and Veronica idly started a contest to see who could toss popcorn kernels the highest and still catch them in one's mouth. Midway through the movie, the shag carpet was littered with missed kernels. Rather than gather them up, Veronica put two more bags of popcorn into the microwave.

Amy grimaced. Her prison gym-generated six pack might become layered in flab if this diet plan continued. Then she laugh-snorted. *However, I'd likely pee all the calories out. Btw, the movie got paused so many times, I lost the plot, if there was one.* Her teeth felt afloat.

At the final credits, Veronica clicked off the movie and, without a word to Amy, filled two glasses with water. She called a pizza delivery guy, not even asking what toppings Amy preferred. Amy was too famished to care and drank the water like a camel loading up for passage across the Sahara.

Meanwhile, Veronica didn't touch a drop. She winked at Amy and then opened a drawer on a side table and handed her a small wad of cash. "Here, pay the pizza delivery guy when he arrives. If he has blond hair, give him a $10 tip, less if his hair is brown."

Amy gaped as Veronica extracted a clear glass contraption that looked like a high school Chemistry class beaker. It had been Amy's least favorite class ever, but she didn't bother to protest. The pizza was on its way to Veronica's house. She served *at the pleasure of* her hostess with the mostest.

Amy startled as Veronica cleared the coffee table top with one swath. She fielded her backpack before its contents tumbled. Used to a confined space with few tools, Amy would hate it if her lipstick, pens, and lottery ticket verification rolled and she had to chase.

Amy set the pack near her feet and surveyed the scene. She'd never seen her new friend move as quickly without a kitchen tool in hand. In fact, Veronica was in such a flutter, it was worrisome.

When Veronica slowly slithered water into the beaker, questions formed. Okay, Amy knew she'd failed Chemistry class, which almost kept her out of college. Something about blowing up the product, but what the heck, no one was hurt.

"Uh, what are you doing?"

"The water cools the smoke." Veronica's words were muted, like Amy knew her remarks had been—on purpose—while she contemplated her misinterp of Veronica's previous offer. She looked at Veronica, her head bent toward her lap, intent on the next step. She'd pulled out a baggie of cannabis and had begun to grind a portion in a small hand held device which resembled a rich woman's compact. "Finer bud is easier to burn."

Oh-h. Now Amy knew the full terrain, but she didn't intend to smoke. She remained committed to the clarity of her lungs, avoidant of an asthma attack. She loped across the room to open a window. Her agreement to meet-and-pay the pizza delivery guy was all right, but hunky firemen weren't welcome.

Amy returned to the couch and meditated to create an out-of-body experience, because she knew the direction Veronica was headed. She was going to get *baked.* Alone. Amy's nose wrinkled against the impending scent. She nearly fell off the couch when Veronica emulated meditation breaths.

Then, she watched in horror as Veronica lip-sealed the glass throat of the beaker. She didn't postulate aloud what the action emulated.

The Bic lighter flashed. The weed flickered then glowed like campfire embers ready for toasting marshmallows for S'mores. So did Veronica's face. Her glower of concentration disappeared, to be replaced by a significant flush.

Veronica took the first hit and handed the cloudy beaker to Amy. She begged off, too much on her mind and not ready to be hookah-looped like Alice in Wonderland's caterpillar. Her next moves required alertness, thought, and real work.

"Before you're totally wasted," Amy said as she grabbed the pizza-delivery cash, "I need an address for a Master Card application. Mind if I use yours?"

"Sure. You'll be able to copy it from one of the envelopes on the counter. Are you sure you don't want to inhale? It would increase your mellow, I swear."

Inwardly, Amy giggled. She imagined she'd heard Veronica say 'mallow.' The image of S'mores ignited Amy's appetite, but not for weed.

"I'll pass, Veronica. I need my wits, not mellow."

Veronica took another long draw, so Amy levered herself from her plump pillow nest and walked to the long kitchen counter. "Quick, give me your full address. The reason is, I've got some unpaid bills and could use a new card." *A solid white lie.*

Veronica reclined on the couch and settled into her solo celebration. Lips in perma-smile but wrinkled by her tokes, laughter loud yet muffled because her lips seemed sealed around an invisible straw. Her glossy eyes slowly narrowed into her inner movie reel.

While Veronica tripped, Amy watched *Bridesmaids* again. She noted the backstory of the failed bakery this time and wondered why Veronica chose it for their movie night. Amy stopped her deep breathing, even pausing to fetch a scarf to cover her mouth Indian style, then laughed at her reflection in the computer monitor. She looked like a bank robber.

She returned to the amble-scramble of papers in her lap and found Veronica's address on one of her bills' envelopes. She made applications to Master Card, Visa, Capitol One, and American Express, half-listening to the movie dialogue to absorb the new language of her age group. Amy felt like Rip Van Winkle with each new term, grateful for her tape recorder memory.. She'd been vigilant to filter her remarks in the few interactions since she'd exited prison, avoiding prison vernacular with Hernandez, her parole officer. She hoped this underscored her intent to stay straight.

Amy hit ENTER on the final credit card app as the doorbell rang. Long and insistent with impatient bleets. Grating. Compelling. She peeped the door's keyhole—to make certain that the ringer wasn't a cop—and saw a lanky pizza delivery guy, a blond. His toes were alternately tapping in impatience inside Converse high tops. *Were those still popular?* After all, they were the same shoes Andy had near-cried to own. So dutiful sister Amy had wired money to him from her college tutoring proceeds.

She grabbed the roll of cash, counting it as she ran to the door and then flung it open, arms reaching through the air for the pizza box.

Not only was the guy blond, but he'd almost left with the pizza, his body angled toward the porch steps. The air on the porch was saturated with scents and good news. Two pizzas.

Amy almost wished she hadn't removed the scarf from her neck. Wouldn't want the pizza guy to think she was going to rob him. She grinned, jammed all the bills into Delivery Blond's pocket, latched onto the boxes, and looked back at Veronica snorting and giggling on the couch. Soon, the monster would need to be fed.

The guy loped to his car, pulled the Dominoes strobe off the top and tossed it into the passenger's seat, and then zoomed off. He was outta-there.

Pepperoni and sausage and robust cheese smells overwhelmed Amy. It was far better than Veronica's smoke and she was famished. She slammed the door shut with her butt, floating inside the small house with the pizzas held like a feast fit for queens. She mimed the cadence of a small, proud wedding ring bearer.

Amy ceremoniously set one pizza by Veronica, who was so wasted, she now snored. Amy put the other pizza on the kitchen counter, sealed tightly.

She tip-toed to Veronica's pizza, opened the box, shoveled the scent toward Veronica's nose, and extracted two triangular slices. She folded them onto themselves and ran to the front porch. She seated herself in one of the Adirondack chairs, and ate both. Wolfishly, lavishly, lustily. Down. The. Hatch. No champagne to wash it down. Hungry was hungry, but she wasn't anymore.

Ideas ziplined through Amy's brain. She felt as buzzed as Veronica, though in a very different way. After a bit, she bid good night with a thank-you-peck on Veronica's forehead and left her inert on the couch.

She sank onto the massive bed in the guest room, unmindful of her vintage clothes, her stilettos still on her tired feet. Soon, she'd own more clothes than could be housed in closets the size of Veronica's house.

But there were tangles in her path. As Amy drifted into a fitful sleep, she hoped solutions would populate her dreams.

Chapter Eleven

BAKED

THE NEXT MORNING'S sky was blanketed in gray, so, out of boredom, Amy baked a cake. Several, in fact, and soon all of the available counter space in Veronica's kitchen disappeared. She banged and clanged as she opened cupboards and drawers in search of ingredients and implements and bowls. She reveled in the noise, the task, and the fact that she recalled how to use a Kitchen Aid mixer, like Jackie, her ex-mother-in-law, had coached. After five years, Amy felt reassured she could still bake.

She splish-splashed in the already chipped sink as she washed and dried bowls and whisks and spatulas and spoons. She hummed as she cleaned the backsplash, counters and floor. Scents of vanilla and butter and sugar dominated—the smells of contentment. Amy felt engaged, proficient, and domestic.

Purpose beyond revenge.

No, she didn't forget Travis needed a *much overdue adjustment*. Amy desperately needed to do more than kneecap that man. She wanted him to kiss her attitude and then some. She wanted him on the killing floor, and she didn't give a damn if the murder wasn't pristine.

The weather remained too hot, humid, and buggy on the perimeter porch, so Amy gingerly carried the final sheet cake to the coffee table, prepared to see the remnants of Veronica's party last night. No evidence in sight—or Veronica either.

Where was that hookah-party animal?

A brief search found Veronica in her tiny bedroom, all business this morning. She looked up briefly, winked at Amy, and said, "Sorry to be scarce. I'm bustling to fill-and-bill wedding cake orders."

Legitimate, no longer as side hustle to WalMart and not a *fakery*. Wow, Amy thought.

Veronica returned to her work, a whirling dervish as she calculated, signed, and shuffled papers. Amy frowned: Veronica hadn't gone paperless for her business, which seemed successful beyond dreams. Wasn't this 2019? Even the prison had gone paperless years ago. Time to back out of the room to assure she didn't scoff.

For now, Veronica's in-need-of-a-coat-of-paint house was Amy's only bunker until she fully became a rich lass. She needed to be polite, not picky.

She knew dope was a deal breaker for parole, but Amy didn't make the rules of her temporary home. *A rock and a hard place Veronica's tiny place is.* She could only hope that the pungent ropey aroma of marijuana didn't infuse her limited supply of clothing. Amy was confined—she didn't have coin for the Laundromat for which she'd have to venture into town.

She also had no wheels to get to the town.

That fact might never change, because Amy was directionally challenged. She'd actually driven little during her life. Neither her childhood's Long Beach streets, nor the confines of a college town, nor the small-town grid where she lived while briefly married, required much behind-the-wheel time.

Neither had riding Travis' motorcycle when she *flew the coop,* nor prison confinement…why even on the 'outside' Amy had traveled only by bus, her own feet, or as a passenger in Veronica's car. Did millionairesses favor Uber or Lyft?

Amy smiled. She possessed the cunning of a cat and the scheming skills of a seductress, two skills she'd put in play soon. She willed herself back to the present set of circumstances. She'd continue to lob her dirty clothes in Veronica's hamper and wash her undies with Prell shampoo in the bathroom sink.

Her nose adjusted to the weed's reek within a day. She fervently hoped there were no repercussions for being a *user*—for either tiny home inhabitant.

Amy didn't mention the presence of weed when she checked in with Dad Hernandez regarding her temporary address. She knew his protectiveness was as unalterable as bronze, but she also knew that parole had parameters. Neither wanted complications under the long arm of the law. Recidivism would look bad on his record and worse on hers.

She sensed she couldn't buy her way out of prison…

During the brief 'check-in' call, Amy didn't seek Hernandez' suggestions for setting up a bank account, the first conundrum on her list. As a former VP, Amy knew something about bank regs. She wasn't going to be able to house her thirty yearly shares of the quarter million bucks in any bank. Her circle of friends in the U.S. was limited, and she doubted she knew anyone in Switzerland or the Caymans or where-ever-the-hell a currently favored money shelter was located. A couple of LLCs would be her best options. Amy knew only one attorney in the world: Judge Blackstone, brother of Fran. She wondered if Fran was retired as principal of the high school, the only woman who had successfully paddled ex-husband Brandon's ass.

"Is Judge Blackstone still practicing law?" Amy asked as she slathered white icing onto a sheet cake. She hoped she smoothed-and-leveled her tone as well as the icing she spread.

Veronica looked Amy in the eye for the first time that morning. "Sadly, he's in rehab. An expensive place on the shores of Lake Michigan called South Haven. Perfect name, huh? It's apparently idyllic, and folks are conjecturing he'll relapse on purpose to avoid the hassles of law practice. I think he hung up his robes in favor of sweats."

Huh. It was great that Veronica wasn't the overly curious type, so that she didn't ask why I asked. But Amy couldn't let go of this line of communication. She needed help. Pronto!

She attempted to maintain her temperate tone when

she followed up with, "Did anyone buy his practice?" Somebody had to be acquainted with the law around here. Though Judge didn't know Amy personally, she felt sentimental about him. He'd been the one who tied the knot between her and Brandon. He was legendary and she couldn't imagine the court house without him.

"There's a new Internet service called LegalZoom." Veronica busily oozed pink icing roses from a white bag with a funnel tip onto a foil-wrapped slab of cardboard box. "It's how I set up my cake business."

Amy watched the rose-making process for several minutes, her tongue metronoming her lower lip. *Girl's got a gift. Maybe I'd fund her business to a higher level when I got my annuity cash. Her kindness deserved a reward.*

Amy pondered employing Veronica to deliver a cake/week to Travis at his bar, to kill him incrementally, insidiously with traces of arsenic or ricin. Though he'd die mysteriously, she wouldn't get the kick of being a witness. And Veronica's implication in the crime would not be a kindness.

Amy shook her brain free of senseless musing, knowing she'd get to the right plan in good time. She'd waited five years, each day secretly wishing Travis dead. Since she worked in the library as an aide, she read books on murder many, many times. Sue Grafton's alphabet series was her favorite, though the murders were seldom detailed.

There were more immediate issues now. Because Amy wanted no bitterness to bleed into her reply to

Veronica, she swished saliva around her mouth, swallowed, and took a deep breath.

She stripped her voice of all color. "Seriously. LegalZoom is a cool name. What are the fees?"

"I'm glad you've returned from your head games," Veronica said.

Amy's head almost fell off its hinges as she swung around to look at the rose maker. Veronica winked. "For a minute you were somewhere else, your face as white as the cake icing. I'm glad you're here. I need you to help me hoist this second layer onto the first."

Silent concentration consumed both bakers. When the layers squared to Veronica's satisfaction, she said, "My charger's over there. Why don't you plug in your phone and do some research?" She smiled and pulled Amy into a hug. "You can call me Ronnie, if you'd like."

Amy felt her face go Technicolor. Her pulse raced as she moved toward Veronica, her arms open wide to embrace her *friend.*

Amy's cheek brushed Ronnie's button pearl earrings as the lengthy hug ended. Rather than weep, she asked her friend about them—the pearls seemed as big as oysters, the likely source, not the pareils about to be mounted on the cake. Veronica, Amy's new landlord, lived in this frumpy, mildly clandestine house. Her pearls were an anomaly whose presence couldn't be ignored. So Barbara Bush. So poignant and shiny and fresh.

"I always wear pearl earrings, because they began as irritations, like us kids were with my mom. These were her mom's pearls, too." Then, Ronnie stern-faced and pointed to the corner of the small open room, where a group of plump floor pillows were stacked, a version of "*Don't ask more.*" "I have to complete and deliver these cakes to the American Legion by 4:00. Can you believe some Auxiliary ladies are having a cakewalk fundraiser, something about boys and clots? Get busy and do your research."

Amy felt excused and tasked. She put her head into her research and didn't come up for air until Veronica came home, two fragrant Polish sausages in a greasy white paper bag held aloft, like first place trophies.

Ronnie looked like a *lunchbox angel,* someone Amy had longed for throughout grade school. Neither of the new friends had eaten since they'd stuffed corn flakes, directly from the box, at noon.

It may have been the loneliness and/or the sudden implosion of her sequestered and highly patterned prison life, followed marvelously, but perilously, with an unfathomable lottery win… Amy realized she felt like a person who'd fallen overboard.

And she didn't know how to swim. She hadn't been drowning, but dog-paddling alone was tiring. Ver-, er, Ronnie's home was the only terra firma she had. Its tininess made her feel safe. Ronnie's huge hug made her feel safer.

It may have been the spicy sausage that forced Amy to belch. It may have been the six-pack the gals shared… Amy let her guard down. She was all in. She told Ronnie about the winning numbers and the LLC plan.

Ronnie shrieked and jumped up to wrap Amy in

another exuberant hug that embedded matching dollops of mustard on both gals' tee shirts. "That's terrific," she shouted in Amy's ear. She gripped Amy's shoulders and gazed into her eyes. "Amy, I'm flat-ass happy for you. I'm not exactly sure what it means, but there's not a drop of envy in the craft beers I'm going to open."

Craft beers? Amy aw-shucksed while Ronnie loped to the kitchen to retrieve two and uncap the bottle tops. Swift moves that made Amy pine for Travis and his bar. There were many levels of unfinished business between them.

Ronnie handed Amy one of the bottles and both of them swigged. The air stilled. Then Veronica spoke. "Congrats, but you're not thinking with a clear head, Amy. People still remember you around here, and not fondly, either."

Amy shook her head and 'researched' the floor, her eyes spying every crack. "I've got nowhere else to go, Ronnie."

"Sometimes the best place to submerge yourself while in a confused state is to become invisible in plain sight. Sooner or later, you'll have to venture out. How 'bout if I go to Watson's Drug Store to buy black dye?" Ronnie ventured. "Like all the heroines on the lam in spy flicks."

Ronnie bounced on her heels as she warmed to her plan. "After that task, we'll drink some of the champagne leftover from one of the weddings I catered. Maybe, proceed with a particular strain of bud that I've perfected out back."

Chapter Twelve

BLACKOUT

WITHIN TWO HOURS, Amy's hair was as black as Ronnie's, chopped into a deranged pixie. Yet, when she looked in the water-splattered mirror above the sink, Amy cringed. A new color palate of clothing would be required, and she'd need new makeup. She hoped the credit cards arrived soon. Her wallet was emptying fast, and she didn't want to be on Ronnie's tab. She didn't know her well enough to project what interest rate Veronica might charge.

Amy's shoulders tightened at the prospect of vicious usury rates. She'd read Shakespeare's *The Merchant of Venice*.

During the lengthy dye process, they'd thumbed through spicy, yet redundant movie magazines. Amy was bored, bored, bored. The beer warmed, which left a sour mash taste in her mouth. And she couldn't imagine the state of her breath after the greasy onion overlaid sausages. She thirsted for champagne and real news to gain firm turf. Watching TV news and soap operas was out.

She decided to ask after Brandon.

Ronnie faked a pout and gave Amy the *Reader's Digest* version. "Interesting timing that you should ask," she began. "I've just visited Watson's Drug Store and Julie, the owner's daughter, with her PharmD from Purdue, was behind the counter. All leggy and career-perfect in white coat, yoga pants, and ponytail. A pert package, if you get my drift."

Ronnie laughed coarsely. "I watched that ponytail flick-flick-flick as Julie whipped about the small closet-like enclave of meds to dispense." She turned to wink at Amy. "I mentally placed bets on how many bottles would crash to the floor but left the store disappointed and forgetting my mission to buy cosmetics along with the hair dye."

Then, Ronnie smirked. There was smear in her tone as she reported Julie had dumped Brandon, the latter seldom seen around town. Something about his parents dumping on him, too, with plans to travel with friends who'd won half of the nearly half-billion-dollar lottery recently.

Oh, my! Amy wondered *what-if*, but kept her mouth shut. Truly a small world.

Suddenly, as in a deliberate topic shift, Veronica Bic-lighted a bong, this time languidly, lavishly, lovingly prolonged.

"Holy Crap!" Amy intoned and quickly looked

around the room. *Did she use her inside voice? How did Jackie Breeden get inside her head? Again?*

She vanquished Jackie's judgmental prissiness by piggy-backing Veronica's ritual. It had been an unf*ing believable couple of days. She reasoned that she felt upside down without the weed, so why not with it?

The burnt rope scent enveloped Amy, evoking a metaphor. Being unable to venture from Ronnie's home was beginning to feel somewhat like prison. Except that the *library* was Google searches on a 4X8 cell phone. Now, energy pushed against her boredom. Her innards gyrated so much, she felt certain the whole house shook. The walls expanded, the universe vast and open to her.

The brainstorming began at midnight and lasted until dawn, fueled by Ronnie's bud. It may have been merely Amy's weed-addled brain, but she swore her friend's dark eyes were alive with the game. Both of them were creative dervishes, wild women of thought. They chicken-scratched and doodled all over Ronnie's worn-edged movie mags, even a few on the recipe pages she claimed never to use, using indelible Sharpies because pencil just wouldn't do. A perfect metaphor to affirm the permanence of their *spendy* and exaggerated plans.

On her Google Maps app, Ronnie located South Haven, the small beach town where the only adult they mutually knew—outside of their tiny habitat—resided. While he wasn't capable of being a touchstone, his presence might anchor them in a newly-chosen town. The young women felt they'd have someone's name to wield, if needed.

Besides, South Haven, Michigan was a resort town,

primed to house a new millionaire and best gal pal. A carefree village, beside Lake Michigan, without undue laud and fanfare.

They schemed to buy Travis' bar, each amped enough to employ the tactics of a cult leader. Work him like a slave, dispensing with empathy for his plight… of having an overlord named Amy. Gleeful, vengeful infAMY.

Ronnie promised she'd gloat, too. "We're a team" she beamed and boasted and high-fived.

We. Amy's gut internally squirmished after Ronnie's spontaneous use of *we*. She tried not to recoil. She tried to trust. She tried to relax into the plans. *Go with the flow* had never been her default paradigm. She'd never shared authority before.

Imagination built a lakeside spa/retreat for the wealthy, maybe women recovering from plastic surgery. Discreet, luxurious, and private, *our* stately mansion of respite stood tall on a hill above the harbor. Should it be Colonial Revival or Grecian Goddess? A Roman Palace with yards of garden paths to meander. A place where well-funded plebeians could relax, as well as patricians. *Our* policy would be egalitarian. Everyone's cash was green. Building and marketing would lap up oodles of cash, so a bank account might not be necessary long term. A ginormous safe on the property could suffice.

Amy chafed as they free-ranged how to spend. While she was chained to Michigan, Andy, her only kin, was determined to remain among the only friends and business he knew, canna cultivation in the Emerald Triangle of northern California, a deeply-embedded culture which had hey-dayed. His last cryptic text suggested the land would be over-farmed because the state was full recreational, no longer merely medical, for product use. An impending market glut foreshadowed wide-spread ruination.

Amy kept that info under wraps. For the future. Canna-infused water and edibles as well as lotions and scrubs would be spectacular spa products. A killing could be made, supplementing her *walking-around* cash. If she told Ronnie, the rockets would roar. For now, Amy kept that tango in her head.

If she imported from Andy and his clan, she could entice Travis to be the motorcycle courier across the U.S. If he had a bike—likely a Gold Wing by now—a bike with a cushy ride and plenty of saddlebags to carry product. Ha! He'd take the rap if intercepted by the feds. YASS!

The serenity needs of the clientele would be served and maybe, as in the case of Judge's semi-permanent rehab, the recidivism would climb higher than the rate of prison return. Amy banked on her business' success to ensure she'd never return to the clink. She earned probation, with five years left on her original term.

Her serenity would be served by tangible revenge on Travis, a potential for him to go down, down while she was up, up. She'd out-capital and crush him to bits. Smithereens. Smash the trash!

Amy didn't wish to follow Prometheus, crashing-and-burning quickly by squandering the lottery cash. She wanted longevity. The clarity that ignited her snap decision to pursue the thirty-year annuity route.

Secret plastic surgery makeovers would be safe—maybe eventually performed on the premises when the business acquired a reputation and the cash flow was intact. A stable of specialists for various body parts' sculpting. A revolving door of satisfied clients who clamored for more. Amy craved panache and a good rep.

Yassss, dollar signs in place of those ssss, penned in Midas' scrawl.

Amy and Ronnie mutually agreed to call the place Lady Bug, though they privately called it Lady Bud. Lady Bug had been Ronnie's childhood nickname. The women giggled and gaggled about the parallel to *the Hotel California*—it'd be a boon to profitability if the guests would check in and never leave. Fees would skyrocket. Profits would reach to the moon.

The Hotel California was already branded and embedded in every consumer's brain, so better selves prevailed. No high-powered lawyers from the Eagles' entourage could/would sue for Amy's mountain of cash. Besides, our Lady Bud would be its own kind of famous. Its own Big Brand.

Soon, the gals agreed, Amy'd snap up ownership of Travis' bar. Nothing good was ever going to happen to him again.

Hey, back up! It was interesting how slyly, comprehensively, Ronnie became embedded in the endeavor. More interesting because she didn't demand a take. Had she gone altruistic—or was she lonely, too?

Maybe, Ronnie was as ready to blow this hick farm town as Amy was to not return to prison, trapped as she was in Michigan.

Chapter Thirteen

ANNUITY

AMY SPENT THE next several days ensconced on Ronnie's couch, allowing her friend to busy-tail bake, decorate, and deliver. Ronnie had long abandoned WalMart employ. After repeated clashes with management over her body piercings, she'd done 'just one more' to get herself fired and collect unemployment. She'd clerked for Uncle Walt at the Feel Good Forever Farmacy, while building her cake business. Turned out that his bud clientele created a reliable income stream.

But Ronnie's mention of including Uncle Walt in their new spa scheme, to become a supplier and/or a referral source was promptly kabashed. In fact, it made Amy's hair stand on end—just like Ronnie's frequent imbibe of weed. Amy was pretty sure that possession on the premises would trigger *interest* and, perhaps, a return to the Pen for her.

The guest room remained claustrophobic, too

reminiscent of a prison cell. The mattress wasn't bad, the bedspread was sweet, but the dresser drawers barely opened because the bed gobbled up the room's real estate. Amy kept her small cache of clothing in her backpack and on the top closet shelf. She wasn't feeling *permanent* yet.

The couch was Amy's island—a life raft in a sea of change. Sometimes, she awoke to find a note about leftovers Saran-wrapped in the fridge. Camaraderie and comfort were growing hand-in-hand.

Amy avoided the mirrors in the small house, still uneasy with the black, quirky-chopped hair. She'd lived thirty years with the power of blonde, and another half of that at near six-foot. Though she wasn't Samson of Biblical renown, Amy was reminded of how scissors savaged his skills.

More adjustment, more upheaval and change, more unsettling than Amy cared to admit to Ronnie, who tried her best. Perhaps prison spawned her distrust and paranoia. Perhaps it had just honed those traits.

Though the nearly empty box's instructions warned not to, Amy dyed her eyebrows and lashes with the remnant product. She refused to relinquishidecisions to an anonymous bunch of researchers—or marketers. Amy was committed to parsing millions on other products, ones that held promises of highly enhanced gains.

Besides, her eyes didn't fall out while she did beaucoup research.

Amy called the manager of Judge's rehab center, pretending to be a reporter for the *Chicago Tribune.*

She couldn't believe that he fielded his own phone calls, with no unctuous secretary as buffer. The two got *chummy* after several seconds—and he offered to take Amy to lunch when she arrived in South Haven. He'd introduce her to a realtor to help her secure the location, location, location.

Amy may have mentioned that she was a *millionaire with influence*. The man salivated throughout the remainder of the phone call.

Amy also kept in touch with Dad Hernandez. Mom, Woolworth Wilma, knew a thing or two about real estate. Mom seconded settling in South Haven. It was private and out-of-the way. A nice, lakeside resort, an untroubled place. "A judge resides there, in a semi-permanent version of a drunk tank."

Amy startled. Was it her Judge Blackstone? The glibly-provided information—twice—gave Amy pause. Had Judge brought the fame… or had infamy found him?

Judge's privacy had definitely been breached. That the local busybodies had ignited prairie fire gossip to reach ears in Lansing, an hour from his residence and law practice, had to be contended with. Amy reminded herself to be on guard. Everywhere. For all time.

As an apparent service to his clientele, Hernandez re-instated her driver's license, Amy discovered. Perhaps the state did it, as a public service, to reduce return to the Pen. Get a job, be a taxpayer. Amy clung to contact with her surrogate dad, Parole Officer payer, an upstanding citizen, get-on-with-your-life.

As soon as her newly minted Master Card arrived, Amy purchased a car. Online, placing *Michigan State Lottery* in the line asking for references. Delivery to Ronnie's address was included—check—within a week. A sturdy, non-gas guzzling Ford Focus with built-in GPS.

Focus. What an apt name for Amy's state of mind. She was on fire, a chickadee in heat, the fever from impending plans.

The car was basic black, like her hair and the banker-tailored suit she purchased. Dignified, simple, direct. Also inexpensive. Amazon was amazing at preserving anonymity and the delivery driver was amusingly cute. He lingered for a signature, a smile, and a bottle of Mountain Dew. His ice blue eyes crackled. He looked good in shorts. Amy was embarrassed when her mind's eye flickered back to Travis' look.

Amy's wardrobe now consisted of alternating *professiona*l uniforms: staid black, vintage, and jeans, yoga togs, and tees. She added snazzy silver sneakers, smiling as she thought of her forthcoming elder spa patrons and the requisite resort wear. She had lots of legwork and needed sturdy shoes, not just stilettos and boots. She also needed shorts and work shirts.

Amy decided to not get ahead of herself and her cash flow,—she'd save resort wear purchases for later.

Not everything was legwork. Though she'd had a checking account in prison, for her meager library pay, that was her old world. She expected that her expenses would be made with credit cash, balances paid in full at a later date. Reward mileage might enable her to zoom out of sight, undetected by Hernandez.

She'd require a bank for the yearly lotto lump sum. Amy found one, interestingly chartered in Indiana and positioned in the clouds. Perhaps it was the Lord himself who administered the accounts. Amy smiled and made **(1Lord!)** her password. It was the perfect combination of lower case, capital letters, and top row keyboard characters. The bank validated it as 'strong.'

The LegalZoom paperwork was Fed-Exed. Amy hoped that no rural folk took note of the delivery truck, knowing that its presence was rare in rural areas. Their team didn't need gossip to spider into local lore. It was enough jeopardy that Ronnie, who baked cakes and catered almost all the weddings in the area, was mixing-and-mingling and might have loose lips.

With the large envelope in her hand, Amy's mind zapped back to the here-and-now-and-future. Her fingers tore at Fed-Ex's tough paper envelope.

Amy's heart was a tom-tom surrounded by a set of snare drums. Her breastbone the capable bass that thumped her stomach's butterflies, jostling her minimal lunch. She felt as if she might heave.

I'm sick and tired of monologue, her sanity exclaimed. Amy shut up and read:

> Our legal team has been at work on your behalf. We understand your needs. We have prepared the preliminary documentation as required for the Lady Bug and Infamy LLCs. Please look

over the documents and sign online with our secure server or print, sign in the presence of a notary, and return special delivery in the postage prepaid envelope enclosed.

Please call us if there are further questions. Thank you for using LegalZoom.

Amy grinned and relaxed. Two LLCs, reliable, silent partners as recipients of the ten million/year lottery dough, swiftly accepted and divvied to her online bank account. No one the wiser—or, suspicious. Uncle Sam didn't need to suss—the state of Michigan had already divvied his share.

Her chin lifted and her shoulders aligned for a plan going forward full blast. She'd corral the rest of her *first rodeo* venture and staff soon. For now, she turned to the explanatory text to determine if all was copacetic according the state lottery pamphlets.

Copacetic? Now Steve Breeden had entered Amy's head. The past as prologue, she surmised. She half-expected to see Brandon stride in the door at any time. She'd have to learn coping mechanisms as contingencies to handle those two's potential interference.

Amy returned to peruse her lottery payment *homework*. It was important to learn and get this right. Copacetic.

A 'draw' is a withdrawal of LLC's earnings. A member usually won't take a draw unless there are profits.

> A 'guaranteed payment' is money that a member takes out of the business whether there is a profit or not.
>
> For income tax purposes you are charged with recognition of your LLC's profits regardless of your draws. Tax recognition and flow of money are two separate things in an LLC.
>
> Example:
>
> If the LLC made a $20,000 profit, then you will report it through your Schedule C if the LLC is taxed as a sole proprietorship. You DO NOT report that same $20,000 a second time due to the fact that you withdrew it during the year as the owner's draw.
>
> In terms of showing your income to a bank, you can show them copies of your tax return, which will have your Schedule C.

Amy gulped. The legalese squawked about "$20,000.00" so she got tangled in math facts. Though she'd been a full-ride collegiate, she'd been an English major. This document's verbiage was legalese, not a language in which she was conversant. The ducks may have been lining up, but they seemed to be scattering. Acting more like chickens without heads. Amy's aplomb tanked.

She intended to be the Alpha, but alpha of what? Too much money, too many nuts to juggle, too much to reconsider, too much to weigh. Too much to torch her ebullient mood. Wasn't rich supposed to be exalting and fun? Not twisted in legalese, protocols, and salutations.

Though she had Hernandez as touchstone, the scope of his lawyerly expertise entailed the terms and conditions of parole. He texted her at 9:00 every morning—to assess her behavior and mood. Amy made certain that she had perfect and perky replies to all questions, especially when he shared that she his favorite among his caseload. Ever.

Dad Hernandez was like an old beater car, reliably starting each morning, using tech as a crutch. Amy was glad that the high price of gas prevented impromptu home visits. The secret of Ronnie's weed stash stayed safe.

Safety. There was warmth in Hernandez' voice. He was Amy's 'welcome back' to the outside world.

Brother Andy texted, though at erratic and highly interruptive times.

Sometimes, she replied. Sometimes, she did not. The duo hadn't been within physical proximity in years, but he was her only conscious blood relative. Schizzy mothers didn't count.

Often, Andy's texts were nutcase cryptic. Still… he was the little brother she'd sworn to protect. Little, maybe conniving brothers weren't privy to the secret of multi-millions in cash. Besides, his texts were hyperactively misspelled and always all-CAPS.

It was time to expand the Dependables, the self-gathered family Amy trusted. It was time for a dose of Amy Ezekiel, her opposite-in-nature, but complicit friend.

On the fifth day post prison release—Amy knew because she'd crossed-off each day on Ronnie's wall calendar—she suited up and practiced her smile. She feared Ezekiel's reaction to her newly-black hair. Would Ezekiel recognize her and request ID?

Amy adjusted and re-adjusted the seats of the diminutive Ford Focus to accommodate both her height and abundance of nerves. She almost requested a Hernandez escort, but knew she needed to go it alone.

With each passing day, though bored, Amy achieved increasing equilibrium. of spending and exacting revenge alternated in prominence, carrying her through. Her mind felt at ease and placid, but her nerves jangled out loud.

Acceptance of being free yet encumbered with responsibilities that rode into her life along with bunches of zeroes, swayed and swashed but didn't buckle her resolve. Thankfully, her blood pressure didn't surge.

A look in her rearview mirror affirmed this, yet she felt the heat.

In addition to transitioning from incarcerated-to-paroled, she *was* addled by thoughts of her mother and brother, consumed by a permanently ingrained sense of responsibility for their welfare. She now operated in a new frontier of millionaire status—back to being the Adult. She longed to be footloose, free to spend as per her own purposes and needs. Free to kill off Travis, one obnoxious cell at a time.

She drove slowly to the lottery office. Slowly, judiciously, and mindful not to get a speeding ticket.

Chapter Fourteen

FACETIME IS FACT

AMY PAUSED AT the lottery office door, hem-hawing because she'd not made a proper appointment. But, once inside, Ezekiel greeted her like an old friend, not like someone who'd dyed her natural blonde hair.

Together they melded Amy plans with appropriate boxes in computer form fields, inserting the tracking numbers of the online checking account and security passwords. Ex-con Amy found it cute when Bureaucrat-Amy averted her eyes while the passwords were keyed in. Bravo for integrity!

The first installment of the lottery win would arrive in Millionairess-Amy's account within fifteen days. Money with angel wings.

Throughout her brief life Amy had scavengered, scampered, worked, set-goals-and-achieved. With utter disbelief, she'd garnered largesse on the dumb luck of a single ticket. A ticket that seemed divine intervention into a hard scrabble life. Having nothing tangible jittered Amy's nerves.

Okay, I'll admit it. I was scared. Bravado means nothing when it's all in your head.

Back in Ronnie's dinky home, the mirrors Amy couldn't avoid reveled in her emerging between-the-brows worry line, not to be discouraged or lotioned away. Wrinkles emerged during her fettered sleep and deepened during the day. The near constant tilt of her head as she thought and imagined and planned tweaked her neck.

Ronnie laughed at Amy. "You look like the Leaning Tower of Pisa!"

Amy texted Woolworth Wilma: HI. LET'S LUNCH. Amy wished she'd thought to walk from the lottery office the other day.

The text reply: OK, soothed Amy. A tangible hug soon. Wilma's voice was sweet as sugar and her advice was sage. It would be good to hear both.

Amy smiled as she drove back to Lansing to visit Wilma, car fueled via credit card. Hernandez was a steady force—a touchstone of truth—but Wilma mothered Amy. Woolworth Wilma was a 1%er. She had more compassion in her little toe than others had in their hearts.

She also had more cash and picked up the tab for lunch. Which was great, because Amy had little *walking-around* money and—with the lottery pay-out she'd select—she might never have. Lottery rich, cash poor. She'd already decided to not have a checking account. No paper trail—and the pre-plans portended skyrocketing amounts of expense, the better to sequester and protect her monetary bonanza.

Amy thought of stupid stuff while she drove. Notably, she'd developed a talent for reading upside down—letters as well as numbers—when bank clients were seated across from her at her VP desk. A handy-dandy gambit, a gift of a talent. Who knew when and how she'd use it in her *rebelutionary* life, but not today during lunch.

Amy and Wilma gabbed about this and that, meandering between politics, local and national, which Amy was learning whether she liked it or not. Climate change ruled the physical world, just as it did the psychological terrain Amy would return to.

They were just about to order pineapple upside down cake, observed in huge slabs in the display counter at the diner front, when Andy interrupted by text. Guilt should have drenched Amy's armpits. Her first thought for a celebrant companion should have been him, but she was unwilling to bring Andy into the loop until she eye-balled him to see if he was 1. Straight and 2. Trustworthy, which meant *reformed.*

Andy hadn't yet crossed over from being a burden to be a brother Amy could rely upon. Actually, he never had been. Not. A. Chance. Amy pictured him now, hopping about as if walking on red coals, lanky legs dressed in raggedy-edged bell bottoms, his blonde wiry curls all dancing wild in her imagination. She'd last seen Andy at age six, when she boarded a train for the Midwest.

She found herself sobbing. She side-glanced as a linen-and-lace handkerchief slid across the table, suddenly aware that she was in public and, worse, ignoring Wilma.

Amy texted Andy that she'd return his text with a real phone call at a proper time…and did he know there were time zone disparities between their states of residence? She stashed the cell into her backpack. She dabbed under her teary eyes with the splendid hankie and lifted her head.

Wilma leaned forward, folded her hands, and placed them in front of her. Amy blessed her for ignoring her waterworks, further thanking her for offering the expensively embroidered handkerchief to wipe away the splatter of tears.

"Why don't you FaceTime your dear Andy? I do it with my grandchildren all the time. So cute. And you feel like you can reach out and touch them."

Amy felt she could die on the spot. She was the younger and Wilma the elder, was more tech-savvy.

Wilma's compassion kicked in. Her eyes crinkled with delight, and she quickly clapped her hands with joy. "Want to see how it works?" Before Amy could respond, two towheads waved at Gramma via her cellphone.

Wilma turned the screen around so the twins could see Amy and wave at her, too. She nearly capsized. One was snaggle-toothed.

Amy openly wept. The screen's happiness reminded her of Childhood Andy and Childhood Her, though she doubted if their faces had been cherubic and scrubbed clean. Nor were their collars crisply ironed.

Woolworth Wilma ended the call and reached across the table to enfold Amy's hand. "Let me offer you another technology update, Dear. You can't look like a proper millennial unless you have earbuds looping across your shoulders and down your front. Let me pay the check and let's zoom back to the store. I have 'em on the front rack along with iTunes gift cards. The gift of both will be on me, just like lunch."

Amy nearly cried again. In front of her was a Person, someone who wanted nothing from her, except that she allowed her to care. The concept of friends-and-family began to sink into Amy's cells. She felt the quarter-century wall around heart start to crack.

The barricade was built with her suspicions, one brick of embarrassment at a time. Amy began to feel she could navigate the tightrope of life, neither falling nor abandoning the equilibrium pole. Tumbling down the brick wall.

Amy's intellect, buttressed by her English degree, was fully cognizant that she was adopting aphorisms and mixing metaphors, but personal will and triteness were all that held her together. Woolworth Wilma's kindness meant more than millions.

Amy fervently hoped she did nothing to screw up their relationship. Warmth would outlast wealth. No matter what.

Chapter Fifteen

WOOLWORTH WILMA, WELCOME ABOARD!

WOOLWORTH WILMA PROVIDED her name, address, and phone number, tearing off the napkin corner on which she'd written them. She closed Amy's fist over the treasure. Amy drew the bundle to tap her heart and blew Wilma an air kiss. She couldn't break character for a public peck on the cheek. She felt both reassured—and frightened.

Amy shivered as she retrieved her cell and input the info. She now had nine people in her cellphone Contacts: Travis, Andy, Hernandez, Ezekiel at the state lottery office, Veronica, Wilma, and the good trio of Breedens. She hastily excised the Michigan State Pen, but retained her own number, lest she forget it. Now she had nine friends—and one singular foe.

To dismiss wistful thoughts, Amy studied her

fingernails. They were mangled, a mess with ripped cuticles. No mani-pedis in prison.

Now the water works began, both eyes, black mascara splashing onto her high cheekbones. Wilma handed back the linen handkerchief, allowed Amy to dab, and swiftly pulled her from the booth. She guided Amy to the nail polish rack in Woolworths. "Take one of every color, my dear." Wilma stashed them in Amy's backpack. She also tucked in a small tissue pack, then patted Amy's butt.

Amy startled and twisted around to see the old lady's face, noting for the first time that her cheeks were peppered with faint freckles. Wilma's eyes crinkled as the grin broadened on her face. Now Amy truly knew that nips and tucks of self-esteem were Wilma's forte.

Next, Wilma lifted Amy's chin with her soft-as-velvet fingertips and smiled into her tragic face. She stood on tiptoe and craned her neck to be as near as Amy's eye level as she could achieve, "You're welcome to stay with me in my rambling old mansion until all of your affairs are in order, my dear."

Blindsided by the impromptu expression of acceptance, Amy fumbled to retrieve her car keys from her backpack. A nail polish tumbled out as she fetched the unfamiliar keys and she bent to scoop it up. She turned the glass bottle over and stared at the polish called 'Revenge'. Could she exact that toll on Travis after such a display of kindness?

She fled, nearly running out, without a backward glance.

On the drive back to Ronnie's place, Amy felt badly that she'd left Wilma with the check. She had coins and credit cards in her backpack—and a bunch more money would soon be banked. It took great will to not add another brick of embarrassment to her wall. Wilma's smiling face loomed before her like the Great Oz. Amy promised herself to live up to Wilma's goodwill.

Amy's insides quivered like Jello. Everything jiggled as if stirred by an earthquake of emotions. About 10.0 on a Richter scale.

She Facetimed Andy but could barely speak because of the novel sense of peace she felt. Andy, now a soul-patched young man with scrambled-egg hair, was chatty. She grinned while he prattled for six minutes. His words made no sense, but she relished the sound of his voice.

Finally, Amy clicked off the call, certain that contact with Andy would continue telepathically. Besides, no time to tear-up now. She needed to move forward. With trust, as she drove to her temporary bunk.

She caught Ronnie, both arms filled with a double stack of pink and a bill clenched between her teeth, ready to zoom out the door. The back of her hatchback was already filled with pink boxes, all with bills, written in her scrawl and taped to their tops. She would be gone all day.

Divine scents, all cinnamon and sugar and spice, wafted from within her gingerbready house. Amy quickly leaned into kiss Ronnie's cheek, but only clipped a wisp of hair because of Veronica's haste and Amy's care to not jostle the boxes. She waved 'bye' at the hatchback's rear windows as Ronnie sped away.

Amy ran-walked to the refrigerator, dropping her backpack on the couch. She flung its door wide, gazing at the contents as if they'd put themselves together to feed her of their own accord. Despite the fact that she'd dined with Wilma, Amy was starving. She wished Ronnie would return to fricassee an egg, fry bacon, make anything at all.

A new scent entered the room. "Hiawassee County is awash with wild gossip and hearsay, but I've done my best to ignore it. It's said that you're back and looking to invest in a spa over at South Haven." Amy froze. She'd never expected to hear that voice again. What the hey-hey? Why hadn't Veronica warned her of this possibility?

Amy dared not turn around. She felt like a statue bronzed into eternity, her arm forever frozen to the open refrigerator door. The voice mellowed with the promise of a kiss and a hug. "I say you look mighty fine to behold—"

Amy wheeled around, pushing off the refrigerator door, both to close it and to maintain balance. Just as she'd never expected to hear the voice, she hadn't expected to see that Spartan Green football jersey again.

It was Brandon, as tall, dark, and handsome as the first time they'd met, a dozen years ago, his teeth still a white picket fence of down-on-the-farm wholesomeness. He looked Amy up and down, settling on her face, not quite making contact with her eyes. He'd hidden his body behind a pizza box and was thrusting a quart of Breeden Dairy milk forward rather than a handshake. "I brought lunch."

He was bringing her food as if were a bouquet of flowers for Valentine's Day!

"Oh," was the single sound Amy could form, her mouth agape long enough to admit pesky fly that had followed Brandon inside, her tongue his landing strip, her mouth his hangar. She acted reflexively to the tickle, then mildly spat. The fly zoomed out of the room. No second warnings for him.

Amy knew she should have fled with the fly. But she felt rooted. Brandon, after all, was her ex. And, he strangely felt like her *home.*

Amy brought two fingers to her wrist, tapping about to find a pulse. She knew that she had one, but hoped those fingers had the same effect as a cold compress. She didn't want to embarrass herself by opening the freezer to fetch one of Ronnie's ever-present ice packs, used to ease her migraines, despite seeming to have an early hot flash.

She didn't tell Brandon she'd already had lunch. She didn't mention he'd slashed a finger through the icing on one of Ronnie's cakes and licked the finger dry. She didn't tell Brandon his presence disconcerted her. She wordlessly swept her arm like Vanna White to invite him in.

Which he already was.

She extended that in-motion arm to accept his peace offering. "Is this Breeden Diary milk, fresh off your farm?" All her man-of-few-words did was grin. The Cheshire cat couldn't have bested him in the moment. His eye contact felt warm.

Brandon set the pizza box on the table, the round one on which Ronnie and Amy seldom supped. He came around the table, pulled out of one of the ladder-backed chairs, and smiled. He didn't say, "What did you do to your hair?" He didn't grab at Amy to make a pass. He opened the pizza box, lifted one of the pre-cut triangles, and handed it to her. He moved with the grace of a former athlete, husband, and lover, unflinchingly maintaining eye contact throughout.

Amy felt as hot as the pizza. She stared as it seemed to suddenly shape-shift into a heart.

Brandon dropped his eye contact and began to chow down. Brandon's appetite had always led his life. His stomach was the most narcissistic of his organs, far surpassing his self-centered mind. All because of athletic prowess—muscles that rippled at will—and parents who super-fanned his ego from his birth.

Now Amy recalled all of the ancient details and her body temperature cooled. Just like the pizza she still hadn't touched.

"You're the only woman who ever got away, Amy." Brandon looked up, his forehead wrinkled in pain. Amy felt guilty when her mind amended, *I got far, far away*.

"When I heard you were incarcerated, I wanted to visit, but Dad stopped me at the door. Mom would have whooped me, with the entire community as enforcers. Time passed—" Brandon's speech, longer than any she'd heard to date, ended in another huge bite of pizza. Amy buried herself, pizza-stuffing to hide the emerging blush.

Outside a mockingbird called. Within seconds, another joined in. The silence filled, she didn't have to voice her apprehension about her spa intentions already circulated the small town. Could the secret of her millions be far behind?

Amy didn't care two bits about the local yokels, though she didn't want to hurt the Breedens. She bridled at the potential opinions and impediments she would experience if she stuck around. In her heart-of-hearts, she knew they'd feel compelled to defend her.

This locale held no promise of recompense—not even from the man in front of her. She felt she owed him something, despite her conviction that she wanted nothing to do with him and/or his limp 'good intentions'.

Amy didn't have time to ponder what to say, because Brandon filled the air. "My folks headed out with another couple. Don't 'spose you recall Bonnie, the church secretary?"

Amy kept her focus on the grub, intent on not over-stuffing on Brandon's 'down on the farm' news. She shook her head "no".

It was the truth and she owed Brandon a bid to be in this conversation. She knew it had taken a lot for him to venture forth. Good men were hard to find.

And, there might be enough of a spark left for him become an ally, maybe necessary down the road. At the present she had more suspicions than allies, so she put Brandon in the plus column and listened as more backstory spooled out.

"Well, another Californian arrived some months after you left, bringing chaos like folks say you did—." Brandon winced when that judgment passed his lips.

Amy let the remark pass.

Gosh, he was calm, informative, and fair. Had he matured?

Did he have a gun stuffed in his pants?

"He took off with Bonnie after she won the Boffo Lotto, dragging my parents along to witness some Vegas shotgun wedding and their honeymoon in Hawaii. My folks flounced off, and I have to run the dairy. Again." Brandon's face fell into a forlorn hound expression, openly appealing for Amy's sympathy.

She choked, gagging so hard that she nearly launched her semi-chewed food onto her new shoes. The odds were so highly improbable of a coincidental monster lottery win, she couldn't deal.

She ran to the bathroom and retched. *Unf*ing believeable*. Amy wished one of Ronnie's millennial slang terms would enter her head, because her polysyllabic English degree was in full-fail mode now. She could conjure nothing to say. No platitudes, no encouragement, no epithet. She just wanted Brandon out of the f*ing house.

Amy locked the bathroom door and did a few yoga asanas, though hampered by the small space. Then, she washed her face, combed her hair, and reapplied makeup. *Unf*ing believable—Brandon didn't even notice my change of hair color.*

When Amy returned to the table, Brandon stood, his face as expectant as his family's pet, the one whose name she couldn't recall, the one that slobber-ruined her army of silk blouses. She surprised herself by flinging herself into his expansive chest and burly arms. Though his belly sported a mild paunch, Amy felt more at home in his hug than at any moment since she'd gotten out.

Brandon didn't disengage from the hug, but neither did he halt his monologue. "The milking operation is semi-automatic, and I got a kid working it for me. My parents and Uncle Carl and Bonnie, the former church secretary, are gone." His voice held the hinting, expectant tone of a teenager proposing a party to a bunch of peers, intent on getting unendingly drunk while his folks were away. And laid.

Amy shoved her way out of Brandon's arms. Though momentarily charmed, she knew their future would be held together by staples, like the term papers she'd written so that he could graduate and make big money in pro football. But. He failed. He broke the *promise* she'd invested in.

The past as prologue.

A dummy Amy was not. She was rich. She'd escaped! She'd rather chew the linoleum of his mom's over-washed floors than return to the bosom of the banal Breedens again.

Her face contorted and she rose above her six-foot height. "I've heard a little community folklore, too, you dolt. You were engaged. It's that spunky Julie Watson, returned to manage her father's pharmacy.

Get her!" Amy controlled her fingers, so as to not stick the appropriate one in the air. "I won't be your *byegones*' roll in the hay. Get out!"

Brandon's shoulders visibly slumped. He shuffled out the door, taking the pizza with him. His instant departure, pizza in tow, assured Amy she'd guessed right. She refused to get played. Dude still thought he was magnetic. She showed him otherwise.

Amy almost felt sorry for him. Almost, but not more or less than Travis, whose bar she'd soon own. While she didn't want or need to eviscerate Brandon—he was a nice lunk whom she'd once loved—Amy craved revenge. She lusted and hungered for Travis' downfall.

He deserved no grace, while Brandon did. The over-grown kid couldn't help that his parents had raised an entitled child.

Amy followed Brandon outside, watched him lurch into his damn red truck. He spun the tires as he backed down the drive. When he leaned out the driver's side window to toss Amy a wave, his expression betrayed his loneliness.

Amy glued her arms the sides of her body, cocking a hip to punctuate the rejection she'd dispensed. It felt good to dump Brandon's ass a second time. A second divorce.

Amy was ready to stomp forward into her giddily-rich rebelution.

Chapter Sixteen

MOVING ON

IT WAS EARLY afternoon, clouds roiling across the sky when Ronnie returned. Amy was ready, her butt perched on the couch, lips sealed around a beer from which she'd taken a huge glug. Ronnie's eyebrows lifted. Amy saw the question marks in both eyes. Ronnie skip-toed in, tossed her keys on the table, fluffed several large pillows to settle in next to Amy, and then plopped.

As if in afterthought, Ronnie shrugged out of her jacket before she swiped the bottle and took a long pull. Soon, the jacket became part of the coat explosion on the over-burdened coat rack near the door.

Ronnie was no more lady-like than Amy,but Amy was thirsty and miffed. She waited for the pause between her gulps before she snatched the bottle back. Dang, it was empty! Frustrated, Amy popped up to retrieve two cold ones from the frig and opened them both with a ruined thumbnail.

The two bottles formed a bouquet of sorts. Ronnie watched Amy take a swig with each step, miming a bride uncertain about her walk down the aisle. Not until Amy returned to the couch did she speak. She folded her hands and leaned forward, sort of speaking to the frig. She didn't attempt to snatch the bottle, perhaps sensing Amy might tomahawk her arm.

"Looks like you are headed for a bender, girl. What's gotten into the newly-minted millionaire's craw? The lottery numbers weren't a mistake, were they?"

Though Amy lowered the bottles, she didn't speak. The fact was, while she'd been bold and decisive before, her determination had crumbled. She wanted to pull the covers over her eyes and sleep into a catatonic state. To cocoon somewhere, anywhere.

Further, Amy was more than abashed. She'd withered under the pressure of being around Brandon, whereas she hadn't when she'd stalked into Travis' bar only a few days prior. Was she still in love with him, still craving the simple respectability of farm life? Where weather was the only chaos in a reliable routine?

She'd shooed Bran away, but still—

Ronnie grabbed a beer bottle, held it to the light to see that it was already empty, got up and shook her head. "This is a symptom of trauma that can't be contained by glugging into an alcohol haze." She turned her head to level-eye Amy. "Whatever it is, it can be solved, and I'm solid with you." Her eyes never left Amy's face, daring her not to dissolve into tears.

Amy hiccupped and looked bleak. Then, Ronnie knew, well and truly, that Brandon had been here. Hell, his aftershave, 'Au de Unwashed Clothes', filled the air. Her face softened, as if she saw something in her friend's expression that reinforced her guess, and she started to speak.

Amy cut her off. She wasn't one for *tea-and-sympathy*. She wasn't one for tea. The taste buds on her tongue were in open revolt for more beer. To wash away the taste of milk.

Amy's head swiveled, slowly, as if of its own accord. She wasn't sure if she'd gone through a metamorphosis or survived a meltdown. The past few days had been topsy-turvy gone-to-hell. Any compass she possessed, moral or otherwise, had vanished.

Ronnie began quietly, as if to mirror Amy's mood, "I'm eager to leave this dead-end town with its extreme lack of eligible men." Her volume rose higher with each declaration. She shouted, "I want to shove a cake in the face of the next stupid broad who orders pink rosebuds, in which I apparently specialize!" She tossed back her raven locks and continued near-whisper, "I felt alive the other night when we brainstormed your plastic surgery recovery hideaway. I want to hideaway with you."

Amy startled. She could feel her eyes bug, her pupils dilate. How could Ronnie be so sure when she wasn't? She was the strong, bold, and brazen one.

Now she felt bewildered—and epically so. Maybe being blonde had been her lone super power.

"Whatever the plans are, I'll go along anyway. I don't know why. Take me away before I change my mind." Ronnie bolted from the couch and leapt toward her bedroom. One-by-one, Amy discerned the rattle-and-roll of three suitcases.

Ronnie rolled one of them to Amy and steadied it against the couch. "You only require the small one, am I right?" Amy sat there numbly while Ronnie packed, occasionally emerging from her bedroom to affirm her resolve to get out of town. "Did I tell you I hate pink?" and "I think I've developed carpal tunnel from slathering icing in rows without visible seams."

She called to Amy only once to struggle a large rectangular lidded bin from the shelf of her closet, now barren of clothing and shoes. While the plastic box was opaque, showing it to be empty, its size worked against balance-on-tiptoes.

"This is to pack my baby bud plants. You didn't think I'd leave them to the next renter, did you?" She whisked out to the porch.

Ronnie was as industrious as Amy was not. The contents of Amy's closet and backpack could be dumped into the small suitcase Ronnie had gifted. Packing would take three seconds. A shocking statistic.

Amy rose from the couch and surveyed the interior of the modest house. When Ronnie paused in the doorway to stomp dirt off her shoes, she said, "Well, if you're intending to leave the house to a rental agency, you might as well leave the furniture, silverware, frying pans, and all."

Bye-bye Bic lighter and beaker, Amy hoped.

Ronnie edged into the kitchen, not taking her eyes off Amy's face.

"We can buy more," Amy assured. She nodded her head for emphasis.

Ronnie concentrated on washing her hands at the chipped enamel kitchen sink. She reached for the lady bug embellished towel, draped on the oven handle, blinking as she rubbed her hands dry. "I like that you said *we,"* she said. "I guess you've just hired me as your spa manager. Let's roll before I smell a rat."

She grabbed a teddy bear lamp, the lady bug towel, and a suitcase, and she headed out the door. The next sound Amy heard was the bumpety-bump of her bag off the porch. Ronnie plucked her car keys from the table and clutched them in a fist. Then she disappeared, soon tramping back for her second suitcase.

Amy dumped her meager wardrobe into the borrowed suitcase after belting a wild whoop-whoop. She had a sidekick. *We* had a plan. She had money aplenty and an inner circle of five or six stalwarts. Life was golden.

Because *we* had two cars, Ronnie and Amy stuffed in a few more things besides the three suitcases, the backpack, Ronnie's tiny weed garden, and the uber-ugly childhood lamp. Like an ice chest of beer and bottled water, boxes of nibbles and other miscellaneous food from Ronnie's refrigerator and shelves.

Each auto interior contained a mixed bag of scents, maybe mirroring mutual mixed feelings for this move.

They'd just closed the trunks when Amy's phone chimed. Her eyes popped at the caller ID. It was Dad.

"Go have one final pee and look around your house. See if we left anything that might come in handy. I've gotta take this call." Ronnie's bladder must have agreed. She sprinted to obey.

Amy walked as far from Ronnie's front door as she could before the fifth ring. She didn't want her parole officer's call to go to voicemail. The timing of his call caused Amy to fear that he had her under active surveillance, and she didn't want him to label her as a flight risk.

On the wide wooden porch, Amy swiveled slowly to scoop in as much sound as she could. Whew! She didn't hear sirens. She shook off her angst and answered cheerily, "Hi, Dad. How's your day going?"

"I'm supposed to ask the questions, child. A little birdie told me you were fixing to leave. That couldn't be true, could it?"

Brandon had ratted on her. Revenge had many paths and one of them was the county sheriff's tip line. Hell hath no fury like an abandoned little boy. Amy smiled brightly into space to avoid grinding her teeth. She sweetly sketched the plan to cross the state, to stretch long legs, get a glimpse of the lake, maybe stick a toe in.

"My bullshit detector is sending shock waves through my body. If I looked in my rearview mirror, I'd likely see my mustache bristling my nostrils at the stench of your lie. Do you want to start over, young lady?"

Hernandez was a pip. Amy wanted to tell him to *kiss my attitude*, but she 'significant eye-rolled' instead. She mimed WTF and the re-settled her face into *pleasant.*

She sighed and leaned back into one of the Italian Cypress trees. Its spikey texture bristled her back, as if Hernandez had hired it to underscore his message. So, this was what was meant by *the long arm of the law.*

"I know that you know I've been staying with my longtime friend, Veronica, while I worked out the details of lottery access," Amy began by re-asserting her *high road* sensibility, then delivered the emotional low, "My ex-husband dropped by and… " She added a chin quiver she hoped Hernandez could hear.

Not because Dad could see. Surely, he couldn't, though he might have binoculars on her. But, in hopes that the words would warble and elicit a level of empathy that would allow Amy to skip over the discussion with Ronnie that had taken an entire night: the plans to invest in a plastic surgery recovery spa, a project that would soak up thousands of hours and millions of cash. There were physician alliances to be formed, marketing, and networking, as well as physical construction that would expend bundles. The duo would be in South Haven for a long, long time, revenge on Travis as a not-so-sideline. Amy had promised herself to be his stalker-for-life. Not until he surrendered or submitted, down-and-out for life.

Hernandez grunted. Apparently, he wasn't convinced with her side-stepping excuse, because he delivered a lecture that he likely had memorized, "I'm mighty uncomfortable with your flighty nature, young woman. You lack discipline, Amy. May I remind you that I have you on a leash? You damn well better give me your address as soon as you light."

Amy seized the opportunity. How could she let such goodwill fly by? He wanted desperately to be in charge, so she gave him something. "Well, we have packed our bags and filled our trunks with with bits of miscellaneous. Know any place in South Haven where we can spend the night?"

When Amy promised to stay at the Comfort Inn, she'd unwittingly checked off a box on his list. Dad knew her address.

Amy knew Dad would be a guiding light in her quest to trust *if/when* she pried the tendency to lecture out of him. He wasn't a man with negotiable values. His voice so even-toned that you could curl up and sleep on it.

Amy had a true North.

Chapter Seventeen

ENTER THE LIONS

AH, SUMMER IN the Midwest! The next day was already sticky with humidity by the mid-morning when the ladies departed Ronnie's ramshackle home. Amy had already pitted out one of her only shirts during the Hernandez call. Now, three steps outside Ronnie's home, its front and back hung damp and limp on her lanky frame.

I can smell my own sweat. Time to high test the A.C. in my new car.

Amy adjusted the air vents—even those on the passenger's side where she'd seat-belted her backpack of belongings—until they blasted straight at her torso. She didn't want one of the few *nice* garments she owned to mildew.

The hyper-chilled air blasted away nerves, so Amy decided to ride without music. This shielded her from regret that her economical Focus wasn't equipped with Sirrius, the music service that Ronnie bragged on. Though Amy had millions, she'd maxxed her lone credit card with the car's purchase—and other miscellaneous purchases—so she couldn't afford the Sirrius upcharge.

She began to go with the flow. Ah-h-h.

But frets returned to smother her. Step-by-step procedure and patience had never been Amy's long suites. She'd have pried the entire winning sum loose if it were pirate booty—she'd have sunk any ship in her path. But the State of Michigan's Lottery Commission was a hard pirate to wrangle. *They* had rules.

Amy couldn't help but think if she'd buddied with Travis, the treasure would be hugged close to her chest, along with his sexy hairy one. Once upon a time…

But the pond scum had screwed the wrong pooch. Amy intended to take him down. She cycled between revenge scenarios and lusty bedroom scenes to handle her confused and over-stressed psyche. Two birds in hand, one in the bush… something like that.

Her jaw often ached after the daydreams—no matter which one—and Amy realized she was grinding her teeth. Again. Like every night of her two thousand while in prison… where she'd never received dental care.

Amy shook her head after catching a glimpse of herself in the mirror. She had to admit that her hair was pirate black, her teeth were a pirate's grizzled set. All she needed was a peg leg and an eye patch.

Certainly, she felt as if one eye had been patched

when she ran off with handsome and dangerous Travis, abandoning the safety of egotistical, yet feckless Brandon. Her inner lusty wench was winning the war about Travis' utility in her life. She might not be better off if he were dead.

Amy reached toward the radio dial, to find music to match her mood, but every station fritzed with static.

She didn't want heavy metal. That would remind her of the prison exercise yard. Country music was peppered with lame, sad stories of drunks, which would remind her of Travis' bar. Sweet Brahms wouldn't do, either. She'd never felt this flummoxed and indecisive. Amy knew her mood was as difficult to gauge as Ronnie's. Each was a lonely ping-pong in her car.

Ronnie had left behind familiar and leap-frogged to the new, but what about me, Amy whined to herself in the mirror. *My jettison from prison was jarring enough, but my heart whiplashed at the sudden circumstances of my wealth. I'd already traveled far up the state and then down again, like a soldier obeying a sergeant who had dislocated his compass, both moral and east-west-north-south. Except for Hernandez, my true North.*

The gals-on-the-run caravanned to South Haven without incident, the country road straight and smooth. For all Amy knew, Hernandez had a surveillance drone whirling above. *At least he didn't insist on attaching a red bubble light atop his car to lead the parade. I needed to slide into my new town incognito, neither marked as a millionaire on the make nor as a felon on parole.*

The duo arrived at near-noon and drove down the main drag, in search of a place for lunch. Amy turned on a blinker to indicate she'd spotted a restaurant that looked down on its heels, yet its parking lot was packed with vehicles. A sign of good eats inside when dedicated locals lined up. A trio of law enforcers' cars assured the kitchen was copacetic with the health inspector.

Ronnie circled the block to locate a parking spot, so Amy checked her hair and makeup and set her phone on silent. Her brother had continued texting wild-ass. Amy needed to channel his enthusiasm and tweak his spirit into line. A tough balancing act portended, but it would be done—as much for her as for him.

Amy shoved her phone deep in her backpack and startled when Ronnie rapped on her car window. She gathered herself and looked up at the restaurant's sign: MISS ELLIE'S HOMESICK GRILL. How apt!

Amy took her time unfolding herself from the Focus, while Ronnie antsy-pantsed outside. Amy smiled ruefully into her side mirror. *I might have to bend and shape Ronnie, too.*

As the business partners moved forward with their mildly-outrageous and wildly-inventive scheme, they would dot many 'i's and cross many 't's.

Deferring to Hernandez's quiet direction, of course. He'd be a good commandant. He'd closed his last call with, "A department motto indicates that the quality of the information shared by a client is only as good as you demand. I set high standards, Amy, to see how high you will jump. Within bounds. Am I clear?"

Clear was good. She'd try to jump, not difficult when one's height is near six feet and half that height was legs, but—. If Dad was clear, Amy could mask her turmoil and inner upset. She decided to feel safe.

When Ronnie walked up to Amy's car, Amy smiled at her scowl and bounced out to join her on the sidewalk.

They marched into the restaurant in tandem, in step. Scents of maple and bacon and buttermilk pancakes tantalized their hunger. They each inhaled deeply and searched for a hostess stand.

Lots of eyes scrutinized their entrance, people probably scanning from the sidewalk, too, because windows spanned the front of Miss Ellie's diner. The men's eyes glistened as they came into close range. The atmosphere shifted from restaurant to zoo, the animals preparing to circle the new meat.

The hostess hadn't gotten aboard the eyeballing train. She stood rigid at her station as if guarding the cash register, all negativity and restraint. Amy had never had to waitress, but she recognized a chip of the shoulder. *Here were two females who'd be demanding and then not leave a suitable tip*. Also, someone to wrest the male clientele's adoration away from her. Ms. Sturdy Waitress relied on those tips. Maybe, she had a child and no child support.

Amy'd made it a habit to refute her *sex-bomb* competitive projection whenever possible, sometimes grabbing the check before her ex could pay it. Women's equality had to begin with women, and Amy always finished what someone else started. A college professor had been at the vanguard when a forward-thinking movement had tried to add the Equal Rights Amendment to the Constitution in the '70s.

"Table for two, please." Amy forced eye contact on the sullen waitress and smiled. Then leaned in to squint her nametag. "Marnie."

The gal's ears perked—and she looked over her shoulder—when a boisterous voice shouted, "Amy, come join us. We're having a membership drive today." Marnie's face shifted from indifference to delight and cemented into a plastic smile.

Ronnie and Amy were IN.

Chapter Eighteen

THE LIONS DEN

A MAN WITH a comb-over and a worn high school letter jacket waved both arms high over his head. The jacket was open to reveal a blue shirt with a Lions club logo on the left pocket. His exuberance toppled two pair of eyeglasses from his shirt pocket, yet he didn't bend to retrieve them. "Amy!"

Because he was already bounding towards Amy. *It's great the man recalls voices, because it's doubtful he can see my face.* The glasses clearly showed bifocal lenses that were as thick as thumbs.

Two other men immediately launched from their seats to recover the glasses, colliding in their eagerness to kowtow. The man must have been some kind of poobah. Outgoing in the extreme, a born leader of the band. Ronnie shook her mane, looking quizzically at Amy. All Amy could do was shrug back.

Marnie thrust menus into their hands, and the

new chickas-in-town moved in imitation of *Victoria's Secret* models. By the time they arrived at the hearty greeter's table, two places had been cleared by a wait staff eager to please, with two blue-shirted men scurrying like rats to other nearby tables, clutching their plates, glasses, and coffee cups at odd angles that defied gravity.

The man had a fringe of red hair. Amy suppressed a grin to not rejoin his hearty "hello" with a remark that flew into her mind: *he looks like a circus clown.* He was clearly the ringmaster here.

The exuberant man extended both hands and grab-pulled Ronnie and Amy into chairs on either side of his. "I never forget a voice, Amy. I'm Phil Lactose, the manager of New Horizons."

Amy looked at Ronnie, and she looked back.

Phil interjected, "The substance abuse rehab facility that the local economy thrives upon." As if on cue, the entire Lions club gathering erupted in laughter and giddy shouts! It seemed each member had made a deposit to reserve a future room in the drunk tank facility.

Phil turned to Ronnie. "May I reserve one for you, Miss…"

Ronnie blurted her name and then put her hand over her mouth, as if to indicate she was nonplussed to be known and truly wished to fall through the floor. Amy avoided eye contact, lest she get pulled into the vortex of regret.

The Mayor gaveled for a full minute to rein in the uproar, then puffed-up his chest to proclaim that he'd retained a suite, an announcement that summoned applause. More rat-a-tat gaveling ensued.

Soon the broader introductions began, each man rising from his seat to introduce himself and then slap a card into each gal's hand. Amy felt grateful that no one genuflected. The act would have reminded her too much of church.

And, I'd have felt compelled to run.

"Order anything you want off the menu," Phil hiss-whispered. "Our Lions Club will pick up the tab." Then he purloined the wood gavel, slammed it within inches of Amy's plate, and said, "Am I right, fellows?"

The ascent thundered like beer hall applause. Amy hung her head and busied herself with rifling the business cards. Eureka! She'd already accumulated a realtor, a contractor, a local banker, an electrician, and an insurance broker within minutes of being in town. All resources to build out the plastic surgery recovery spa.

Holy shit! The local pastor of the Episcopalian Church had slipped his card into the bunch. Amy's revenge-on-Travis plans traipsed away.

The meeting proceeded jovially during lunch. Amy avoided listening to the various and sundry issues, such as who would ride the National Blueberry Festival float in the annual August event, and should the parade route be altered to pass by the Episcopalian Church where parishioners would be lining the curb with collection plates.

The pastor was the group's treasurer and held a lot

of sway. His shirt was as deeply creased as his elderly face, shirtsleeves rolled up to his elbows, the better to gesticulate as he jawed. It was apparent his Sunday sermons were a huge draw. His style seemed more Holy Roller than staid Episcopalian. He probably morphed into John the Revelator before his parishioners' eyes.

Amy rolled her eyes back into her head and concentrated on keeping the grilled cheese from oozing out the sides of her mouth and looking-not-looking at Ronnie. Both positioned paper napkins properly on laps and kept their elbows in, so as not to bump bodacious Phil. Each chewed quickly and thoroughly, trying not to plop on blouses, to draw any more attention to bosoms by wiping and scrubbing at stains.

After lunch and lots of promises to return to the meeting next week, the new gals-in-town climbed quickly into their vehicles and drove to the Comfort Inn, refraining from tossing kisses as cajoled by the male hosts' body language.

They dual-GPS'd to the Comfort Inn on Lake Michigan's shore. The vista rushed to welcome them, the waves gentle, unlike the Pacific's insistent surge. Amy wondered if the gentleness would rock her to sleep as the Pacific's rock-and-roll had when she'd slept under the Long Beach pier.

The waves may have been gentle, but Amy's attitude wasn't. As soon as the ladies snuggled their rides into spaces in the lot, she jumped from her car, loped to Ronnie's, and motioned her to scroll down the driver's side window. Amy commanded Ronnie, in the most severe terms she could muster—even shaking her finger in Ronnie's astonished face—to leave her weed patch behind, covered by jackets and obscured by the butt-ugly lamp. The hatchback had a lot of glass on its backside.

Ronnie gained new awareness of the perils of ganga. Hernandez knew Amy's precise location and could appear for a sudden inspection of their temporary abode. It was, after all, *the* motel he'd suggested, so the inn keeper may well have been a spy. Amy couldn't chance the parole violation, especially when it was not her personal violation, but the company she kept.

When Ronnie began to whimper, Amy softened her bluster with a promise to replace the stash if it withered as its plastic coffin heated in the summer sun, crossing her fingers behind her back.

Because Amy's plan was to trash the stash, using her well-honed childhood dumpster-diving skills in reverse.

As soon as they'd checked into their shared room and unpacked their meager wardrobes, Ronnie and Amy strolled to the concrete pier, wearing light jackets. Amy's body ached from bending into a small space and her right foot complained about the constant, stiff-legged position of the several hour drive. Her toes threatened to remain clenched inside her boots.

A pier beckoned them to walk.

The air was dank, the sun still clawing to get

through fog. Amy fingered her rescue inhaler in her jacket pocket to assure that she'd be safe from an asthma attack.

The air cloyed with its sweltering heat. A mildly acrid odor of fish and flotsam filled their nostrils as the duo looked from the red lighthouse in the water just beyond the pier, and then back at their temporary resort. Amy thought that the lighthouse at the end of the pier resembled a bucolic red barn silo, its presence on the horizon unavoidable and stark. Until now the only silo she'd 'met' was blue enamel, on the Breeden Dairy Farm.

She began to deep-breathe, but soon shallowed her respiration, remembering her tendency to asthma attack. The act led to a yoga calm, the first Amy had felt in years.

Suddenly, Ronnie abandoned her to run to the end of the pier. Though the lake was far below the pier's stilt-like legs, Ronnie abandoned her shoes and wiggled her toes. The sun sparked her toe ring and her hair was a-sail. Even Amy's short, black haystack flickered her ears, as acrid air tickled her nostrils.

The lake water gently slapped the concrete and a few sea gulls screeched. Amy may or may not have heard a distant dog bark. Maybe someone's pet as it scampered in the waves down the beach. There'd been several cars parked in the lot, so other people had to be about, but the stillness was complete. The sense of calm infiltrated her soul.

Incomprehensibly, Hernandez called. His timing continued to stun Amy and, not for the first time, she believed he possessed either the eyes of God or a drone.

"I think I've found the spot, Dad. South Haven's it."

"Good, Amy. I've longed to put a fence around you in the few days since you became my case, but I'm not allowed. My role is to contain the chaos that, I sense, bubbles inside you at all times, like lava in a volcano ready to erupt." He paused. Amy imagined a calculated hand pulled up to his chin. "Now you've given yourself a boundary I don't have to monitor. The lake, am I right?"

"How did you know I can't swim?"

"I'd heard it's a common Californian malady, to grow up in proximity to the ocean but never acquire the skill because the water's too dang cold. Anyway, thanks for helping yourself out. The state of Michigan is tired of paying your room and board."

To which Amy bit her tongue so as not to sass, "Did you forget that I'm a millionaire, with enough money to buy the state?"

Chapter Nineteen

HOUSE HUNTERS

THAT AFTERNOON RONNIE and Amy gave each other mani-pedis in their dinky motel bathroom while watching silly soap operas alternate with far sillier talk shows. Amy was glad that she was yoga-limber so that she could stretch her legs skyward to use the sink for soaking her mangy cuticles. Ronnie sat on the side of the bathtub to accomplish her soak.

When Ronnie told her the color of the OPI she was about to apply, "Put It in Neutral," Amy insisted on glitter polish on her toenail tips, to bely that subliminal message. She was a star with millions to spend. She was golden and did not to intend to put anything in neutral. NOO-O-O.

While Amy typically despised such girlie-girl routines, the stinky polish masked the aroma of the bedraggled drapes with bedspreads that matched. The thin carpet had been laid directly on the concrete slab, so the ladies tread lightly in the functional-and-conjoined bed-and-bath room. They mutually agreed that *their* spa's accouterments would not be this spare. Splendor would be expected by a hyper-rich clientele—and them. Splendor was going to be fun to squander beaucoup bucks on—as necessary camouflage for her ultra-large amount of cash to splash.

With that inspiration, Amy fast-forwarded their splurge, to start today. On themselves.

She duck-walked, her still wet polished toes spread apart by rolled bits of TP. Amy surveyed Ronnie's eau de parfums and selected 'Far Away' because that's how she felt. She sprayed the bathroom, she sprayed the bedroom, she sprayed upward, at the dingy ceiling tiles. She sprayed until her forefinger ached.

Ronnie's nose revolted. That girl screwed up her pretty face and moved to open the mini window in the bathroom. "There are days that not even chocolate can make palatable," Ronnie said after she settled on the rank bedspread and admired her toes. She extended her toes to the ceiling, wiggled them to-and-fro and then stuck out her tongue at Amy, as if to say "I have yoga moves, too."

Amy retreated to the bathroom, where the 'Far Away' fumigated the room, almost gagging her. *I overdid it again.* She drew a 'Skin So Soft' bath and settled in for a full body soak. When it came to other people—especially those forced into close proximity—you never knew when you were going to hiccup or hit a landmine.

Amy hum-de-dum-dummed and reclined into the

bath. She was ready to relax 'Far Away', up to her chin and down to her soon-to-be withered toes. When Amy broke into "We are the Champions," Ronnie poked her head into the bathroom.

"The hubris and humidity in this room has melted your make-up and you sound like a walrus giving birth!" Amy watched Ronnie rip the tissue from between her toes, toss it into the trash, and then slam the door.

Amy heard the jangle of grabbed keys and lurch about the bedroom gathering up a change of clothes. Soon she heard the outer door slam.

"You'll hate the look of your face, too, when you glance in your hatchback's mirrors," Amy shouted after her. "And, your hair has staged a rebellion! You're not going to impress anyone in this small town…"

She and Ronnie had shared a fledgling friendship of giggles, make-up, and rants a day over two weeks. Ronnie's double door slam indicated what stage they were in now. They were bonded to the core via many threads of coincidence and those coincidences were slim. In the moment Amy might take a sword for her compadre, but doubted Ronnie would take one for her. Their friendship was *fragile.* And truly, Amy knew in her heart of hearts, she would take a sword for no one.

Despite the chill of the bath water, Amy remained in the tub. It calmed her spit- fire reverie and retorts.

Amy's millionaire spirit writhed, itching to spend. But Ronnie had insisted that they store energy for the ardor of scouting suitable locations in thin building pickings, staving the search for another day. They might have to shuffle up/down the Lake Michigan shore. Nearer to Chicago's Gold Coast, which had already lapped up Indiana's brief stretch of coastline and was reaching for the Michigan state line. They might even have to consider Holland, a popular resort that mined people's fondness for tulips and folklore in exchange for stories of stupidity to recount during the off-season. Tourists never failed to disappoint their antics and cash.

Tulips. Ha, many of their future patients might have two lips done, too. Plumped up in fakery to help camouflage a chin tuck or divert attention from a face lift. Amy amused herself with a few snide remarks she'd never be able to say aloud, once the spa opened for business.

Further, Amy didn't want recent girl bonding rituals to mellow her snark and bite. Brain-bitching had been sport in prison, and she didn't want her well-honed skills to slide. Her skin could soften via the leisurely bath, but her wits needed to remain sharp.

The Lions Club realtor/member Elvin Goodrich called at 4:45. "Hiya. Am I speaking with Amy?"

Amy had already input the names, phones, and addresses of each of the potential helpers into her phone contacts, but she played shy. How'd Elvin get *her* phone number? Was Mr. Lactose, the Lion's Club President, already pandering to his members' businesses?

"I'll see if she's available. Who is calling?" Amy had seen a movie or two. Didn't want to gain a stalker in this sparsely-populated town. Being on Dad's leash was enough encumbrance for her independent spirit to abide.

In addition, Amy-the-Lottery-Winner had been coached by Amy-in-the-Lottery-Office to keep a low profile. Though her win was officially private, newspaper headlines in the racks at Miss Ellie's Homesick Grill were bold and speculative. Didn't want locals to catch on and ply me for loans. Especially not when she'd landed in the laps of the Lions Club, where gossip was a hobby called *networking*.

"I'm certain she'll remember me. This is Elvin Goodrich."

Amy pictured no one from the sea of faces at the lunch meeting, though she did recognize his name from her instant Rolodex of business cards. The aligned perfection of his God-given name and her lottery win almost knocked her flat, but Amy gripped the side of the tub so she wouldn't drown.

Unf*ing believable. Amy felt like a winner all over again. Life as a Michigan millionaire was gonna be golden.

Just then Ronnie burst into their motel room. When she saw Amy's smug look, she grinned. *Maybe she was merely imitating me, Amy thought, but she looks happy all over. Especially with her spectacular toes and fingernails.* Amy barely noticed Ronnie's humidity-curled locks, the frizzed-up hair she'd gaffed Ronnie about earlier.

In truth, she felt relief that her friend had returned. Maybe Ronnie's hissy fit was a sign of homesickness for her gingerbread house. Their departure *had* been sudden.

Amy gestured Ronnie to the business card stack on the bureau. Ronnie went over and rifled the stack, stage-whispering each name until Amy nodded at Elvin Goodrich and his title, Realtor and member of the Millionaires Club for Coldwell Banker.

Ronnie howled, dropped the card, and rolled on the floor. She giggled and wiggled and laughed, but not overlong. The carpet was crumby—in not much better shape than when she'd walked out an hour ago.

"I'm delighted you called, Mr. Goodrich. I was planning to come by your office tomorrow morning."

"Well, there's no time like the present to start. I was about to head home for supper. Would you like to join me and the wife?"

Amy mouthed 'supper?', gestured the question with a lift of her shoulders, and pointed to the phone. Ronnie caught on quick and nodded. There didn't seem to be an abundance of restaurants in town and they'd failed to grocery shop—or fish when they walked the pier.

They'd both forgotten about the weed in the hatchback.

Well, Amy hadn't forgotten. She had plans that were all good. It'd be golden to be free of that temptation.

"Thank you," she replied, smiling in hopes that Elvin would see it through the phone. Amy was relieved to have to miss a meal.

"Pick you up in ten minutes?"

Amy raised her eyebrows and flashed five fingers

twice to Ronnie, who tested her fingernails, and then flashed back fifteen. Apparently, she had seen her hair because she plugged in her hair straightening device.

"Make it fifteen. And thanks, Mr. Goodrich."

"I look forward to it. Please call me Elvin."

Amy hung up and dashed to the closet to put on one of her suits. She'd never, ever abandon calling him Mr. Goodrich. The name was better than apropos.

Amy needed to snicker about something, so she did, engaging her image in the mirror in a prolonged high-five. It was time for some relief from all the mania attached to the millions, the plans, the methods, the investments, the responsibilities. Amy wanted the spree of spending to begin! To at least purchase the most outrageously expensive morning coffee drink the local barista made!

What would Travis, the barman, make for her? Something delicious and dumb? Something she could imitate and surreptitiously dump Roofies, the date rape drug, into—and cart him to The Rack installed in the basement in her new abode.

CHAPTER TWENTY

GOOD AND RICH

THE CLUNK OF a car door thundered outside their hotel room. A quick look at her cell told Amy that Elvin had an elastic relationship with time, meaning he was late. It was all good because she and Ronnie had needed the time.

It had been hard to apply makeup after swigs of the fledgling and watered-down coffee made with the machine in their room. She longed for the best Starbucks confections money could buy to celebrate the start of her rebelution life.

Ronnie touch-up/smoothed her dress as well as Amy's suit, with her hair straightener.

Elvin flashed each young woman a fresh business card and squired them to his Cadillac, somehow opening both doors to impress.

A realtor's Cadillac more heftily built than Amy's new Ford Focus and Ronnie's old Pinto, a High Roller ride. The Starbucks stop felt imperial when the sthe barista personally trotted the coffee confections to the car. Amy began to enjoy the cushy accoutrements of being good and rich. Elvin paid.

The lack of road noise or radio allowed Amy to sip and swivel-head as the vehicle drove the single street downtown and into quaint neighborhoods. The streets had names, mostly trees of the locale, Elvin related. Amy knew none of them. The placid simplicity hinted that it might be easy to get lost within the confines of this town, to feel forever safe and blessed.

Amy began to doubt that this area—away from the shore lined with shoddy bait shops and motels—was amenable to their purpose. Sleepily stuck in the '50s, it seemed stifling and insular. Their elaborate spa, no matter where placed, might attract questionable infamy and gossip. Especially because they'd hire staff from among the local population.

Elvin's voluble nature nonplussed. Ronnie handled his endless prattling while Amy studied the horizon behind her giant sunglasses. She watched him tick-tock his eyes across the rearview, between Ronnie and her seat-belted into his back seat, to suss the source of the money and how much was at play? His squint-eyed visage reminded Amy of a weasel.

Suddenly Veronica boomed, "How do you know where you're headed, Elvin? Everything looks the same!"

His laugh was immediate and boisterous. "Folks do get lost. Get lost all times of day and night. It gives the only cop something to do. He pulls tourists over when they bob-and-weave. High dollar tickets if they're texting or using an app to find a location. South Haven's constituents valued their privacy and their never-raised taxes, something achieved when the law shivs the tourists with tickets and add-on fees."

Amy looked at Ronnie and Ronnie looked back. While *privacy* was desired for the spa, *sequestered and dull* wouldn't suit. It was obvious that all supplies, maybe even food, would need to be ordered from Amazon. Time to establish a Prime account.

Elvin pulled to the side of a street without sidewalks, put the Cadillac-as-limo in park, and brought his arm across the back of the seat. He looked at Ronnie and Amy and smarmed, "Now what did you say your price range was? And, how many bedrooms do you seek? Do you wish to purchase a rental property, a summer home, or a permanent residence?" He rat-a-tatted inquiries like a Gatling gun.

Amy didn't know how to field this flurry or finesse the B.S. She hadn't perused prices of real estate in the area. Caught off-guard, Amy telescoped inward.

Ronnie must have seen it, too, because she reached over to grasp Amy's hands, as if to save her friend from careening over a cliff that wasn't there.

"Oh, you gals are gay. You'll be cohabiting, sharing expenses and bed and *things*. Don't worry, your secret is safe with me. Locals don't mind. Even gays' money is green." He chortled and turned off the car. He no longer seemed messianic. Instead, more like a demonic Charles Manson.

Just then a chummy blonde yoohooed from the

bric-a-bracced porch. Who knew how long she'd stood there. She seemed untroubled by Elvin's lateness and/or two extra lipstick-laden mouths to leave smudges on her glassware.

Elvin bounded out of the car and ran to open the Cadillac's back doors. He yelled over his shoulder, "Sorry, honey. These are the two ladies I texted you about. We aren't too late for supper, I hope?"

Linda beamed. "Honey, there's always room for two more prospects." She smoothed her frilly white apron. She swept back into the home, leaving the entry door ajar. Her apron and actions reminded Amy of Jackie Breeden and a sense of forlorn longing entered her soul.

For a moment. *Forward. I must look forward, not back.*

When the realty trio entered, she chirped from the dining room, which seemed to round the bend and down a hall. "Be sure to wash your hands. The powder room is reserved for the ladies, Elvin. Mind your manners, Dear."

Ronnie and Amy looked at each other and shrugged as Elvin swooped into the dainty small room and slammed the door.

When the newcomers peered into the dining room, long lavender tapers were lit and other guests were seated at the mahogany table, their plates strafed of food. Supper had apparently begun long, long ago. The mashed potatoes were half-emptied from their fine china bowl and the platter was depleted of ham. Other guests?

Elvin slipped into his place at the head of the table and tucked a large linen napkin under his chin. He looked ready to lunge at the biscuits but held his manners in check to make introductions. Hands were shaken and then everyone at the table returned to scarfing the meal. Ronnie and Amy, his supper guests, effectively disappeared into the woodwork and paisley wallpaper.

Elvin may have neglected to share that his home was a small B&B, but he wasted no time proclaiming that it was for sale—in front of his guests who looked at each other, questioning if they should pack now. Conversation collapsed while the guests shoveled what might be their last meal.

The splash of water in crystal goblets and knives and forks occasionally clanging swelled as Ronnie and Amy reached to serve themselves and eat. The remainder of the meal, including devil's food cake, passed silently except for Elvin's drone and his wife's amenable titter.

Suddenly, abruptly all were excused, Elvin waltzed his realty prospects to the door, handing each another card before he escorted them back to the Hush-Hush Motel.

Twenty minutes later, Ronnie and Amy exited Elvin's boat-of-a-car, eager to return to the safety and sleep of their suddenly very comfy room. Dude had issues. Neither liked surprises, and he'd pulled too many fast ones for one night. Starbucks seemed the only plus.

Elvin bounded around his car, almost impaling

himself on the hood ornament, pumped their arms, and began to bid goodnight. He looked haggard and ready to hit the hay.

Then, unaccountably, he began to gush about The Asylum Inn. Its historical significance couldn't be overstated, he said, and it was for sale.

Amy snuck a look at Ronnie. *Our supper was for sale?*

The Asylum Inn had been an institution in the '30s and blah-blah-blah, the deal blighted. While Amy had never shared the intimate details with Ronnie, an asylum had once been her schizzy mom's abode. The Asylum Inn would be forever off limits.

Besides, Elvin had blah-blah-bored too long. Ronnie and Amy winked at each other and backed away, agreeing to meet Elvin at his office at 10:00 the next day.

He said. "You can't miss it! It's next door to the laundromat. I often sell homes to tourists who come to do a weeks' worth of laundry…because I've conveniently ringed the room with 8X10 photos of properties for sale."

Then, it was his turn to wink. "I also own the laundromat and provide all the single bills in change for the machines. I'm raking in as much money as those damn Indian casinos upstate."

With that, Ronnie and Amy dashed to their motel room and keyed the door open without a backward glance. They slammed the door, literally and figuratively on their diverse welcomes to South Haven.

CHAPTER TWENTY-ONE

WEED BE GONE

THE PLACE DIDN'T seem like a haven yet. Ronnie readied for bed—in five minutes. She pulled the bad bedspread over her head, an affirmation of Amy's thoughts.

Amy hastily brushed her pearly whites and gargled a bit of Listerine. "Night, Ronnie," she said, and began to tiptoe toward the door. She had an agenda, so she hoped to depart alone. At the tippy top of her list of things to achieve was trashing the plastic storage container of weed.

Amy texted Hernandez bid him a good night and to outline the next day's plans.

He texted back a thumbs up.

Amy whispered, "I'm going WalMart shopping."

Ronnie bounded out of bed, grabbed her car keys from the ashtray, and headed for the door, dressed only in an over-large tee shirt. "What?" she said to

Amy's look. "We're in a beach town, for gosh sakes! Let's pretend I have my bikini underneath this shirt."

Ronnie had misinterpreted Amy's dubious look, but the genie would not return to her bottle.

It was actually great for Amy that Ronnie drove. This teeny-tiny plot twist could work out well. She merely had to be stealthy in a WalMart parking lot, not switching the weed between the hatchback and Focus within feet of the motel door. Amy put on her black jacket, inhaler still in the pocket along with the room key, slammed the door, and marched to Ronnie's car.

Ronnie drove with purpose via the directions Siri gave, eager to see how another WalMart looked. Amy smiled, too. Peace of mind, food, and beach sandals would soon be hers. And, Amy knew that the box store was known to have gigantic dumpsters located in the shadows somewhere.

Amy pointed to the perimeter of the vast parking lot and directed Ronnie to park. She bought the excuse that they needed the exercise, if Amy promised to fetch the car and park closer to the front door when they had bags and bags full.

They bought cereal, bananas, apples, and chips. Milk, juices, and bottled water, but no beer. They inquired about a health club, both used to workouts to balance their calorie intake, but the clerk just shrugged and kept her eyes focused on the cash register punches. She looked too bored to have the items memorized. Perhaps it was a symptom of how boring and staid this town was.

Amy got vibrant pink beach sandals with glitter for a dollar. The upper soles were adorned with flamingos.

She left Ronnie with the numb-nuts cashier as the endless line of cardboard and produce and plastic bottles marshaled across the conveyer belt. Ronnie didn't object to payment on her credit card, which further blessed Amy's plan. More smiles.

Amy would make good on her part of the bargain, returning to push one of the over-large and very full carts to Ronnie's car, making certain she'd be the hatchback packer, grabbing the paper bags from Ronnie as she hefted them to the top of the cart. Amy would hustle, bustle, and assure Ronnie didn't notice that her coveted plants had vanished.

The busy women stashed the groceries and slept like babies.

While she didn't know what Ronnie dreamt, Amy's dreams were populated by hundreds of ways to avenge herself on Trav.

She could drop him with a b.b. gun, stuff him in a plastic container, and then haul him to a WalMart dumpster. If she were lucky – and he was not – it would be trash pick-up in the middle of the night. Every little boy's dream was, in Amy's experience, to ride in a trash truck, but Travis' experience would be decidedly different.

Travis could pound all he wanted on the semi-transparent plastic container, but the noise of the trash truck would compete and no one would hear. Travis would have plenty of time to rue the day he'd set her up, he'd rue the five years of days when he didn't visit her and give her hope with his return. He'd rue the days…because he'd be in a ginormous container on a slow boat to Singapore, where he'd be buried along with the rest of America's trash.

Ashes to ashes, dust to dust, there was no revenge better than to have Travis vanish from Earth's habitable surface. Perhaps he'd enjoy a one-way ticket to Mars.

Next morning, the real estate partners ate their light breakfast, and dressed, vowing to save time—and to collect quarters—to wash underwear and other clothes at the end of the day. The clothing section at WalMart had been picked over and—as ever, there were no slacks long enough for Amy's legs—yet glitzy sandals twinkled her toes.

Elvin's office was a contrast to his bombastic personality. Big ideas and big sales didn't show in any of his simple furnishings. The walls were faded pink and the carpet worn thin by voluminous traffic. Corny and tattered travel posters were scotch-taped to the walls and two upright chairs lined up against his desk, where Elvin haggardly shuffled slag heaps of paper. Ronnie and Amy stood, as if at attention, for several seconds and then slumped into his chairs. Each grabbed a copy of the Multiple Listings, which were larger than suspected, and included pictures.

There wasn't a coffee pot or dispenser of mountain spring water in sight. A smoldering cigar stank up the room. Bet his wife didn't allow cigars in the house.

Somehow cigars and taper candles didn't mix. Amy tried not to gag or inhale.

Ronnie snuck the smoldering cigar to her lips and dragged, exhaling smoke into Elvin's face. He bolted upright, dropped his fountain pen, and grinned. He didn't notice that ink blotched one of his important papers—he launched into a spiel. Clearly, he didn't recall his clients' names any more than he'd recalled their appointment. But he was here to sell.

The Stones' classic "Start Me Up!" resounded in Amy's ears as she stayed him with her hand. She extended her arm across the desk to shake his and re-introduce herself, then Ronnie. Elvin's eyebrows raised in recognition of who had the money and, thus, the lead.

Elvin took a deep breath and started up. H crooned his way through presentation of two properties that left them unimpressed.

"Let us have a look around the area," Amy said. "Let's get out of Dodge."

Ronnie winked at Elvin and then at Amy. Ronnie shrugged a question, "Should I go along." Amy suggested that Ronnie do the laundry. She said, "Good idea" and left.

Elvin ushered Amy out to the Cadillac, freshly polished and gleaming in the sun.

Chapter Twenty-Two

PROPER SEARCH

"I'VE DECIDED UPON a country manor," Amy said. "I've seen enough of this resort town to assure myself that it does not meet my privacy requirements. No buzz of boats, no impertinent gossip, and no cigar smoke."

Elvin had the grace to choke when Amy glared directly at him. She now possessed the upper hand and helped herself into the front seat of the Cadillac. There would be no cigars in the car.

Elvin didn't balk when Amy grabbed the MLS and began to thumb through the pages, letting herself in on realtor secrets and prices and deals. He merely put the car into gear and drove as if he were accustomed to being bossed by a woman half his age. Her adamant and headstrong manner may have disconcerted him, but he didn't disrupt her study. There would be no chatter in the car.

Amy looked up from the catalogue of home-for-sale listings when the Cadillac turned off Ash Street and slid into the driveway of a mansion on the outskirts of town. She looked at Elvin, who beamed at her, and then at the two-story brick building, with an impressively statuesque facade. Elvin urged Amy out of the car for a look, acquiescing to the fact that she wanted to lead. No preemptive swash-buckle of opened car door this morning.

When her silver sandals sank into the high-piled carpet of grass, Amy felt luxurious. Then the chiggers or 'no-see-ums' or fleas bit. She hopped back to the car, lickety-split. "Absolutely not," she spat at Elvin. "Slapping at bugs and/or spraying them does not fit into my business plans."

"How about that place?" Elvin pointed to an abandoned estate-like building across the wide street. It was not persuasive either. The two-story shamble needed many coats of paint and the cornices were crumbling near the uneven roof.

The house's thicket-of-weeds lawn daunted, too. While Amy knew a contractor by his Lions Club-proffered card, she was eager to begin her business rather than devote a year to construction. She wasn't certain that thong underwear under skintight slacks would be the bet motivation for a huge construction crew. Especially because she didn't own any thongs. Yet.

"Let's jet!" she said. When Elvin looked querulous, she explained, "I mean, let's drive further into the country."

As soon as the Cadillac headed out of town, the two-lane road began to swoop and gently curve and was sided by mature trees. Though the vehicle's windows were rolled up tight, Amy swore she could hear birds.

She began to feel that their team was on the right track. She and her ladies would be miles from lights and noise and commotion. Surrounded by quiet, secluded in the country. They would see the Milky Way Galaxy and star-gaze as long as they pleased. Even recover-lounge in the nude.

Elvin suddenly, discreetly rolled into a lane that seemed to emerge from nowhere.

He slowed to ease onto a gravel driveway, driving between golden brick columns on either side. There was no gate, long gone in history, but the stately effect of the entry suggested the way to great things. Amy was entranced.

The two-story mansion sported evenly spaced rectangular windows with green shutters and capitals on the outside and lace curtains flirting within. A sunroom addition on the front side of the expansive front door winked with its window blinds drawn halfway up/down. She glimpsed people moving about, china cups clinking on return to saucers, fork tines adding their music to morning. Positive energy bustled and hustled her toward the door.

"What's the address?" Amy asked. After Elvin complied, Amy texted Ronnie. DUMP LAUNDRY & GET HERE AS SOON AS YOU CAN.

When the hatchback rolled into the lane ten minutes later, Ronnie looked wide-eyed. She jumped out of her car as soon as it rolled to a stop and strode toward Amy and Elvin.

Now Elvin looked wide-eyed and led the way. The long-legged duo strode in on the wake of his goodwill, fervently hoping this wonderful place was listed by his firm. Neither wanted to dither with locating another realtor when there likely wasn't one. Nor did they want to lose a potential ally in this small town.

Elvin knocked on the door, awaiting the proprietor's welcome, and then squired Amy and Veronica into the stately home to begin a silent tour. He'd apparently learned not to clutter good looks with commentary. He didn't hover either, his hustler moves closeted for the day.

There were five tastefully decorated guest rooms, mildly Victorian but appealing. The near floor to ceiling windows were evenly spaced and shielded by gauzy lengths of peach cloth, proclaiming privacy for those within from those without. Filtered light filled the space with ambient peace. Sumptuous drapes suggested Scarlet O'Hara's Tara.

Instant comfort for a woman who'd just undergone surgical repair, the envisioned spa's clientele. There was a large living room with a fireplace bricked to match the exterior. Because it was summer, there was no fire, but Elvin assured them that it worked.

Glory upon glories there was a library with books

and movies. Amy envisioned multiple guests cozied into the many overstuffed chairs. Tasteful chintz with china roses in muted pinks, so feminine-wiled. A window seat with cushions…and a view of a screened in gazebo with a swing hanging from century old rafters. Amy's heart sang in synch with a grandmother she'd never had but imagined. In the constant daydream Amy read book after book, castle-building her way out of her squalid childhood.

Amy felt as though her head would explode with joy when they walked onto to a flat patio that led to a series of interlinking nature trails, paths lined with peonies and daisies and bees.

She'd forgotten Veronica's presence, deep into her daydream. She startled when Veronica screamed, "A bee is buzzing your ear! It's probably attracted by your hair spray!" She ran ahead.

Ronnie screamed again at something yet unseen. She ran back to grab Amy's hand, almost wrenching the arm from its shoulder socket as she darted away. In a clearing, near what Elvin reported was a well-stocked one-acre lake, stood a log cabin fronted by a screened-in porch large enough to accommodate a wood picnic table. It was like those seen in a park near the harbor, only these weren't populated with families eating.

So, Hansel and Gretel. Except for the aluminum screen door and redwood shutters latched harshly over the windows. To save the occupants from the wicked witch or bears?

Ronnie had fun musing aloud of this… Amy

didn't join. She busied herself running numbers and writing copy for brochures.

While Elvin didn't seem like the type to offer candy to children, he did sweeten the deal. "This place has been on the market since last summer. One of the sites pluses is that it's on city water and sewer, local utilities that one of our Lions manages and the rates for usage are low, low, low. Furthermore…" He paused for effect. "…the property's price has been lowered twice."

Though she inwardly smirked that Elvin would call this town a 'city', Amy outwardly beamed at the lowered price of the property. Ronnie was obviously overjoyed, so this would be a score, score, score.

Prepped to buy, Ronnie and Amy glided into the log cabin, heads swiveling to assimilate all details. Their eyes met. Each could tell by the look on the others' satisfied face that they agreed. They needed a more permanent place to live than the Hush-Hush Motel. This cozy cabin with its two bedrooms and full furnishings, complete with dusty linens and a few hundred cobwebs, would suffice. It could have been straight out of the fifties, except the TV had a remote and a DVR. An Air Wick provided a pleasant scent, as if Grandma had just put chocolate chip cookies in the oven. Golden.

A fireplace across the room was the solid feature, a welcoming wall, a boundary along one side. Its stones held a covering of soot to show that the cabin's incumbents enjoyed warm nights in front of its glow. It looked like the kind of chimney Santa Claus actually slid down, and Amy wanted to dash to WalMart to buy stockings to hang.

Ronnie and Amy converged at the fireplace. Ronnie whispered in her ear," This place is cute and cuddly. We can hunker and be kind."

Amy mouthed, "What?"

Ronnie cleared her throat, as if to prepare herself—and Amy—for a bold left turn.

'This place will accomplish your plans of moving forward and allow you to abandon your backward-looking revenge plans. Why taint your new life with bad plans? Haven't you ever heard the statement, 'Living well is the best revenge'? Forget about Travis, forget about the years you lost, and focus on what you'll gain. Let's splash some cash and have fun!"

Amy turned abruptly to shake Elvin's hand. She beamed. "I'll take it. What, again, was the price?"

Elvin whipped out his iPad. Amy signed on twelve lines on twelve cyber-pages. $485,000.00 cash. Amy's first hotel, her first home, her first renter, Veronica, and there would be many, many more.

Travis only had one dumb, drab-building bar. Don't look back, Star Amy.

Chapter Twenty-Three

CONUNDRUMS DRUM

THE HONEYMOON DIDN'T last. Though the log cabin was twice the size and configuration of Ronnie's home in Hiawassee County, somehow the fung didn't shei.

The cabin dated from the mid-1800s. Maybe the two hundred-and-fifty-year-old logs were warped. Perhaps the karma of early settlers, who'd battled Indians and clear-cut the land incited a kind of restiveness to which Americans are uniquely prone. Amy had a particularly bad case of restive.

Maybe it was a flaw in her moral stamina or her money burning a hole in her soul. Amy had been housed in a small space for an uncomfortable number of years and longed to get her show on the road. She'd endured a lifetime of hard scrabble, and she wanted to shed it, had the means to shed it, and didn't want to lose her steam.

Maybe it was the fact that she'd trashed Ronnie's baby weed plants, though guilty pleasure ruled. Amy declined to reveal where the plants were dumped. She knew mad-as-a-hornet-on-steroids Ronnie would retrieve them and coax them back to full health. At present Ronnie and Amy argued over contractor selection—as if they had a choice other than the single card shoved into their hands by a Lion Club member. While Amy agreed it would have been great to barter or persuade him to lower his bid with competition, in a town of 4400 people, one had little position other than abide. Who knew Ronnie was more contrarian than she? Who knew she expected to be half-boss?

Who knew she expected to be paid? A lot.

The gal pals-not-pals bickered over the list of luxury amenities and the local architect's renderings of what could be done to double the capacity of the Lady Bug Lodge. They squabbled over whether to call the Lady Bug a lodge or an inn. Whether to add the word "luxury" or to assume it was understood. Amy swore the turbulence was pushing her hair to grow. She had blonde roots—and her artful polish sported nicks and chips.

The glitter was gone.

By the time the thirty-day escrow closed, and all of the guests potentially relocated to other lodging, Amy wasn't in the mood to build. Ronnie was supposed to have been Amy's improvisational "Yes and" cohort. Instead, she'd become Amy's oppositional "No, but." Ronnie had ignited Amy's full-metal sass.

Because Ronnie morphed into a night owl who

elevated the TV volume as if to raise the dead, seemingly on a regretful quest to watch the entire video library in the main house, the last straw had been bent. Amy attended the next Lions Club meeting alone. She had several roles to fill: lawn mower, hedge clipper, a handyman who could handle plumbing. She also needed a cook, because Ronnie refused. "I retired from baking forever." Amy didn't know how. Spaghetti, ramen, and cold cereal had worn thin as rotating menu items, even with a pliable guy like her ex-Brandon.

Amy hated to admit it, but thinking of Brandon brought a smile to her lips.

The local Lions Club provided a well of resources for all necessities and needs. They were the community activists, with fingers in every pie. There always seemed an accommodation or solution among the band of brothers she'd gained.

Little did Amy know, the guys considered her the golden calf of jobs and cash, a resource to use and/or abuse. They'd supply free lunch as long as Amy remained.

In turn, Amy enjoyed the free lunch, sometimes taking leftovers to Ronnie to repay her kindness in the early days of couch-squatting. Amy reasoned—and was proven right—Ronnie wouldn't hold a grudge when there was grub.

They both gobbled the casseroles that began to show up so that local gossips could observe, first hand, what was going on. It was the best scene in town, and one they couldn't shut down. The women's hunger matched their curiosity, cores of daily life in a small community unfettered of crime and anger and angst.

The lookie-loos over-pooped the potties during their surveillance visits, maxing the century-old plumbing. The Lions Club lead turned out to be elusive to Amy's calls. A common contractor ailment, the small town voyeurs agreed. When a contractor said, "No problem", there always was.

Amy blubbered to Hernandez, who allowed he might know another parolee in the area, a plumber, who needed employ. He'd get back to her on that.

Amy had no doubt. Dad was a man whose promises one could set a clock's time on, whose persistence and punctuality were fanatic. He wasn't a man to tread uneven lines, a propensity she didn't know existed.

On Lions Club Tuesday, Amy attempted to sidle in, but a six-foot single woman couldn't get ignored amidst the crowded hyperactivity of local civic pride. Elvin Goodrich stood, gathering his belly in an attempt to stretch his height. Amy tried not to laugh at his posture, arms spread to assure impediment to her path. His yellow jacket flared, an extension of his paunch, to reveal a satin lining that matched his slacks as well as a black Lions-logoed shirt. He looked like a very busy bee.

Elvin started to speak, but her cell interrupted. Andy. She mouthed "I have to take this" Amy strode out of the diner to hunker by the side of the building to answer his call.

"Michigan. I think I might have a problem."

"Oh, great." Amy loped to her car for the privacy she sensed would be necessary for the rest of this call. If Andy had become a stoner, she might kill him herself. "Hold on," she said, "while I settle myself in my car. I sense I need to be seated for what you're going to say next."

She should have known when he called rather than texted. Clue one.

Amy clicked off, edged her keys out of the backpack, and got into her car. She adjusted the rearview mirror and re-positioned her seat. She rolled down the windows, adjusting until each one had the same sliver open to cross-stream air. At last, she folded her arms across her chest for a half-hug, gathered her resolve, and met her own eyes in the side mirror. Amy nodded to herself and returned to Andy's call.

"I tried my best. I truly did," little Andy said, diminishing to dwarf stature in Amy's mind's eye. The pitch to which his voice climbed suggested his skivvies were in a bunch. Clue two.

Amy began to visualize a samurai sword on which he could fall.

His whining was seriously pissing her off. It soured the air. Amy made a mental note to purchase one of the pine tree air fresheners the diner sold to fend off bad juju in her Focus. She didn't need another mess in her lap.

Amy took a deep, deep breath before she spoke. "I know you did, Andy," she cooed instead. She'd overheard Jackie Breeden handle her son Brandon's inane and incessant calls with soft-spoken, placating aplomb. She'd never experienced such love-laced ego massaging from her mother. Jackie excelled. Amy added role model to Jackie's list of titles.

"Lester said we deserved a celebration." *Deserved*? When had this entered Andy's lexicon? Had the self-esteem demands of California's culture fractured into her brother's jargon?

Amy breathed deeper—and almost gagged at what she heard next. She knew her brother to be long on image and short of facts.

"The green haze began at dawn. By dusk a fire had consumed his entire green-housed crop."

Amy bit her tongue to suppress her gasp. At least it wasn't her profits that had gone up in smoke.

Be careful what you wish for, the devil whispered in Amy's ear.

For several minutes, Andy blah-blah-blah-blah-blahed while Amy held her phone between her knees, wishing she could place her head there as she fought dry heaves.

As if Amy didn't know the calamities inherent in any Andy plan. She was not an initiate and he was not a prophet. As if.

As if Amy didn't already have enough problems with Ronnie, who was still pouting the loss of her crop. Holy calamity! Now Amy had several more leeches for her cash.

Amy could already smell the acrid, ropey smoke, the pungent odor of Andy's business proposal going up in smoke. She also envisioned the rangy outline of her mother. Amy bent her head in honest-to-God Catholic prayer, gripping the steering wheel for support. "Bye, Andy, I wish you all the best." She hung up and turned off her phone, wondering how many voicemails and texts Andy would send in the next few hours. She intended to *ghost* him for days.

She cantilevered out of the car, mentally calculating how long before she'd be able to trade up to a larger vehicle, and then heaved a sigh. Amy gazed at the diner with its unique blend of caution, ambivalence, and charm. She leaned into her next chore: schmoozing its pride of Lions. She needed a lawn mower, hedge clipper, handyman, and cook. Maybe a long-distance babysitter for her brother. Hernandez was the best, but he couldn't be loaned out. He was Amy's keeper, her minder, her dad. He was Amy's absolution.

Amy returned to the diner. She needed new shoes, maybe work boots.

Amy lifted her head. Sheesh. Elvin had waited for her at the diner's door. *Not golden after that disturbing call.* He held a menu in one hand and put his other hand in the small of Amy's back. He guided her to a booth, a bit apart from the pack. The scent of maple syrup and scrambled eggs and burnt coffee assaulted Amy's senses. All of the members turned their way to wave and raise their eyebrows. Phil grimaced, but turned back to the business meeting.

"To what do I owe the pleasure, Elvin? I'm not exactly comfortable being cut off from the herd." Amy focused her attention to the menu.

"We'll get to that in due time, Missy. Right now, I'm in need of protein."

Amy declined to touch that remark for all of the money in the world, so she bent to silence her phone. Maybe she should palm it in case she needed 911 in the next thirty minutes.

Naw, nothing adverse is going to happen in full view of all of the influential men in town. Half of the men wore their former service jackets. Some of them may have been armed.

So was she, so there. Amy was six feet tall and not long from the weight room in the Pen. Though no health club seemed available in this tiny town, she and Ronnie had kept up their tone. It was ethic in their generation. Amy's biceps bulked, her abs enabled for any kind of fight she chose to mount.

She and Elvin ordered and then ate in silence. Small talk would have interfered with the business that was being carried on behind Elvin's back. Perhaps he'd learned that if he didn't eavesdrop and pay close attention to the rumble of the group's gossip, he'd be in charge of some committee. Oh, well.

At the close of the meeting, all of the men shuffled by the booth, again placing their business cards on the table top in front of Amy. She spoke with a few of them that might have promising leads for her renovation jobs list. Some of them scribbled more names and numbers on the back of their cards. All were deferential and polite.

"Want to go for a ride in my big black car?" The

voice was familiar but warped with classic 'dirty old man with candy' sneer.

Amy jerked to attention, flickering Elvin's face. No malice there. And none in his voice. "No, but I'll follow your car in mine."

He grabbed the bill Marnie dropped near his coffee cup, paid it, and they set off, Elvin in the lead.

They drove north of town this time, following the Lake Michigan shoreline. Every now and then the road wiggled and tall grasses and sand appeared, with a faint gray hint of lake. After each touristy glimpse, another juicy bug or bird splat dotted the windshield. Amy had not missed that aspect of driving while she'd been in the pokey.

Chapter Twenty-Four

NEW BUDGET DRAIN

AMY WAS GETTING edgy, her leg numbed from twenty miles of maintaining a constant 35 m.p.h. on the gas. Amy had trespassed her own caution. Allowed herself to trust. She longed to believe Hernandez truly and actively surveilled.

Elvin abruptly turned on a blinker, and she followed him left onto uber-bumpy Pinnacle Drive. Wasn't that prophetic of her situation?

The lane was curvy and plump with trees, touching each other's branches like longtime friends. The forest of maples and pines matched the fresh scent of the Focus' interior and, for the first time in a half-hour, Amy began to relax.

She opened the sunroof and craned her neck, hoping for a glimpse of a bird… or a drone. Amy counted to one hundred forward and backward to keep her pulse well-paced. She drove within two car lengths of Elvin's his big black car, astonished that he left no candy trail to entice her forward.

Suddenly, there it was. Not peppermint or Red Vines or Tootsie Rolls, the lust of Amy's childhood candy dreams. Nor the entrapment of the wicked witch's house for Hansel and Gretel.

Amy's eyes popped. Her heart skipped a beat. YA-A-AS. A ginormous block-and-gray stucco house. Stucco in Michigan? While ubiquitous to California, Amy's home state, this castle had to be an illusion. What drug had Eldon put in her to-go coffee?

The house had *scope*. Expansive, sequestered, and awesome, but too reminiscent of Prison with a capital P that Amy almost choked on her shock. Her body went rigid in protest and every swear word she'd ever heard, said, and read flashed through her mind.

Amy stomped the brake so hard, she almost launched herself through the sunroof.

Elvin loped to Amy's car and opened the door, using both hands to fan her face. "I knew you'd like it, Amy, but I didn't think you'd faint." He looked like a bewildered parent, who wondered why a child didn't like the elephant ride he'd just plunked down forty bucks for at the fair.

Amy burst into tears. Now she wasn't worrying about soaking her shirt. Now she fest overcome with jubilation-tinged self-doubt.

"This place has five bedrooms and five+ baths," Elvin oozed as he leaned past Amy to punch her car into park. "It's secluded, private, and serene. Wait'll you see the view of the lake."

He wedged his strong arm behind Amy's back and began to winch her out of the car. He was good, maybe a volunteer fireman. Smooth. She didn't even hook a heel on the door's inner ledge nor catch her purse strap on the gear shift. The jam of the steering wheel didn't disrupt her breath.

But the house did. It was eye-poppingly huge. Interest swelled her chest and Amy knew she'd never let go. The edifice was an assembly of giant gray boxes, stacked like a child's wooden block set, with vast windows carved into each. She may have initially balked because the home looked stone cold, too similar to the gray bar hotel, but her heart was stolen from its frost. This house equaled perfection for a rich ladies' getaway.

And through the vast windows Amy saw enormous modern art installations, low Italian leather couches—and a granite fireplace that hung like a chandelier in the center of a great room. She was beyond intrigued.

She was in lust as much as when she'd first laid eyes on Trav. Brandon, too, though she'd stalked him longer than Travis, who came next. *Why did images of my past men excite me so much?*

She was a lady with a plan. Bolstered by millions. She didn't need a man.

Amy swiveled to fully absorb the further enticing tidbits that emerged from Elvin's mouth. "Want to get back in your car, so we can enter on the three-car garage side? Inside one of the bays is a Porsche, which comes with the house."

Amy almost wet her pants. Yasss. Her Focus would like to meet its new brother, a sleek and shiny Porsche.

It didn't matter what color it was, though Amy prayed it was not arrest-me red.

It was. Amy's instant lust was perverse, her pulse rushing to convince her mind to follow her heart. Elvin pointed her toward the empty center bay, while he parked his realty *limo* on the left. As soon as they got out of their respective vehicles, he began his realtor patter. Amy let him do his job, which was to talk her ear off until she relented and signed.

The home was a weekend retreat for a former mob boss, a Chicagoan of Italian descent, who had run with the I.R.S. into a small problem and needed to unload. Fast. Liquidate assets. His horses, his Porsche, his house. The paperwork would be kept hush-hush-rush-rush by Elvin Goodrich, and a cadre of complicit Lions Club members. A nearby horse farm had already consigned the horses.

Hmm, Amy thought. She wondered if the mob boss was a card-carrying Lion. Certainly, his lawyer was. While she'd felt constrained in a prior close-knit community—when she'd attempted to fit into its preset—Amy now felt embraced.

Was it the millionaire glow? Surely all of these men didn't want to smother her…or date her…was she their *prime* business bait? Maybe molesting her millions was the ensemble's intent.

She and Elvin walked companionably into the lower level of the house…and into a brand-spanking new kitchen filled with gleaming aluminum-faced appliances of significant proportions. When Amy opened the oven door, it was also apparent that the appliances had never been used. She opened the double-doored refrigerator to see a bottle of champagne. Elvin winked and pulled an opener from his suit coat's inner pocket. He leered like a street person hawking stolen watches or young girls for sex, while Amy felt like a homeless person on house arrest.

"I knew you'd like it! And I figured, if you were good for one house, you'd be good for two!" The champagne popped, its cork flying into the atmosphere. "I can see you now, soaring in that ultra-fast Porsche," Elvin exclaimed in-between slurps of the bubbly as it splashed out of the bottle and onto the floor.

Suddenly azure glimmered just beyond Elvin's head. Amy strode toward a pool whose water shimmered with pixie light. When she gripped the sliding glass door handle and mildly jerked, the glass rocketed back. She became one with the outside. Though she couldn't swim, the water beckoned. She already felt replenished. Lake Michigan's water lapped gently on a beach far below this promontory. The sun shone golden. Amy felt richer-than-rich. She felt blessed.

A dozen gray lounge chairs aligned the wide, otherwise bare concrete patios, which lined the large rectangle of pool. Not a shimmer of shade. One had to be a full throttle sun worshipper to flop around that pool. Amy wondered if chlorine bothered post-surgical incisions. She wondered if she cared,—or if her future clientele would either. There were a half-dozen low tables for pool-sized drinks.

Amy's heart felt massaged. She was golden beyond redress. She could almost feel her skin tan.

CHAPTER TWENTY-FIVE

PURCHASED!

"DOES GUIDO HAVE a cabana boy? A full-time groundskeeper and house cleaner? Or will I be finding my staff among the Lions Club members and their progeny?"

The matter came up because gangrene had set-in, the shrubs overgrown, the flower beds bereft of fresh blooms. In fact, they looked like fresh graves of mob-hit men, women, or children. God perish the thought, maybe even the past owners' pets.

"We'll have you covered, Amy. Service is our aim. Even a build-out to serve your preferences, needs, or whims. No worries," Elvin said.

"I'm glad there's no diving board." Amy shook her head. Her neck bristled as the sun baked it, so she turned to walk back inside. Amy began to recall the expenses and responsibilities of home ownership. Like insurance, repairs, electric bills. Let alone the cost of renovations required for an ultra-luxurious spa.

Then, a lady bug landed on her hand and Amy knew she'd be okay. Her guardian angel had glided into view.

"Oh, I forgot." Elvin marched downstairs, beckoning Amy to follow. "The basement is one vast room that begs for build-out."

Did he wink at me again?

Amy, glad for young knees, thought a large number of steps would hinder an elderly clientele. She sized up the area, adding elevator installation to the list of enhancements.

Back up the stairs, Elvin hastened. When they got to the top of the stairs and moved directly into the open space, Amy almost collapsed with vertigo. She twirled once to the left, and then once to the right. She didn't want to be wound too tight when she asked for the price. She glided to the couch after a glimpse of the view, sank into the leather and kicked off her shoes. Amy wanted to be seated when she heard the amount.

She looked at Elvin and he looked at her. The silence stretched the already vast space. He slowly withdrew one of his realty pads, walked to the coffee table, and wrote on the pad.

There was an extraordinary bronze sculpture between them, a sort of idealized horse head or a god, Amy couldn't tell which. Elvin slid the pad past it, closer to Amy, then stepped away as if it might sting.

It did. The paper grew a set of lungs to shriek.

$4,750,000. The house and its 5.5-acre lot price was nearly half the sum of her yearly draw from the lottery annuity. Though the money was burning a hole in an LLC account—and earning a daily interest amount that might equal some Michigan citizens' yearly salary—it hadn't been in her hands overlong.

And, she'd already purchased a half-million-dollar house, a compact car, and incidentals. Amy's past-banker math went mad.

But. She ached for this modern house. It felt like home, the status she'd longed for, and was resplendent. Fully furnished, ready for residence, and primed to be the location of her future hyper-rich clients' surgical recovery. The business wasn't even up and humming, but Amy'd already secured property #two.

Secluded, protected, and an outlier, like her. She belonged here.

I could breathe and be myself. I can ignore Andy's idiotic pleas for money, maybe leave my phone in permanent silent mode.

Amy turned to Elvin, her body already feigning a mobster moll lean. She mentally wondered how the posture was going to look while driving a Focus, since she wouldn't afford new clothes—or even food in the near term. Luxury build-outs would take priority.

"Elvin, you've done well." Amy began with the *sandwich* approach she'd learned from Jackie. 'First you compliment, then you jab, and then you end on a perkily positive note.' In that manner, one's audience was more receptive and less likely to feel the stab.

Amy moved her hands behind her back, so that

Elvin wouldn't see them shake—and to cross her fingers against a white lie. "I haven't established a checking account or credit history in this locale."

"Not a problem. I can walk you into the First Third Bank and have it all handled by noon."

"Elvin, I've got no collateral to finance a loan of this size. It's called a double quadruple jumbo loan where I come from." Amy smiled like a sunbeam and nudged Elvin's side, to evoke a return smile on his face. "And back to my prior point. What about comparables, so that I know this is the best price? I know you Lion's Club members do business with a handshake and a slap on the back, but I haven't been in town long enough for that attitude to fit. Got any data a girl can look at?"

"Well, I hadn't considered bringing the MLS with me. Besides, when you paid cash for the first home, I thought you were a 'whale'."

Amy snapped back, "This house is the size and color of a whale, yet nature's wonders are free. What the hell is a 'whale'? Are you playing me, Elvin?"

Elvin hemmed and hawed but offered little meaning or gist. The term 'whale' had apparently been heisted from the club's monthly poker game, to which the Lions always invited at least one out-of-towner from the lakeside motels. Phil, the New Horizons manager, often brought one of his recovering alcoholics as a reward for the person's good behavior. The whale's purpose seemed to be to lose bundles of cash.

But he'd never, never, never tell Amy. He was surprised at his gaff and pinched his wrists.

Amy frowned and folded her arms, letting her body language signal her distaste, but Elvin plowed on. He was full of suggestions, but he wouldn't lower the price below $4,000,000. The former mobster client was in dire need of the quick sale and the cash, he said, artfully neglecting that he was in need of his commission, which was already spent.

Amy bridled. To avoid a snit-fit, she began to imagine new colors for the stucco. Not blue. Not green. Maybe yellow? The color would be seem sunflower fresh, yet might conjure a giant canary in people's minds? With a helo pad on top, Sesame Street's Big Bird with a grad hat?

Maybe she should consider a red polka dot house, to honor her silent mentor, the lady bug. Amy wished she had wings to float and fly away, too.

Amy's heart jack-hammered, her skin clammed, and her brain reacted as if struck by a hot poker. She attempted to conjure an image of Dad—his eyes invisible behind the tint of his glasses, his inscrutable smile crossing his face, ear to ear. Amy longed for his presence to steady her.

It felt patronizing—and conspiratorial— when Elvin side-hugged her with one arm and thrust a business card into her hand. "Dan the Man" the painter's card announced with a phone number below. Like Elvin's recent gesture, the locals had her going on all sides. Her lottery win was surrounded, as was she. Uncomfortable. Encumbered. And fit to be lassoed into the local economy.

"How am I going to afford buckets and buckets of paint when the house cost four million?"

Elvin's blink showed that he was surprised, but a second blink seemed to indicate that he would drop the price. Morse Code for Buyers 101.

"Four million. In Michigan," Amy blustered. "I didn't know that was possible in a hick state?"

"Hick state, you say, Lady Bird?" Now Elvin was angry, posture rigid, fists clenched. Not a good mood. The sales price of the house spiked higher.

Political maneuvering had never been Amy's forte. She longed to beam herself back to the prison library to research negotiation ploys, er strategies. Though she had once possessed elegant verbal skills, those had downgraded in prison. She was left to rely on blondeness, her wits, and her six-foot height to command. Her forthrightness was a bluff, and she largely brain-bitched. Amy was in shock.

Suddenly her kindergarten nun's voice sprang to mind, "Use your words, dear. Use your words, not your fists." It was good advice at the time—because she had a bloody nose—and it was good advice now. Amy should do it. She could do it. She had an English degree-enabled dictionary in her head, that should be recoverable at will.

Amy realized that was her true super power: what was locked inside her head. Between her ears and not the hair covering them. Amy had never had to rely on blonde, so it didn't matter if her hair was dark. With blonde roots. Ronnie had taunted her, "You look like a Goth gone white with fright."

Ronnie labeled Amy thus when she looked in her mirror after brushing her bangs. Jealous? Amy patted herself on the back. She hadn't retorted at the time. Ha! Her educated brain now housed a catalogue of what not to say…to several people. Amy knew she'd rue the day when the cork came out, and she sprayed the universe with invectives and stored retorts.

Amy vowed not to drink or binge on the spa's subliminal products like Ronnie had implored— not even canna water seemed safe. Those stimulants loosened primed lips. Maybe she could beseech Woolworth Wilma to ship cases of real water, maybe mountain-spring, via Woolworths. Amy trusted Wilma more than she trusted herself.

Amy wished she could call Wilma by her first name aloud rather than the nickname that stuck. She owed Wilma that tribute. To not link her name permanently to mercantile purposes.

To be kinder, especially to Wilma, and to not remain her ritually conniving self.

Chapter Twenty-Six

NO EASY DAY

ELVIN CLEARED HIS throat several times to regain Amy's attention. She jerked, wondering how long she'd folded inward for her self-scolding and promises to reform. She realized she was lucky for his small-town manners and allowed him to lead the way to their respective vehicles. Elvin needed his *big dog* moment, and she needed to be demure.

Elvin turned to zap the mansion's front door and slider locks and then zapped his keyless entry car door. He zapped on the Cadillac ignition and placed his cell phone on the dash.

He squired Amy back to town and into the local bank, just as she was, unkempt and uncombed. She felt like his victim, rather than an esteemed client. A whipped millionaire about to harness the home of her dreams/not dreams. Her lust for that house was irrepressible, so Amy succumbed to his lead. No matter that she was a former small-town banker. Mortgages were not her forte—she'd been burned for inappropriate tasks.

Elvin shook hands with the banker man and introduced Amy. They sat in two damask-covered chairs, so country manor in pedigree. Amy folded her hands into her lap, so that the two deal-makers couldn't see her shining eyes in her non-pokered face.

Elvin blithely guided the banker into a second mortgage on the country squire property for which Amy had impulsively paid cash, mere days before. No one was judging Amy but herself. The men were too consumed with greasing her path, to collect their share of the dough—via fees.

Amy gasped as she provided the routing number of her online bank. She'd invaded her own privacy. Amy hoped that client privilege applied to bankers as it did to lawyers' clients and news sources. She was so very, very far above her head and her means, her emotions holding sway. Her heart thumped in her chest and her skin tingled as if it had been sunburned while previewing her new property.

Elements were tumbling into place faster than a bank vault's locking system. Amy just hoped she remembered the combination to the safe. A ginormous loan secured by a cute little property that was a tenth of the castle's valuation, the poor cousin saddled to serve the court, similar to the serfs in medieval times.

$4,000,000. A figure that could have been scribed by some demonic pencil lead, but it was the discount

Elvin and Amy apparently negotiated. Given on a handshake, a flutter of the eyes, and a flick of the wrist.

As if. Details were likely a bit more complicated, but help was everywhere in a small town. Slickened by goodwill.

Amy had intended not to hyperventilate, an occurrence which the banker matter-of-facted when he handed over his lunch bag with remnants still inside. He covered over mutual embarrassment when he hastily shook out the contents and modeled the bag's use.

Amy vampishly sucked in her breath and tried to avoid the giggles that lurked—for the act reminded her of smoking dope from Ronnie's bong. Amy hoped against hope that Ronnie would never-ever discover her gone-gone weed. The *equipment* required was gone-gone. Ronnie might panic—what Amy felt now—relapse and seek pot's refuge as the burdens of spa partnership moved forward.

Amy eased. A few moments passed. Documents were printed. The banker handed Amy one of the bank's logo pens. She signed like a queen with her magic wand, hoping that magic would continue as the big house germinated the Lady Bug Inn. Banker Man told Amy she could keep the pen after he whipped all the papers into a file.

Amy felt Hernandez' presence levitate over her, his attitude almost gallant in its trust that she would do *righ*t, and that he approved of her path.

Life was one curvy, rock-filled lane. Groovy and epically insane. Not fully golden yet, but emerging. Amy realized that this might be her last easy day.

Secured was the palace of perfection for the ladies recovering from their secret plastic surgeries of choice: secluded, protected, modern, and posh. A place in which Amy's personal comfort was immediate, too, though not her net worth.

A palace with a monstrous mortgage. Amy envisioned stacks of hundreds filling the 6000+ sq. ft., if she'd elected to pay cash. There'd have been no place for her ego and dreams, now threatening to deflate under the weight of responsibilities. Amy grew dizzy, her nerve undermined.

Calamities could wipe out her full bank account, still housed on a cloud. Amy wondered if the direct deposit she'd signed to pay the mortgage would truly work— how and how soon? The monthly mortgage amount was thousands. Her credit cards were maxed.

Amy quaked in her resort sandals. She felt mired in monetary quicksand.

Amy paused to rehearse in the driveway of the first building she'd impulsively purchased, between the tall brick pillars that foreshadowed the substantial house, now fully burdened with a mortgage higher than its bricks. What had looked grand and abundant for her and Ronnie's scheme now looked like a shrimp.

She drove carefully down the gravel drive, as if this would prevent dings to her car. As if this was more important than the dings in her hide that Ronnie might inflict.

Yikes! *Hide* had multiple meanings. Amy gulped

and swallowed involuntarily at her word choice. Which meaning threatened her most? She had to turn this around to think long term and not be remiss. She couldn't afford to self-obsess, a habit reinforced in prison, but embedded early in her life. Amy knew she needed to become an *other-directed* adult, who could accommodate any and all well-heeled guests. And a not-so-well-heeled, but appropriately talented, sidekick.

Her pride was what Amy had to swallow to assure that Ronnie was aligned. This country cottage—yet to be named—needed to become the workhorse property in the stable.

Amy smiled. She now had her lead.

She parked the Focus in front of the log cabin. It was shut up tight, with both bedrooms' swamp coolers clanging noisily. The clatter and hum should have been enough to scare mosquitoes and other bugs, but Amy started to scratch one of her ankles.

Note to self: purchase bug spray for this abundant artifact of Michigan's heat and humidity. There'd been no bugs in California, none in prison, none in the bank where she labored as a business-suited VP. Amy could only recall flies—lots of them—when she and Brandon lived on the Breeden Dairy Farm.

Amy tiptoed lightly across the broad wood porch, reminded again of how like Ronnie's former home this cozy cabin looked. She squared her shoulders and entered.

Ronnie was ensconced on the couch, burrowed into yet another DVD. Amy sat in one of the chairs and tried to blend. It didn't seem proper to startle someone who'd already stated that her growing-out roots looked a fright.

Then Amy had an idea. She tiptoed back into the kitchen and microwaved a bag of popcorn, nervously monitoring Ronnie's mood over her shoulder as the bag twirled on the microwave carousel. During the two minutes of popping corn and popping can tops, Ronnie never moved. Fully absorbed and even mouthing dialogue, which Amy knew would be sprinkled into future conversation without intro or clues. Amy's mind was hopped like the corn, her legs dancing to the beat, while Ronnie remained inert.

Amy sought an infusion of single-minded focus to help harness her hip-hopping brain. She needed a sidekick she could rely up on. While Woolworth Wilma was a good sounding board and Hernandez was a great parole sitter, Amy needed someone by her side who'd known her longer than a month.

"If a rat were to walk in here right now as I'm talking, would you treat it to a saucer of your delicious milk?"

That voice! Amy's eyes darted to the screen to see the pouty, perfectly formed lips.

*Inglourious Bastards. Ya*sss. She couldn't take her eyes off Brad Pitt, not even when he was mean. As a kid—on the back streets of Long Beach,—she had snuck into Saturday matinees. She'd imagined Brad Pitt as her dad.

She stumbled to the kitchen to arm herself with two popcorn bowls, a horde of napkins, and two drinks, vising the cold cans to the food tower with her chin.

The buttery popcorn scent swirled the room. Amy saw Ronnie's chin lift to follow her nose.

She realized, too late, that she shouldn't have opened the cans. One small snafu to a magnificent entry. Apparently, she wobbled, and a beer came tumbling down, fizzing the entire floor. Amy placed the items on the grungy countertop as gingerly as her nerves allowed and hastily swooped a cloth from the sink. Its wetness slimed her palm, but clean-up had to be done. Amy squatted to swab the deck.

Now Ronnie was alert. Wide-eyed and mid-shush against the noise that interrupted her communion with Brad Pitt, she began to laugh and laugh and laugh.

Amy tossed the wet cloth into the sink, not bothering to rinse out the beer.

She edged into a seat near the TV, not taking her eyes off the screen. Soon, the only sounds in the room—besides the movie characters, actions, sound effects, and plot—were she and Ronnie shoveling and munching and swigging.

It felt companionable. It felt right. Amy imagined they'd just slide together, like a long-married couple.

Amy's blinked in slow-mo. Brad in a tank looked good, but the dirt and grime appalled. Egad, like Brandon in *farmboy* days.

She willed her mind back to the movie, but saw little of the men in uniform, heard little of the inglorious dialogue. After a day of plot twists, Amy was tuckered.

As always, she hadn't figured out the allies from the bad guys. Her eagerness for prowess had imploded her innate vigilance. She needed to get to her new safe place.

Chapter Twenty-Seven

RONNIE GETS A TURN, YET NOT

YOU AWAKEN AT oh-dark-thirty, uncomfortably clumped on the wrong side of a bed. The light switch isn't where you left it, so you stumble as you get up for relief.

The terrain changes, yet onward you march. You remain upright, sensing the goal is near.

But it's a clothes-cluttered floor, unfamiliar to your feet.

A voice intrudes on your sleepwalk, "Hey, don't pee in my closet!"

What's Amy doing here?

Somebody rattles your shoulder, almost shaking the stream loose.

Your eyelids flicker, obedient servants they be. The

first to guide and defend on your behalf. Uplifting, that's what this dreamscape needs.

Now you're all eyes, into it. Adrenaline is your friend. A shadow separates from the dark.

"Amy, what are you doing here?"

No response. Her eyes peer as steely dominatrix as her voice was commandant. They're burning a hole in your head.

Did you stick your head in an oven? You recall retiring from baking, don't you?

Am I on the right path? You remain befuddled and nonplussed.

"I brought you to a sleep-over in my new property. You've been sleep-walking again, Ronnie. Are you ready for me to switch on the light?"

Your inner Kindle reloads, and you are familiar again. You vaguely recall a drunken discussion. You'll seek clarity after you pee.

She claps. You blink. The cycle repeats.

She'll jump, you'll follow; she'll juke, you'll apologize.

"Sling on a robe or a shirt, maybe some shoes. There's plenty among the piles. Help yourself. I'll take you on a tour of the new manse."

You startle, but it's her money, so you remain mum. You traipse, stopping momentarily to peek in the refrigerator and grab a bottle of tonic. You thirst for knowledge, but this fizzy stuff will do. Bubbles settle the stomach, your mom always said.

"Isn't this ab-fab!" Her arms sweep like the appliance salesmen you've seen on TV. "It's larger, more secluded, and more prestigious. The price we can charge the customers just sky-rocketed. I'm thrilled, and I know you will be, too."

She grips your head to swivel your face into view, almost wrenching your head from your neck. With your jaw held firmly, your mouth is unable to form "no". She moves your head in a nod, modeling an encouraging smile.

"Ronnie, I'm inviting you back into the business. You can stay in your own place. I cede the log cabin to you, rent-free if you hang with me to become the spa manager of the Lady Bug Palace."

You can feel your eyes widen.

"Okay. Okay, I cede the point to you. We'll call it the Lady Bug Inn."

In spite of your hangover, you laugh, "That's funny. We'll invite customers to bug in, but not bug out. Ha-ha, but I'll never get over your trash of my stash. Perhaps I'll mix cannabis plants among the new landscape I plan. It'll be golden." You wink broadly at Amy, but she waves you off.

"Speaking of golden. Should we re-do my hair, or let it return to blonde?"

You know you may have had your one moment of control, when she went along with your initiative to alter her hair. Well done, thou good and faithful servant.

Your mind begins to noodle details, not insurmountable, but the shit pile will be delegated to you and it's best to be prepared. What about the first hotel/inn—the inhabitants already deported, rooms ready to rent to new customers, er clients?

"No problem," she says. Gonna be filled to capacity as soon as brochures are shipped to famed plastic surgeons on Chicago's Gold Coast.

Brochures to write…no, wait, Amy's the one with the English degree. She'll claim that rite. She photographs well and likely has a printer already aligned via Lions Club contacts. You heard some Travis dude will distribute via his Harley, a noisy presence better than airmail or snail. Gonna shake up the neighborhoods in all ways.

Travis? You thought he'd already been sized up for his coffin in Amy's mind. Dead to her like Brandon Breeden, her ex. Dude had a target on his back.

Now was not the time to remind Amy people were to be loved and not used. She hated that guy's guts. Best not to add yourself to the cross hairs. Best to abide and let Travis carry his own cross.

"Living well is the best revenge," you'd counseled Amy. Wonder if the message could inhabit her soul?

You shift topics from that dead end, to surmise a price differential between the two properties, how to price a week's stay. While you may not have sway in the decision, it's good mental exercise. A lot of zeroes to balance. Room rental prices will be affixed by suite size, view, and ambiance. You place a bet. Both on the price and the size of the staff you'll be enlisted to manage. And hire.

You've never hedged your bets on anyone else's

success before, being a go-for-it girl. Gopher was not your intention. You'd done combat for Brandon, but what did you win? Now that you've cut the bride and groom off of the cake, there's no return.

You're hitched to Amy's parade, ensnared in her plan, your wallflower fly in her spun-up web. Living well might be a challenge.

There are two spiders tangled in this web.

CHAPTER TWENTY-EIGHT

MAN TROUBLES

AMY HAD MAN problems, too. Multiples. Andy, Hernandez, Travis, maybe Brandon, her ex, who'd spooked her with a visit when she resided in Ronnie's gingerbready home.

Nah, not Brandon. He was catastrophically soft. His day was done.

Thank goodness for the band of Lions Club brothers, I can rely on them as good and noble men.

In actuality, the Lions Club in South Haven was no different to any other club in its international data base. The group's premise was to build business relationships as well as building a community, tenets that were essentially the same. Community service as veneer—to make each man useful to all citizens—to assure that each man's name was the first and only call a small town's citizens made when expertise was needed. There was no *who you gonna call* in South Haven.

Amy Breeden was every members' mark. She had more suitors for her money than she'd ever had for her long-legged height. But she wasn't afraid: she could out-run, out-whip—and out-wit—any of the men 365 days/year. A few of them had come tom-catting around with adventurous schemes. While none knew the extent—or the source—of her largesse, each was eager to help Amy help them *improve the community.*

The leader of the band seemed to be the local banker, who'd boldly told her he'd Zillowed both of her properties. Would she like to buy a broken-down bar, which had formerly anchored the tiny town's tourist draw? The owner had bankrupted the business and flounced to another resort town up north, maybe Traverse City with its relatively new Indian casino.

The first man to arrive at Amy's door, hat in hand, was Pastor Weems.

Elvin had warned her that the man tended to be moody, remote, and vain. He seldom

spoke—except when in full battle cry for the Lord on Sundays—which made him the

perfect Treasurer of the Lions Club. The pastor was a weasel to watch out for, Elvin

confided.

When Pastor Weems knocked at the Lady Bug Inn door, Amy locked her heart

and closed her lips, then thought of an alternative ploy.

"Now's not a good time—nor is this a good place—to chat, which I assume you wish to do, Pastor. How about if I attend your church on Sunday?"

Dumbstruck, the Pastor backed down the steps, grinning, almost snickering with glee and clasping his hands in prayer.

As if, Amy thought. As if he had already bagged a millionaire's tithe to his church. But Amy knew, via Elvin's share, the church was chronically hard-up, as was its pastor. It was rapaciously rumored that Pastor Weems was the source of the church's indebtedness due to the fact that he siphoned off a little of the budget to pay personal expenses.

Amy would be good. She'd arrive at the 10:00 service, in the loudly-red Porsche, and showily drop a dime in the silver collection plate. She knew, because the Catholic nuns had told her she had a 'relationship with God'. While He might have missed her for a while, she'd missed him, too.

Amy shifted her mouth from a frown to a smile. Perhaps God hadn't gotten sidetracked with His other sinners around the world. He'd given her a sumptuous lottery win on the first day she'd escaped lawfully, out early for good behavior, a state that certainly had God's provenance written all over it. Amen. Golden and epically so.

Link N. Law utilized a different approach on/for Amy. Mountains of paperwork. Glamorous brochures and pamphlets of possibilities and more ways to squander millions hither, thither and yon. All composed in the *slitherese* adopted by snake oil salesman throughout the millennia. Tax dodges and shelters and flim-flams of all kinds. More ways to elude Uncle Sam's taxes than Watson's Drugs had varieties of potions and lotions and pills.

Elvin Goodrich, the realtor Amy loved because of his name, most persistently pursued Amy's money. After all, he'd sold her once. He'd sold her twice.

His commissions were elegant.

And the Asylum Inn was still for sale.

Amy didn't like being the *Mecca of Money*, the sole mark in South Haven. It was a notoriety she did not enjoy. Even the manicurist of the local shop hit her up for big coin when she and Ronnie visited her shoppe for mani-pedis.

She'd even received a hundred texts from Uncle Walt of the Feel Good Forever Pharmacy. Amy largely ignored him after his initial text: A LITTLE BIRD TOLD ME YOU'VE MOVED INTO BETTER QUARTERS THAN PRISON. YOU HAVE A HUGE, PRIVATE PROPERTY AS PER ZILLOW. WANNA CANNA-CULTIVATE?

Ha! As if! Amy refused to risk recidivism for anyone else's benefit. Now was not the time. Nor the place. Perhaps when all aspects of the plastic surgery recovery building were complete, she'd invest. To serve the needs of her clients and nothing else.

Perhaps she'd tell the skank Uncle Walt about Hernandez' active surveillance, and Walt wouldn't come sniffing with the law around. Hernandez had become more than a dad. He was a friend with protective benefits, deterrent to bad influences, including Amy's own.

But Hernandez' presence might be a mistake, too. Amy had blurted her intention to rent to wealthy inhabitants recovering from plastic surgery. She could envision his wince over the phone and the blast of his voice percussed her eardrums. "You don't have a medical license—and I seriously doubt if parolees can get one!"

In that moment she realized how much she needed Hernandez. He was always informed and always around. While sometimes he might drive Amy crazy with facts, she needed him to put his foot in the door and kick her out of stupidity. He was a worthy watchdog and as ever-present as the hidden cameras in the prison.

She felt certain she drove him crazy with her false starts and fits of good intention gone awry. An inner thought startled Amy, making her cock her head in contemplation. She fell to her knees, prayer-like, with the realization that one had to have a stake in something to be a judge of it. Hernandez' blazing reaction told her that he had taken a stake in her future. He'd be her guard and guardian forever.

She was golden.

Dante Thurman entered Amy's life like a manic bull, leaning on her doorbell and pawing at the welcome mat.

When she flung open the door, ready to bluster, he charged first. "What took you so long to answer the dang door? Where the jack were you?" he blustered while she blinked away his bad breath. "Elvin sent me. Told me to be here at dawn, but I had to sleep off last night's drunk. The bar where I worked for seven years closed, and I got no savings or severance."

Uhm, even at 8:00 in the morning, Amy could tell what's-his-name was bad news. A ton of bad news in a 200 lb. sack. He towered over her, a circumstance she wasn't used to. He wore the shredded remnants of a muscle shirt, his dirty blonde hair similarly rent, surfer flip flops, and what seemed like out-of-fashion olive-colored board shorts. He swayed back-and-forth, perhaps intending to hypnotize Amy. Maybe he was still drunk.

So, instead of retorting in return, "Who the jack're you?" Amy stuck out her hand. Dude gripped it, pumped it over-long, as if forgetting the act. When Amy was able to extract her hand, she discovered his business card in her palm. DANTE THURMAN, PAINTER in laser-raised print.

She noted his inner arms sported demonic tats. She read the name and then pointed to the tats. "What's your damage?"

Dante squinted at her. "You an ex-con, too?"

Amy blushed, but didn't take the bait. "I meant, how much do you charge, Dante?"

"Enough," he said. "My dad is your realtor. He said you've got two properties

to spruce up. I'd like to start here. This concrete monster reminds me of prison. We've got to get rid of the gray."

Social acumen was not in Dante's toolbelt. After

his blunt words, he spun around and darted from the doorstep, almost flip-flopping in the process. As he neared his monster truck, Dante shouted, "Don't dither. Soon it'll be too hot and humid to apply paint, let alone to allow it to dry."

Well, hello/goodbye, 'Dan the Man'... Christ on a bicycle! Will my millions survive the onslaught of the Lions? What have I gotten myself into?

The Lady Bug Inn was supposed to be peaceful and serene, a sanctuary for rich post-plastic-surgery inhabitants. How could Team Ronnie-and-Amy achieve their purpose with this whirlwind and his potentially-expensive rehab?

I'll need a purge of sage and incense before guests arrive. Costs spiraled in a flash of inconceivable amounts of zeroes and dollar signs. And the paint wasn't even dry, let alone applied.

Amy hadn't slept well while alone in the house. That was why she'd urged Ronnie into one of the many fully-furnished bedrooms. If impressions of this property were that it looked like a prison, the inside felt like a bat vault. Things bumped in the night. Pre-Ronnie she'd bounced between the bedrooms and the couch, but the copper of the fireplace glowed with fire that wasn't there. She'd begun to ponder the downside of having 6000 square feet.

The downside was further underscored by the estimate of time and money that Dante eventually shouted overloud, stretching out his delivery of the price until it echoed inside Amy's head. $15,000.00! Her edginess didn't improve when she understood that the estimate was 15, and not the 50 that she initially heard. Amy agreed, knees so wobbly she sank to the couch and napped.

In a tortured dream, she shouted at Dante, "Delaying customer bookings isn't the option I need. Get your head out of your butt and paint!" Soon an army of painters, plumbers, and other contractors would swarm the future inn like ants. Dante's painted-pocked truck was parked between the Porsche and the Focus and sixteen shades of paint blotched the underground garage walls.

Amy awoke, startled by the all-too-realistic dream. She wanted to wad up the mortgage and go drown herself in the lake.

Instead, she lounged by the pool, completely forgetting that she was naturally blonde and subject to sunburn. Already red with frustration, she added calamine lotion to her purchase list. Amazon declined to deliver to her door.

Amy dreaded the upcoming construction worker catcalls that would harass her leisure. Ladders and catwalks gerry-rigged and co-mingling with steel scaffolding, like a lean-to addition to her luxury spa. Before her daydreams spiraled down to Dante's level, Andy texted. ALL IS LOST HERE. HITCHING A RIDE TO MICHIGAN TO LIVE WITH YOU.

My life was going to hell because of a chance lottery win.

This was not how Amy had pictured her happy-go-lucky multi-millionaire life. This was not the intention when she and Ronnie sketched/planned a spa. This was not golden. This was not star-worthy 'People' magazine material. This seemed more like a 'People' article about a lottery win gone wrong.

And her vengeance on Travis remained undone. Amy was beginning to feel like a failure in her own rebelution.

CHAPTER TWENTY-NINE

MAN UP, BROTHER ANDY ARRIVES

ANDY NEARLY FARTED his way onto Amy's doorstep courtesy of his arrival on the back of a Harley with tailpipes jitter-bugging to the rumble of the bike. The black-leathered driver revved his machine a few times to eject gray clouds of bad-smelling smoke—and to announce that HE was here. Driver and passenger squinted at her, though Amy faced the afternoon sun, the direction from which the Harley must have come.

Amy watched from inside her home while her now-adult brother tucked a renegade strand of scraggled hair into the red bandana triangling his head before he dismounted. He wore no helmet. *Trouble with a capital T had just arrived.*

Amy snatched her phone from the waistband

pocket of her yoga pants and hastily texted Hernandez: MY BROTHER'S HERE.

His reply: YOU HAVE A BROTHER?

Amy contemplated her reply to Hernandez' text while she continued surveillance. After Andy waved off the motorcycle driver, he turned to look at Amy's prison-like home. The scowl on his face said it all. He took off the red bandana and shook it, sending a wheeze of dirt her way. Andy looked like he's just awakened from a long-term nap.

Though he couldn't see her, Amy returned his scowl with one of her own. She'd recognize her brother anywhere. Still lean, and sporting a stupid 'soul patch', which resembled a dead upside-down pine.

How had he found this house, sequestered by so many layers of privacy, including her small pine forest? A rural delivery outpost with a mailbox at the end of the curvaceous lane deliberately left unmarked.

I CAN BE THERE WITHIN MINUTES, Hernandez texted next. REPLY NOW.

MY ONLY SIB LIVED IN CA. HE'S DOWN ON HIS LUCK. NEEDS HIS BIG SIS. I'M ALL RIGHT. Amy almost stowed her phone but decided to add FOR NOW.

She smiled as she pocketed the phone. The additional message would keep Hernandez on red alert. If family fireworks started, she would text HELP and he'd arrive pronto. His car was probably already idling amidst the evergreens, Hernandez either listening to the police scanner or Broadway show tune albums on his iPhone.

Andy became the second stranger to lean on Amy's doorbell. She hoped he had needs, not demands.

Amy flung open the door, so wide its handle banged the wall. She struck out her chest, steady in superhero stance, prepared for hugs or fists, whatever Andy led with.

Her brother stumbled toward the door and collapsed at Amy's feet, as if his spindly body could no longer bear wearing Desert Storm fatigues with heavy multipli-laced combat boots. He thrust his arm up to beseech, "My butt hurts, and I'm famished, Sis. Got any grub for a brother?"

Amy threw back her head and laughed before she braced and extended one of her arms to pull him up from the doormat. "You always were a chatterbox, Andy, even in Catholic School where comportment was key. You and I probably vied for most time spent in the Head Nun's office, though for differing offenses."

Now Andy lunged at Amy, bear-hugging her. In this sibling embrace they began to bounce like pogo sticks, a toy coveted in their youth. After several minutes/lifetimes, they collapsed through the door and into the house in laughter.

Andy picked himself up first, slammed the door shut, and shouted, "Show me the kitchen!" Amy scurried behind him, wondering what the heck to feed him and, again, wondering *how the heck* Andy had found her new house. He'd been less clever than she in the ways in which he'd been consigned to the Head Nun's office. While he'd hard-scrabbled at recess, sometimes hiding from those he'd beaten, she'd provoked nuns with smart-ass remarks. Thank the Lord for the teacher who'd convinced her to pour her words into the essays that earned her a college scholarship.

She knew her brother was indifferently educated. He'd never gained a mentor like she had. Now, seated at her small kitchen table, he radiated gullibility and Amy felt guilty. Without a champion or protector, the roles she performed in their youth, his life nose-dived and topsy-turvied.

A truth shushed the guilt and compassion forming in Amy's mind: *Hernandez will hate him*. She knew she must assure the two men never met. A mental list of retorts, if/when they did, began with this line, *"You're not mad, Hernandez? Fine. Well, tell that to your eyebrows."*

Eerily, Hernandez texted in the next moment: EVERYTHING OK?

YES, she replied because the popcorn was already in two plastic bowls. She began to munch idly while Andy finished a shower. She'd used air freshener to remove the stench that clogged the air and was pondering what beverage to pour him, when Andy ambled into the kitchen with one of her bath towels wrapped like a toga.

He was toking. Nope, everything was not going to be okay—and it never would be again. Amy knew Andy was invested in being combustible—a potential blowtorch to her dreams. He'd been a hellion since birth, a son of anarchy.

"Put that out!" Amy couldn't help herself. She'd

intended to approach Andy softly, but this was her house.

She slapped both of Andy's cheeks, hard, and pulled on his stupid soul patch. She would not let him violate her parole for her. Travis got her into prison, and she got herself out with prudent behavior. She might kill Andy if he bounced her behind bars.

Andy shot her a long look and moved to within an inch of her face. He leered as he exhaled a length of smoke directly at her nose. Amy whirled up and away, running to open a window and suck in clean air before the buffoon's act caused an asthma attack.

Andy had always been a lungy type of guy, as if he had a bungee cord attached to his waist. He'd once hit me—in a joking way—and sent me to the E.R.

"What the heck is going on?" Ronnie padded into the kitchen in her nightgown and slippers, boobs bouncing. Halfway to the refrigerator before she lifted her head from behind the waterfall of her bedhead hair and looked sharply at Amy. "Who the hell is this?" She pointed at Andy, who was still chimney-puffing dope smoke. "Amy, I thought our planned guests were wealthy post-surgery women."

Amy hung her head, too spent to fight or explain. Andy did his lunge thing and pressed himself into Ronnie's breasts.

"Don't bury yourself without permission!" Ronnie yelled after pushing him off her chest. She whirled on Amy. "If I can't grow weed, I don't want this dope's smoke in this house! Who wants temptation here?"

"No one," replied Amy. "Ronnie, meet my brother, Andy. He's, uhm, just passing through."

"Well, if he straightens up his act, he could move into the other bedroom at the cabin—" Ronnie ventured, apt to be kind to a relative of her friend. He was kind of cute in a doleful way. She almost pitied him, his pain, his suffering…his hairy, slim chin.

"No!" shouted Amy. "No way, no way, no way!"

Andy began to chuckle as he looked back-and-forth. "Well, I hadn't counted on two women fighting over me when I saddled up for the several thousand-mile trip on the back of a bike. But I am liking it." He winked a naughty wink at each of the women before he looked Amy boldly in the eye. "I choose the long, dark-haired heathen, Sis."

He stubbed out his doobie in a bowl that didn't yet contain food. "Now, where were we? About to have a bite to eat, I believe."

Amy stomped one foot. "Ground rules first: This is my house and Ronnie's place is my house, too. I make the rules and the rules stick, or you are OUT, Andy."

Andy looked at Ronnie. When she nodded, he nodded, too.

"Ronnie, I'm rousting you to the cabin where you can resume your duties as manager of the original spa."

Though neither dared to look at the other, Ronnie and Andy blinked as they absorbed the boss' commands. Neither had seen Amy this adamant for a long, long time.

Amy snapped her fingers to break the spell. She

softened her voice and turned toward Ronnie. "If you'd please make breakfast, we'll share a civil meal. After the dishes are done, you can pack. Andy will join me while I drive you back to your place." Then Amy absorbed herself in her phone.

The next half-hour passed in silence, with only the sounds of cooking and chewing then clean-up filling the space. Andy fidgeted and squirmed while Amy said nothing. She felt out-of-sorts, flustered and mildly fearful about what might come next.

Chapter Thirty

WHAT THE HECK NOW?

ONLY AFTER THEIR return from stowing Ronnie in her rent-free cabin did Andy learn his fate. Clearly, he desired to cohabit with Ronnie and not Amy, the latter his grown-up/overlord sis.

Amy rolled the functional Ford Focus into the garage beside her upscale Porsche. She could see via side glance that Andy lusted for the sports car. Before he could even ask for the keys, she cut him off with a bark, "There's a pool with this house. Go look at it, but don't jump in. I need you to clean it, maintain it and, maybe, if you get lucky, to keep future guests well-oiled. Now get out of my sight."

Amy cantilevered from the small car and watched Andy do the same. "The pool's around back. Go!"

Andy followed her point and giant-leaped to the back yard. Amy tailed him and watched his expression as he surveyed the terrain. She wasn't certain what pool cleaning entailed but she figured he'd get the gist. While *mi casa es su casa*, it was clear her brother understood there would be conditions to gain free rent and food.

"So, I gather that I'll never drive the Porsche. Got any transport for me?"

Amy shook her head. "No matter how much you hustle, wheedle, or whine, the keys will be stowed beyond your reach. Understand also that Ronnie and weed are out of reach, too. I'm tapped out of cash, and I *will* toss you over the cliff and into Lake Michigan rather than return to jail."

He seemed to grow smaller and shorter with each word she bit off. Her body language made it clear she'd bite off his head if he did or said anything outside her bounds.

Andy scratched his soul patch. "Well, I guess if you go away to the pokey, I'd have no home." A little-boy shiver ran through his body, and he kept his eyes to the ground. "Okay, Boss Lady, I agree to tow your lines."

Amy crossed her arms to connote her triumph over his intended turmoil. *Where there was a will, there was a way*. Andy had lived a self-determinate life, just like Amy—only he'd turned left after she'd tried to turn right. Could she trust him to comply with her plans?

Both siblings had zigzagged. Their situation was complex. Definitely not golden. Epically surreal. Amy used her head to signal Andy to get to it and returned to her manse. Arms crossed, she watched him through the wall of windows that overlooked the pool and patio.

Andy ambled to the pool, looked around for some things that seemed to be the proper implements to clean a pool. He found, propped against the stucco, an aluminum-handled implement with a brush. With a twist of the handle, the pole lengthened to at least sixteen feet. Andy held it aloft like a champion weight lifter and then angled up-and-down the pool sides, taking giant steps sideways. As green slacked from the sides of the pool, murking the pool water more, Amy hoped she'd done the right thing.

Amy wasn't one for tedious baby-sitting, so she Googled 'swimming pool care' and ordered the necessary supplies on Amazon. She hoped a large purchase would be delivered Prime. Costs were mounting on her boondoggle plan.

Rather than slide into a well of questions that might make her soul ache, Amy slipped outside and turned on the pool pump she found on the far side of the pool. The equipment jolted to a start and the water in the pool began to roil. At this point, all she had was hope.

The repetitive motion of the pool brushing lulled Andy. He soon became restless and bored. This body of water wasn't a pool—it was a lake! Monotony was not his game, and he longed for a toke.

A loud rumble-rattle broke the silence. Andy stuck his head around the corner of the gray-stucco home.

A rangy guy spotted him. "Hey, you!" Andy reeled around. How could this broad-shouldered punk be one of Amy's friends? Further, was the sloppily dressed dude looking at him?

"Get the jack down here!" the guy roared, his shout reverberating against the stucco. "Do I have to come back there and yank you by your soul patch?" Just as the guy began storming, as if to grab him by his collar, pants pocket or worse, Andy bolted toward the guy and his motley truck.

As he neared the truck, a giant hand thrust in his general direction and a voice boomed, "Name's Dante. Do what I do!" He then hooked each forearm through the handles of two gigantic cans of paint and marched off.

As Dante ran for the pool patio, Andy blinked and wished he'd brought the long-handle brush, instead of dropping it when he hopped to help. He coulda run the handle through two cans of paint and lifted like an ox. He winced, then reached into the truck bed, hooked his right arm through one can handle, and lifted.

He nearly fell backward due to the weight. He rubbed his forearm and tried again. Without success. He knew he was malnourished—would benefit from chicken-fried steak, biscuits, and gravy like the crew's cook at the grow farm, but dang those cans were heavy. He rolled the can nearer and looked at the label: 5 gallons. Of canary yellow paint? What the heck was Amy thinking?

Andy was just about to run inside and ask Amy

what-was-what when Dante returned. "What the jack!"

His path to the house impeded, Andy reflexively guarded his flank. He'd barely acceded to Amy's rule, and he wasn't about to be bludgeoned into work for this man. Andy had known a guy like him in prison, and instantly feared Dante. That other man had been a slack-jawed Cajun and took no crap from anyone, not even the prison guards.

Andy ran to the pool and jumped in, not minding the still murky water. Inside the house was a sister who wouldn't coddle him, outside a man who wanted him to heft gigantic cans of paint.

Andy dogpaddled and watched and listened, remaining in the deep end of the pool. Dante cursed and swatted in his direction for several seconds, then thrust both middle fingers in the air, and returned to some vehicle. Over the course of fifteen minutes, he unloaded 40 enormous paint cans and stacked them next to the house, cursing the entire time. It was obvious he was furious. It was also obvious at whom.

Andy dog-paddled well. He also read character well. A great defense mechanism to cope in many milieus. He surmised that Dante would paint his sister into a corner. Not today, but someday. So he bolted into the house to snitch.

The house was quiet. Andy called out Amy's name. He tiptoed, though he couldn't say why.

Fifty steps inside the house, Andy located his sister in a back bedroom. She was staring into space, her hand still clutching her phone. She looked like she'd seen a ghost.

That looked scared Andy. He tiptoed to Amy and snapped his fingers in front of her face, as if he were the antidote to this trance.

She startled, looked him up and down, and clenched her jaw. Her mood was not discernible until she opened her mouth and shouted, "Why did you come in here soaking wet? You ought to know by now that water is wet, and you've dribble-tracked water into this house! Have you no respect? These are solid mahogany floors!"

Andy wanted to tantrum. Andy wanted to pout. Instead, he dropped onto the fully made up bed and rolled himself up in the covers, writhing like a dog.

The big sister rant ended. Andy felt himself consumed in the best hug of his life, not squirming out of the wet cocoon.

After Amy ordered the pool chemicals, she took a deep breath. Time to check on the lottery influx. She needed beaucoup bucks to cover her credit card purchases. After all of the home renovation expenses to which she'd indebted herself, she hoped sufficient cash remained for groceries.

She counted to ten—evenly and slowly, timed with even, slow breaths. Amy walked through her 6,000 square feet and did a few yoga asanas before she powered up her phone to go online to check her bank statement. She cracked her knuckles and crossed her heart, then began the reality check.

Amy didn't know what to expect, but it was time to know. It had been a couple of weeks, as Ezekiel had promised, so the state of Michigan had to have made good on its yearly deposit from the ¼ billion lottery win. The sum she'd receive once yearly for thirty years.

Amy knew she'd be financially secure even if she went through the entire lottery amount, spend-thrifting and thriving and having a brilliant life… because she'd be nearly Social Security eligible soon after the lottery payments ran out. But knowing that math and feeling that security were very different things.

Andy, Ronnie, and the Lady Bug Inn X two portended a trifecta of cash drains.

Amy clicked screens and more screens. She looked back and forth between the Notes app where she'd stored the lottery ticket number, the date of her win, the tracking numbers and other necessary info to gain her rightful share. Numbers began to bleed into numbers and her fingers grew numb. Her concentration faltered, her eyes began to cross and she wondered if she needed glasses or if she'd missed a stop or—

Holy! Holy! Holy! Zeros and zeros! Unfathomable amounts! She rubbed at her eyes as if to clear them and looked again. Yaasss, stardom amounts of cash.

Amy knew she'd never be able to spend all of that. She sincerely regretted not being able to leave the bounds of Michigan. Even with two palaces with plans and ambitions to spend—and clothes closets to fill and every conceivable sweet treat to eat—she might never be able to spend that amount of money in one year, let alone thirty! She couldn't 'money pit' her mansions enough. But there was that other matter…

Travis would eat shit and die. Spectacularly!

Amy decided to drive the Porsche to personally exact many pounds of his flesh. Her arrival would be stealth, her revenge would be brilliant, her *rebelution* would surmount all of her personal guilts.

Chapter Thirty-One

CHANGE OF PLANS

AMY CAME OUT of her *money spell* with her arms around a huge wad of sopping wet fabric, squeezing with all her might as if to wring out all of the water. The expensive set of white linens were saturated with pool water, she guessed. She remembered seeing a skinny, near-naked Andy jump into the middle of the bed. He was shivering under them, she knew, because she could feel the vibrations and hear his sobs. Like the never-ending earthquake that shook the earth when she was ten.

She dug at the covers as if mining for gold. In truth, she knew she was mining for gold—her real live little brother was here, in her house, and soon to be in her arms. All of her uptight bitchiness dissolved.

To hell with Travis. To hell with Revenge. Heaven was here. Family! The past be damned!

Amy quickly hugged Andy and then grabbed his

hand. She signaled and the pair cooperatively scooped the sopping sheets and covers off and dumped them into the bathtub. Then, they hauled all of the towels off the wide, shimmery bars and used them to wipe the trail of water through the house.

Andy hustled to the bedroom he'd been assigned and shed his wet clothes. Since he had no others, Amy rummaged through her closet for tee and jeans and belt. She urged Andy into them and then waltzed him to the kitchen. She seated him at the table, poured him a glass of water and proceeded to order pizza online, saying that she'd meet the delivery guy at the end of her lane. She hoped the guy took Apple Pay or Pay-Pal, because she had no cash on hand.

Amy searched the cupboards and drawers, opening-and-slamming each one, while Andy silently glugged the water.

Amy shook her head at the state of each drawer. One held fifteen pens that didn't work and fifteen pens that did, but not a piece of paper in sight. So much for being able to call the pizza place to find out when the driver arrived.

Millionaires despised cold pizza.

She dug into the cabinet under the sink and fished out the Porsche keys, certain Andy had seen the hiding place. She would deal with that later. On second thought—she tossed the keys to Andy. "Wanna drive?"

Andy flashed a smile and bolted upright. Though he had to hike the pant legs up and hitch-step, he was barreling downstairs to the underground garage in seconds.

"Wait for me!" Amy shouted after him. "Don't leave without me. I've gotta pee first and then we can mosey to the end of the lane…"

Andy was already seated behind the wheel, his hands fondling, slithering over the dials and leather seats when Amy reached the garage.

As soon as she put her hand on the car door, Andy started the engine and revved the sleek beast. Amy deliberately slowed her pace, hoping he would slow his. When she was seated in the passenger bucket seats, she took his head in both her hands to swivel him to direct eye contact. "Look and listen. I have five words for you. Andy. Are you ready?"

Amy shook his head 'yes' with her hands and uttered her three words forcefully. "Seatbelt." Andy nodded. "Slow-go." Andy nodded. "Garage door open." Then, she depressed the automatic opener.

Amy put her hand on his knee. "Now you may proceed. Slowly. This driveway is an incline, the lane is curvy, and—though I know you are hungry—we don't want to go spitting stones on this highly-polished paint."

Andy tapped the pedal, accelerated gingerly, slowly backed up and out of the garage. He guided the Porsche down the lane. He parked jerkily but solidly at the end of the lane and stopped beside the mailbox. Not until then did he speak. "Are you really painting this giant house yellow? Do you really want it to look like that Big Bird on Sesame Street or like a contraband bar-and-brothel?"

Before she could renig on her intention to never bridle her brother and smack him upside the head, the pizza guy arrived.

He did use Pay-Pal. He did accept a tip via Pay-Pal, too. He dropped the pizza in Amy's lap and left.

Andy and Amy ate the pizza in silence. In the car at the end of the lane, looking in the rearview. What now?

They'd consumed the last piece of the large meat-lovers pizza when Amy's cell chirped. She licked her fingers and clicked on the call. She could feel her brow furrow as she listened for several seconds. She squinted and her ears began to ring when she glimpsed the murky photo that had been messaged. She shook her head in disbelief.

Though her brother's eyes were wide with hope to soon be in the know, Amy clicked off and stuffed the phone in her pocket. She slammed the pizza box closed and tossed it over her shoulder into the Porsche's minimal back seat. "Drive!" she shouted.

"Where?" Andy asked. He looked wide-eyed, exasperated, and unclear. There was no target in sight. His hands flew in the air as if he'd been shot, and he almost lost the keys as he jerked.

"Turn right onto the blacktop and go like a bat, though we must be wary and cool. There are speed traps and Hernandez to contend with."

"What?" Andy shrieked and raised his hands held

even higher as if he was already under arrest. "Hernandez is who?"

"Hernandez is the state of Michigan's guardian of my actions." Amy smirked and translated to Andy, turning to look him in the eye. "In other words, he's my ever-present parole officer. I've begun to suspect he has eyes on me at all times via drone as well as the tracking achieved via iPhone. It's like he's my moral compass, because he doubts I have one."

Amy sensed Andy was ready to say something crude, so she reached over and yanked his soul patch. His mouth startled shut. "Here's something to truly and thoroughly understand, Little Brother. Though I may feel as if I'm locked-down, Hernandez cares about me. At times it feels claustrophobic, as if I'm his only parolee, but he keeps me safe from myself. It's a pure form of love that he swarms me."

"That's kind of creepy," Andy said, lowering his hands to his lap and then to the leather-wrapped steering wheel of the Porsche. Rather than contemplate the potential that Hernandez was a perv due to his eyes on Amy at all times, he started the car. Rumble-rumble, purr-purr, the car announced that its enormous engine and its sleek lines were in control.

Andy drove expeditiously, though Amy barked, "Hurry! Hurry!" in between "Turn left, turn here." driving directions. Soon Andy turned into another sumptuous home's lane and guided the Porsche between tall columns made of the same brush-painted bricks as the house.

Andy swore he heard the automobile curse when

he shut off the engine. Before he could ask what was next, Amy handed him her phone and earbuds. "Stick these in your ears. We're a long way from any radio station here. Though Chicago's WLS comes in scratchy and faint, I suggest that you cue up Spotify."

Before he could ask more what-the-hells, such as what the heck was Spotify, Amy bounded out of the Porsche and disappeared behind the stately house.

Chapter Thirty-Two

THE SHIT HITS

BASED ON HER brief glimpse of Ronnie's video, Amy was afraid to enter their initial guest house. She thought about the plush carpets and the deeply cushioned couch as she fast-forwarded to the smeared walls, the brown-brown-brown, upside and down, that she'd glimpsed. The fact she couldn't smell the shit was the only reason she didn't vomit.

Amy thought about the floor-to-ceiling windows with drapes that hush-hushed sound as she tried to suppress a scream. She tried not to think about the extensive library of videotapes Ronnie had watched hour-upon hour. Tears flooded her eyes as she trudged. This couldn't be happening—

When she finally arrived at Ronnie's log cabin, Amy burst through the door like a bullet.She grabbed Ronnie's phone from her hand and punched it on.

"Don't look," Ronnie implored. "Don't look again.

It's true. All true. A guest room is mucked up. And it stinks!"

Naturally, Amy opened the video on Ronnie's phone. She'd never looked away from any disaster, and she didn't plan to start now.

Amy watched again, as if her second view of the lurid details would be any different than her first. As if a rewind button or an *erase* would emerge. Within several seconds, she said, "That's not so bad, Ronnie. While the furnishings, window treatments, and damask-covered walls were expensive, I'm certain we can hire one of the local motel maids to put in a little overtime and clean up the mess.

Ronnie shook her head. "You don't understand." She slumped again for several minutes.

Amy was aghast at Ronnie's behavior. Was she truly independent management material? This site was supposed to be the workhorse, creating significant cash flow until the second spa was opened with great fanfare and filled to capacity with well-heeled surgery recoverees.

Ronnie lifted her head to report. "One of the guests skipped without paying her bill. When I entered her suite to clean it for rental to another occupant, I discovered she'd smeared the walls, furniture, and drapes."

"Smeared?" Amy recalled the video footage. "You mean the mud?"

Ronnie whimpered and involuntarily cowered. "Not mud. The stink suggests the thick brown stuff was her shit."

Now Amy sank to the floor. Dumbfounded, she wondered what to do now? Her entire cell block been moved once because a convict had smeared her cell. Anger over a meal cooked poorly.

"When did this happen, Ronnie?" she creaked. "During the night?"

Her friend nodded. The rest of the guests needed to be packed and cleared out before they notified the Health Department. The mess needed to be cleaned up and quick!

Christ on a bicycle, Amy thought. I wish my ex-mother-in-law, Jackie Breeden, was nearby. That singular housewife would know what to do! Her use of Lysol was legendary.

Amy put in a call to the Hush Hush Motel and spoke with manager. She hired the entire Housekeeping staff and gave the address to the manager, promising to pay the cab fare and the women's pay for the day.

Joe Quick lived up to his name. He screeched into the driveway, marched up to the front door, and knocked-knocked-knocked within a half-hour. She knew because Andy texted her—good boy! She'd forgotten him in the Porsche.

Amy abandoned Ronnie, weeping helplessly with her head in her hands, rocking and swaying to the beat of *good grief.*

Good grief! She rounded the large home just as the

khaki-uniformed man put his hand on the doorknob as if to enter the place.

"Hello, how may I help you?" she asked sweetly, emulating Jackie's farmwife tone. She was grateful for her long legs and her ability to recover rapidly without feeling winded—and without provoking an asthma attack. She had no time to pause for her rescue inhaler. She needed to make *nice* and head off this inopportune person's entry into the blighted establishment.

Khaki Man looked officially like a hassle. When he handed Amy his card without a hello, smile, or other form of courtesy, he proved he was an *official hassle*.

Joseph Quick was the county health inspector. His demeanor set a tone of rules and governance and no-way-back. His posture was rigid and official, imperious even. Amy wished she knew how to finger-text her phone in her pocket. She had many rescue-interveners: Andy, Hernandez, Andrew Machinist, the lone South Haven cop. Maybe the Mayor, who was President of the Lions Club.

Amy remembered her squeamishness around germs. That stopped her, but only for a second. Then she remembered that cleaning meant gloves… and baggy overalls… and a hat, maybe one of Ronnie's…

Joseph Quick suddenly at-eased. He reached over to slide his card out of Amy's hand and smiled as soon as he'd replaced in his khaki shirt pocket. "I remember you, young lady. You've been to several Lions Club meetings." Now he extended Amy's hand to pump it.

Nonplussed, she took his hand. Would the creep kiss it or slap a fine into her palm?

"I received a call about something suspiciously *aromatic* in this place. I came to inspect and write up legendary citations and fines. You see, the town coffers are a tad low and rumors were spreading that bills and salaries wouldn't be paid. As a member of the Council, I was inclined to do my part. Rumors had it that you were *flush*, young lady. What was your name again?"

Amy pulled her hand gently out of *The* Health Inspector's squeeze. "I'm Amy and, if you help me to relocate my guests quickly and without repercussions, I'll bless your town appropriately." She hoped her smile was demure enough to prove her sincerity. She was, indeed, flush. Needy, too. Her desire to make all of the mess disappear as rapidly as possible. She didn't desire business death via Yelp. If flashing cash prevented that, she was in for whatever dollar amount was required.

Mr. Quick's eyes rolled back in their sockets. Could this six-foot Amazon really achieve all his, er, the town's goals simultaneously? If so, he was all in. He needed his paycheck. The Lions' annual dues were due soon and his mortgage payments were five months behind. He could no longer slide with the local banker, who, of course, was a fellow Lion. The man semi-threatened to blab to the other brothers about his financial instability.

Amy watched Mr. Quick's face and knew she had a deal, but she needed to act quickly. She'd thwarted a Haz-Mat clean-up, but soon alarm would spread among the guests. What to do, what to do? Think, think, think.

A text buzzed her phone, mid-think. Amy sort of apologized to Mr. Quick, who stepped off the stoop in a small-town manners move that wasn't necessary. Texts could not be overheard. She began to think less of Mr. Quick.

No, it wasn't a text. It was a FaceTime request from her nominal mom, Woolworth Wilma. For this Amy would need to step away from Quick's earshot, so she opened the door and stepped inside quickly, so that the Mr. Health Inspector couldn't get his foot in the door.

Amy whirled around, intent on walking into the secluded library to chat with Woolworth Wilma. However, there were eight grim-faced ladies ensconced in the living room. Their luggage surrounded them in stacks. Their combined demeanor proclaimed a wall of discontent.

Amy almost whimpered, but instead she ceremoniously held out one finger. "One moment while I take this call from my mom." The ladies faces' softened, so Amy tiptoed to the library to chat.

As soon as she saw Wilma's face filling the screen, Amy let a flood of tears go. Wilma's soft coos and encouragements intervened so that Amy revealed details of the ugly-upon-ugly messes she was in. Blurts and bleats and sobs may have obscured the message, but Wilma was a skilled interpreter of messes.

She also had a solution. "I'll clear out my stock of

Lysol and be at the home within the hour. You know I have a pen ready, paper here by the register, so give me the address, Amy. I'll be able to help you clear the worst mess—and give you another embroidered linen handkerchief to wipe away those tears."

Amy felt her shoulders relax and lower a full inch. About to say "Thank you" to Wilma, the elderly soldier-of-fortune intervened. "Don't thank me, dear. Merely make certain that there are plenty of towels and buckets and rags to properly disinfect and clean."

Amy promised, clicked off the call from her savior, and then backed into the living room filled with livid creatures who collectively fidgeted and held their noses. Fierce. One woman seemed to have elected herself as spokesperson. She spoke with the furious energy of a former administrator, and Amy was reminded of Fran Blackstone back in that small-town she'd fled seven years ago.

Though Amy was scared, she did not allow herself to be intimidated. She had the backing of millions and knew that everyone had a price. She would meet these ladies' price, exceed it, and sign them to secrecy forever. There had to be a lawyer among the Lions.

"Please raise your hands if you have your own transportation, ladies?" Eight hands shot into the air. Still grim-faced, no smiles yet. Amy needed to pull out more stops to sweeten the pot, not stir it.

"Raise your hands if you'd like to return home?" Four ladies vehemently raised their hands. "Would you please step into the dining room, ladies? You know the way. May I have someone serve refreshments?"

"I demand Scotch," one woman smarmed. This set the flock aflurry. Amy summoned Mr. Quick. Under-age Andy couldn't bartend. Further, he might be inclined to whip out some weed and get the guest house inhabitants stoned.

No one noticed when Amy stepped outside to hiss-whisper to Joseph Quick, "I need you to come in and pour some stiff drinks." Mr. Quick nodded. "Wait, before you step inside, I need another favor. Call the Lions Club member who's a lawyer and tell him to arrive quick."

Chapter Thirty-Three

FACTS AND FIXES

AMY STEPPED INTO the home with Mr. Quick in tow. The ladies, none of whom had abandoned their squabbling comparison of conditions and demands for booze, began to search for their purses for implements to freshen make-up. After a brief search Mr. Quick ducked into the kitchen. Then the ladies returned their faces to pout and recrossed their arms. Amy didn't know what to say, so she just smiled, hoping to sunbeam the atmosphere.

Within moments Quick motioned Amy into the kitchen. He looked at her sternly and began listing health violations. Amy's eyes widened—and she knew her pocketbook would, too—while he whispered. The final items almost made her gag. It seemed that 'Stunned Mouse is a Dixie Cup' and 'Dwarf Bites of Rat Poop" were menu items in the pantry. There was no chilled wine, no Scotch to be found..

"Perhaps the liquor and wine are stocked in the dining room," Amy said, suppressing her gag with a gulp. "Help me grab goblets, glasses and ice and we'll glide the ladies to the dining room."

Joe jumped to open all the cupboards while Amy found a pitcher for water and a bucket to hold all the ice cubes in the freezer. Amy found a tray, assembled the items, and held it high like the waitresses she'd seen at Miss Elly's Homesick Grill. Mr. Quick held the door open for her to pass and directed the host of mad-as-hornets ladies to rise and follow them to the dining room.

There she left the assemblage, assuming the Joseph Quick knew how to uncork and pour wine—and to make Scotch drinks. She fervently hoped he'd pour one of each while she awaited the Lions Club lawyer at the front door. She texted Andy, asking him to stay put.

He texted back: HAVE TO PEE.

HOLD IT OR PEE IN A BUSH. DO NOT PEE IN THE PORSCHE. And, as an afterthought, DON'T LEAVE ME HERE. I'VE GOT A SITUATION.

OK. DO YOU NEED MY HELP?

NO! Amy replied before Andy even completed his text. She already had more trouble than she could handle and didn't need Andy to haul his wreckage inside.

She looked up as another Porsche rumbled into the parking court, selecting a spot on the end of the row to avoid dings in the door of the ab-fab expensive driving machine. A slick-haired, bespoke-suited man with python-leather cowboy boots climbed out of the car and zap-locked it. He clenched a black briefcase that almost made him look like a doctor on a house call. Well, actually, he was.

Amy looked down at her yoga apparel, wishing that she'd worn one of her two suits. She hadn't had time to amass a power wardrobe yet. Things were moving faster than fast.

Besides, her Master Card was maxed.

As soon as she opened the front door, she knew that she needn't have been concerned about her garb. She had the advantage of height—probably 18 inches, including his butched-up hair. His card indicated his name was Link N. Law.

Amy almost giggled. Matthew McConaughey had played Lincoln Lawyer, and she was certain he wasn't this short. She quickly ushered the attorney in the door and began to briefly describe her needs.

Mr. Law asked a few questions, nodded a few times, but said little. Amy began to prattle, knowing that she may have sounded foolish, but she needed to thwart tears.

In that moment, Woolworth Wilma stepped into the home and extended a superbly-soft and daintily-embroidered hankie to Amy. Then, Mom wheeled on the short man. "Who are you, and why are you here?"

"No worries, ma'am." He nodded to Amy and said, "I'll be a moment. I have a printer in my car." In reply to Amy and Wilma's stunned looks, he said, "Yes, my office is in the passenger seat of my car. In this way, I'm totally mobile and can serve the needs of clients from Chicago to Ann Arbor and Detroit in a flash." When he smiled, Amy knew his teeth were veneers. Impressive.

"I'll return with nine copies of a binding document for the ladies/guests to depart without comments. Their forever-silence will be purchased, too. The documents will be notarized within the hour and messaged to your door. Shall I use this address?"

Amy was too stunned to speak. She and Wilma followed the attorney to the dining room. The path to the room was easy to discern now via the open laughter and guffaws. Apparently, the Health Inspector entertained with dirty jokes.

The room was stunned into silence by the entry of the short attorney, Amy, Wilma who incited instant sympathy and rapport, and soul-patched Andy, who'd never pass for a gardener anywhere.

No worries, however, Andy waved a tiny hello and scampered outside to lose himself in nature. Amy knew he intended to pee on every plant in the large yard.

The health inspector seated himself at the head of the mahogany table. At the lawyer's finger snap, he exited the room. Amy suspected he intended to find more health violations to assure the entire South Haven town budget requirements would be met. Not having to raise taxes would satisfy the 4000 inhabitants and the hoteliers and bar owners, too. Everyone would prosper at Amy's behest. Maybe even herself.

Wilma held Amy's hand as they stood in the corner of the dining room, trying to remain silent and out-of-sight. Amy had to admit the lawyer commanded the room despite his slight height. He was a classic example of 'baffle them with your bullshit."

Within a half an hour he left the house with his briefcase. But not before pausing to whisper in Amy's ear, "Haven't seen you at Lions Club meetings in a while. You ought to return, because we have a hunk of a new member. Name's Travis. He's re-opened the bar. He's our newest economic hero…and he's a hunk that's your height."

All of the air sucked out of Amy's lungs. She scrambled for her inhaler. No-no-no! Noo-oo-o! She'd intended to hunt down Travis, and he'd landed in her lap. What a plot twist!

The wind currents changed swiftly as the horde of former guests hurried after the fixer-as-messenger, loaded their own luggage in their respective vehicles, and roared off. It was not the respite they'd expected, but an adventure to be expanded into great stories later. But no talking to reporters. Ever. Adverse publicity was forbidden. Forever.

Wilma sighed. Amy echoed her sigh. All the liquor was gone. Not a drop in which to drown sorrows. A good thing, because the shit smell had begun to leak from the angry guest's room at the end of the hall.

"Help me bring in the cases of Lysol, better yet, fetch that lanky kid and put him to use," Wilma exclaimed. "We have some righteous house-cleaning to do, and I have just enough hankies to stuff our nostrils while we scrub. I've done this before, by the way, with those cuddly grandchildren you waved to as we Facetimed. Turns out that 'terrible twos' can be terrible in too many ways."

Amy wondered if Wilma always smiled, no matter what—

"By the way, let's squelch this episode. Promise you'll never tell Hernandez, the parole office, so help me God."

That was an easy promise to make. And while Amy scrub-a-dub-dubbed, she wondered how much this was all going to cost. Lawyers of that magnitude charged a lot, but he'd salvaged a bad situation, which made him worth every cent.

Sometime during the several hours of cleaning, Amy decided to sell this stupid residence. She had better plans, an assembly of helpers, and a dream to achieve.

As soon as the scrubbers had scrubbed the room—and then themselves - she called Elvin the Realtor to *fire sale* this place.

He agreed after two caveats: 1. to not alert the bank that she'd sold the collateral on which the jumbo jumbo loan for her soon-to-be-sole property, The Lady Bug Inn, was leveraged, and 2. that his full commission would be used to fund the Blueberry Festival Float. He would become the community hero, because the club members would not have to endlessly fundraise.

Entrepreneur Amy planned to ride atop the float. From there she could toss hundreds of spa brochures into the throngs that lined the streets. A publicity genius with long legs and a tan. Hernandez would be proud of his parolee.

CHAPTER THIRTY-FOUR

MOVING FORWARD WITH MONEY

HERNANDEZ' CHECK-INS BECAME less frequent as the weeks passed. It was likely his alpha-assertions decreased when Amy's increased and solidified around correct, law-abiding steps. Trust was a beautiful thing, and Amy grew daily amidst her community of family and friends. Brother Andy remained a wild child, but hunger—and the need for a roof over his head—kept him under Amy's thumb.

While she missed Dad's daily interjections, Amy figured it was likely Hernandez had improved his pre-detecting of her schedule and moves. It was certain he had an extensive roster of parolees, with new fires to extinguish. She wished him well, knowing that she had him on speed-text if she needed him. His number was etched in her heart. She knew he'd never forsake his prized parolee.

The attorney's bill arrived, and Amy nearly collapsed. She waited a week until she Pay-Paled payment, savoring the thirty-nine reminder texts she received. Though he'd saved her ass, the little weasel could wait for that many zeroes to plump his bank account. Where was there to spend that amount of cash, anyway?

Amy almost laughed (but didn't) when Elvin related he had a buyer for her initial property. It was an irony, yet not. What came around, went around—

Of course, it was Link N. Law. Predictable, yet not, the bespoke-suited guy was a remorseless weasel. His skin was the color of liquid brass, as well as his car. To hide in plain sight must have been his monochromatic credo.

Her counteroffer excluded the log cabin and an acre—and Lincoln graciously granted the request. Ronnie needed a place to live—apart from the dynamic and spacious Lady Bug spa she'd manage for Amy. Andy as roommate/cabana boy was problem enough for Amy to handle in-house. Amy felt, as owner/greeter of future guests, she needed to reside onsite.

All life elements were under control except Travis. Her quest for revenge, never at bay, lurked and breathed down her neck, filling her back with tension. Hernandez warned her to back off her thoughts of revenge: "You don't need murder on your rap sheet, my favorite parolee. It'll look bad on my record, but worse on yours. There's no way to spend millions when you're behind bars."

Still Amy slept little at night. What if Travis was stalking *her,* like she was stalking him?

One day Amy received a text with pictures and video that almost made her eyes fall from their sockets. It was a gyrating male stripper, staged-named Tiny Tarzan, as per the gigantic letters affixed to a shimmery curtain behind him. Though her phone's screen was small, she could tell that Tiny put on a lengthy, sensuous show. She couldn't help herself—she watched it many times, including while she showered, hoping that her iPhone was waterproof. She didn't bother wondering who sent the video and body shots. She finally had an inside joke for herself, one none of the locals enjoyed.

Though the video was dark and moody, in the light of the disco ball above his head, Amy was certain that the satin-bikinied man with the grinding attitude was Dante. Amy decided that she needed Ronnie's corroboration, so she forwarded the pictures, moving and non.

Amy considered it improbable that any other small town in Michigan had a painter moonlighting as a male stripper - her realtor's son. This was rich! If she chose to forward the video to Elvin the Realtor, the cache of blackmail would assure that he'd never reveal she'd sold the property out-from-under her jumbo jumbo mortgage. She knew she'd never have to blackmail him out of his soon-to-be legendary status as the hero float funder.

And thus, it became less of a trial to endure Dante abruptness, short workdays, and lack of finesse. Amy had come to know him as a dribbler and a drabbler, so that she feared the house, with its interior of 6,000 square feet clothed in a stucco exterior might never be done. He seemed disinclined to end the job or worry as he drained her bank account. He seemed to be as much of a resident as Andy. Thank God the two ignored each other.

Dante made every day interesting. Amy adopted a thick skin regarding his crude remarks and sexist attitudes. She merely smiled, dug out her phone, and stuck her head in his online videos.

The videos reminded Amy to remain fully clothed as she roamed about her home. There were many, many windows and sliding glass doors, and one never knew when Dante was inclined to peek or let himself in for a snack.

Further, Amy never stocked beer in the frig. She feared Andy's and Dante's paths would intersect and their shared cluelessness would combust. Each man-child was confrontational to a fault. Dante continued to insist upon painting the giant house yellow, calling it "Big Bird" whenever Amy was in earshot. Andy demanded a helicopter pad on the roof.

As Hernandez had warned, she knew, well-and-fully, one didn't *need* to make up characters. They just inserted themselves onto her stage, causing Amy to feel like the servant rather than the served. She did not enjoy control of the situation. She did not have any guests to pay the bills. Though Elvin had sold the other property and she had a place to live, Amy began to itch for something to do, rather than pad around her roomy house, fully attired in clothes bought online.

After she'd expanded her wardrobe and built a respectable one for slacker Andy, who no longer looked like a ragamuffin beggar, she needed more to accomplish than twiddling her thumbs. Ronnie oversaw spa start-up supplies: linens and massage tables and essential oils. Listening to Ronnie—or even reading her texts—nearly hypnotized Amy.

She controlled the big bank account. Due to auto deposit, nothing remained for her to contribute to the business beyond cash. She avoided the Lions Club meetings, so she practically became a recluse. Too Howard Hughes or Little Girl Rich.

Suddenly it occurred to her that, while spa supplies were being ordered, and the rooms upstairs had been parsed into six spacious in-suite bedrooms, the lower floor contained only a vast pool table. With that much space, there could be more post-surgery guestrooms. The business was about to expand.

Because she trusted her Dad, coupled with the simple fact that she missed him, she texted him for a contractor referral. Her dependence on Lion's Den resulted in one of the banes of her existence, a painter who seemed to consider himself eligible to move in, rather than move on, with the house painted in a color which she, the owner, didn't like.

Her alpha certainly didn't daunt him.

Dante had a constant 'chaw' and, throughout the days that he did paint, she noticed that his brush strokes were timed with his chew. This made her snicker—but the man's indolence caused a cramp in Amy's spleen. She needed to move forward.

"NEED A CONTRACTOR TO BUILD OUT HOUSE."

"HI TO YOU, TOO. WAS JUST THINKING OF YOU. NEED COFFEE WHILE WE CHAT? I'LL BUY."

"A ROOT BEER FLOAT? I'LL BUY."

"DEAL."

Hernandez was apparently quite encumbered that day. He arrived a half-hour behind Amy at 50's style A&W in South Haven. She'd already swilled a root beer float and was about to order another. "Welcome to the land of gigantic onion rings," Hernandez said.

"What?" Amy startled, then re-settled after his entrance.

"Onion rings the size of your hand," Hernandez replied. "It's guaranteed you'll gain a pound a bite." Hernandez winked when Amy reared back. "I'll buy the next round of root beer, with the fried rings on the side."

"As long as you get me a plumber and a contractor, I'm game," Amy replied.

Hernandez raised an eyebrow and gave her a long look before he left to place the order.

Amy twiddled her thumbs and tried not to chew her nails while she waited for him to return to their table. She counted down from 100, marching among her fingertips. Would he help her source the help? She disliked her Lions Club leash.

She just flicked her final pinkie when, out of nowhere, an onion ring shot onto the finger. It was hot and greasy and smelled more delicious than anything she'd ever eaten. Decidedly more delicious than prison basics.

Though the ring was hot, Amy moved it to her ring finger. "Hernandez! What are you proposing?" she fluttered her eyelashes, dipped her chin like a starlet, and smiled benignly at her parole officer. It felt good to be near him again.

Amy swore Hernandez flushed beneath his ultra-bronze skin, more leathery, yet less smarmy than Link N. Law's. He took a seat across the picnic table from her, taking a moment to regain proper composure.

It took several moments before Hernandez met Amy's gaze. "Eat that thing before it cools. Cold onion rings taste like all the grease that they are when they're cold." He popped two into his mouth and began to earnestly chomp.

His grin widened as he chewed, so Amy forced the high-calorie ring into her mouth. She fought back imagery that her molars were sliding across the grease. Before he downed two more, Hernandez said, "I'm fairly certain that flirting with your parole officer is a misdemeanor, Amy. I can still bounce you, you know. I've got the ball, er law, in my hands."

"But I've got the cash to buy all of the onion rings anyone could want, hot or cold and forever," Amy retorted as she reached for another onion ring to nibble. She wanted to practice her millionaire-fueled authority.

All explanation regarding Amy's contractor needs, and/or Hernandez' ability to fulfill them, ceased—put on hold in deference to chewing. Only flies circled their heads, advance to the vapid 80s tuned piped onto the A&W patio.

Soon, the container was empty. The greasy remnants of the paper liner attested to the fat content of the scrumptious food. Across the table, Hernandez folded his arms while his facial expression said, "What's next?"

Amy gave him the short version of what had been a very long and overwrought sequence of events. Hernandez' expression changed so many times she was glad they'd eaten first. As she described the rapid turn of events and observed the whiplash of emotions on Hernandez' face, Amy realized how tumult-filled the last few days had been.

Hernandez took a long swig of root beer to clear his palate. "Good!"

"Good?" shrieked Amy. "How is any of that good?"

"It's good, because I can finally place another of my parolee's in a job. It's good that you two, among my most dangerous, will be within proximity and easy to monitor. It's good, because I know you are solid, and will you will keep him away from the many bars and brothels in this seaside tourist trap."

"What's the good part for me?" Amy swiped Hernandez's frosted beer mug and began to alternately sip his between turns at her own, daring her parole officer to object.

"What's good for you is that you'll be able to help your fellow man. It'll also be good because you'll be distracted from exacting revenge."

"Revenge?" Amy shrieked. "I'm living well, I don't need revenge. What are you talking about, Dad?"

"Remember that I know all and see all—and what I don't see others report. I know that Travis Castro is the new town saint. He's also the dude who prepped you for a ten-year prison term. I know you well, my child. I know you'd love to *off* that turd. Here, front and center in your new turf."

Hernandez stayed Amy before she could stalk off. He gently pulled her closer, so that he could look her in the eye, up close. He emphasized each word as he said, "Know this, my favorite parolee, if you bring someone else down, you bring yourself down with them."

Then Hernandez shook his finger and tapped on her nose. "Don't do it. Don't bring yourself down. You are golden. You are a star. Believe it."

CHAPTER THIRTY-FIVE

THE PLUMBERS

HERNANDEZ' GUY WAS short and burly. His cheeks sported the perpetual red of an alcoholic and his pug nose looked like a cherry in the middle of a red velvet cake. His close-clipped hair appeared to be slurried with grease. Perhaps he'd forgotten to comb after a short shower.

However, due to his grimy body odor, it was probable he hadn't showered since being incarcerated. According to Hernandez it was a plausible theory, because, like many ex-cons, he had no discernable family or friends to take him in when he was cut loose. Hernandez' hapless guy, named Tony King, was the type who did petty crime just to return to the comfort and routine of a 6X8 cell.

When Amy asked Hernandez how he knew the guy had plumbing and building skills, Dad laughed. "Because Tony dug his way out of prison with a serving spoon, slowly widening the plumbing of the communal showers in his cell block. Of the team of three men who did the deed, he's the only one who succeeded twice."

"You're harboring a felon?" Amy set their mugs down so hard, root beer splashed over the sides.

"Easy, Amy." Hernandez laid his palms on her hands, pressing hard when she attempted to free herself. "You've got no right to moralize." He returned Amy's gaze, fierce-for-fierce.

Amy broke the stare-down. Hernandez had the law—and a gun—on his side. "Try to relax. We're all under pressure here," he calm-voiced his favorite scoundrel.

Amy squirmed, but relented to listen. Nowhere else to go for a while.

"Trust is a remarkable beast, Amy. I know because I've ridden its back with hundreds of parolees like you."

Hernandez winked and flashed his 100-watt teeth when Amy winced at his claim. The word 'trust' made her itch, and she'd chosen to believe that she was *singular…* Now she knew she was *a dime a dozen.* Not golden, not unique, not special—despite being armed with a quarter-billion bucks.

"My man was pressed into public service, aka prison, to bear the burdens that belonged to someone else, like you, my dear."

Amy's eyes widened in empathy. That final burden she knew. Was Tony King bent on revenge—like she had been until a better deal surfaced? Her monthly share of zeros had diverted her killer thoughts. Perhaps she could extend a hand to Mr. King.

"Okay, I'll meet him."

A surly-faced man, with a thick and muscled neck, rose from the picnic table next to theirs. Since there were only two tables—and no other people—on the A&W's tiny outdoor patio, Amy wondered how she'd missed noticing the guy. His footsteps were leaden, yet he was beside them in seconds.

Tony's hands were clasped so tightly in front of him, he looked like a weightlifter attempting to swell his mountain-goat chest in order to win a Mr. Atlas title. The chest you'd never see before he punched your lights out in a bar fight. She should drag this man with her for Round Two with Travis.

Ah, so I haven't denounced my killer thoughts to take Travis down.

"P-p-pleased t-t-to me-meet you, Amy. Her-hernandez has told me about your homeowner needs. I p-p-promise that I can do it-t-t all. And for a pi-pi-pittance."

Amy's eyes widened further. Mr. King's accent was British, but his stutter was American made.

"M-m-mind if I bring me a p-p-partner?"

Amy looked at Hernandez, who nodded.

"It-t-t takes two to carry a toilet, Miss. No need to ask me how I know that-that-that p-p-particular fact."

At some unspoken signal, Hernandez swiftly scooted along the picnic table's bench to allow Tony a place to sit. A space wide enough for two men, though Tony was the only one present of the Construction/

Plumber team. Amy knew her construction project was in good hands, brute-force hands, expedient hands. Should she call Dante or his Realtor father to pull the permits for her? Or Phil Lactose, the Lions Club president, or the mayor of this small town? Amy was pleased to roll off the number of influencers she knew in this town—a fistful.

"I can see your eyes roll back in your head, my protégé parolee," Hernandez said. "There's no need for construction permit applications, because I've already handled that matter. Our mutual friend, the Mayor of South Haven, has already completed the paperwork—and his fellow Lions approve—soTony and Tiny can begin in the morning."

Bada-Bing. Bada-Boom. Clang the cymbals and bass drum. Amy's spa would quickly expand and be available for the business of a dozen post-surgery peacocks, er patients, while its stucco facade limped along without the essential curb appeal.

Perhaps she could get Hernandez to give Dante a kick in the pants. She was tired of his excuses and complaints about the humidity, lack of shade, and general diddley-farting around. Perhaps she should forward Dante's male stripper video to the Mayor or to the town's only cop, Andrew Machinist.

Amy gulped and thought better of that bad idea. Rather than focusing Dante on his task of painting *her project* rather than the town, Machinist would badge up and jail Dante's ass. Indefinitely, piling charges upon charges so as to fill the town's meager coffers. Such commotion that followed, incarcerating the realtor's only and bad-ass son, would rob her of the only painter around.

Better to call Hernandez in on the warranted disciplinary action. While "the weather was impossible to trust" (Dante's favorite complaint), Amy would put her money on Hernandez any day of the week. She was learning exactly who to trust and it was all good. She reached across the table to shake Mr. King's hand, "See you tomorrow morning at 9:00."

"If you don't m-m-ind, ma'am, my buddy and m-m-me will start at 7:00 a.m. We'll b-b-be testing the timbers and such. D-d-don't want the demo dust to mix with the midday humidity. Or the painter's paint."

Now Amy began to stutter, "B-b-but—"

"No buts about it, Amy," Hernandez interjected. "If we are done with our drinks, I think you'd best be researching plumbing supplies online. I don't recommend American- made crappers."

Amy wrote Notes on her phone, hoping to keep the toilet info straight and not giggle too loud—or at all. She kept her head down, concealing her smirk.

She'd barely caught up when Dad relaunched his monologue, "I do recommend Harbor Freight website for good prices on shipping. The ferry comes directly from Canada into Ludington, Michigan, so the plumbing products are simple to pick up."

Amy noticed that Tony vehemently nodded his agreement with each suggestion, especially at the "easy pick-up" line. She was glad that Hernandez was in control. She'd better polish her pencil and shine her Master Card.

P-p-pronto!

The presence of the two men hefting and lifting and installing—body odor ceasing in proportion to their efforts—seemed to goose Dante into action. Perhaps his day job became more important than his night time gyrations. He circled the exterior to paint and paint and paint.

At any rate, the Lady Bug Inn build-out portended more business, enabling Amy to endure. Noises of the basement buildout buzzed and sawed from 8:00 a.m. until 4:45 p.m. Only a lunch break brought peace and serenity to the palace.

Amy watched proudly, plugging her ears against the cacophony. She felt as if she resided in a three-ring berserkus, riding atop an elephant as an observer without a ticket—and it was her tent!

Actually, everything was copacetic except Andy, who seemed to slack more in direct contrast the other men's dedicated energy-and-effort. Rather than being invigorated by work, he seemed to be allergic. Nothing Amy said mattered. It was time to bring Ronnie in a string bikini to swish her sway in front of his draggy ass.

The first words out of Ronnie's mouth: "See the macho

men accomplishing something, Andy! Your loafing is an ungainly mess! A trespass on your sister's good will. Do something! Get your rear in gear!"

Andy merely blinked and dog-paddled to the other side of the pool. Amy, who'd commissioned the take-down, shook her head. *I've got a good family: Sister Ronnie, Mama Wilma, and Hernandez Dad and one untrainable goon.*

Amy quickly separated Ronnie from further confrontation with Andy. She couldn't afford the fisticuffs that would sideline the better half of her work team, Andy being the lower-than-low man of that totem.

Since that plan went bust in a hurry, it seemed best to leave Ronnie in her cottage, while Andy languished at the big house, his rumpled clothing tossed about to overload all available surfaces. A 6,000 sq. ft. house suddenly seemed more than small. His inherent antipathy for work cramped her *honey 'em up* style and his cabana boy moves weren't impressive so far. She felt compelled to oust him when post-plastic surgery guests filled the rooms.

Which would happen soon.

Ronnie's bustle, though often unseen because she worked in her home office in the cabin, was enviable. Amy preferred to remain hands-off to prevent the clashes that might bend their relationship and her millionaire-boss mindset. Ronnie, her reliable manager, kept busy with ordering necessary guesthouse items and hiring staff.

While Amy relished the constant delivery trucks filled with bathroom fixtures and parts, bedroom furniture, linens, and drapes from her expanse of windows, delegation-by-cash had its perks and she never volunteered to help. Ronnie arrived to watch a movie with Amy, just as the work crews left each day. Her reports were thrilling and succinct. She prepared supper for three and stocked the refrigerator with drinks and snacks and leftovers. Otherwise, she'd shimmied out of Amy's presence. She was a good sister/sidekick.

Amy hoped her blood brother shifted his oppositional streak to join hands in cooperation. She hoped her dreams tonight proffered a plan to curb his enthusiasm for mayhem.

And perhaps her dreams would summon the method to move forward from her patiently aggressive stance with Travis now in *her* town—without offending *her* Lions Club mates. Maybe it was time to employ Duct Tape and Tupperware, the secret weapons of her former in-laws, Steve and Jackie Breeden, to keep her millionaire mindset safe.

CHAPTER THIRTY-SIX

PRESERVING TURF

AMY WAS GLAD she'd abandoned her vindictive plan to *out* Tiny Tarzan, the stripper about town. Dante had amended his dilettante ways and resumed painting with fervor, as more interior guest suites were built. Best of all, Hernandez convinced Dante to re-mix the paint, so that her 6,000 sq. ft. Lady Bug Inn resembled a civilized and cultured place to reside, albeit temporarily, for high-dollar guests.

While the final color was khaki, like Hernandez' daily uniform, Amy decided not to buck what worked. Hernandez was happy, so she tried not to notice that her building might resemble an Army barracks.

At least it didn't resemble a prison, a hen house, or an egg yoke—nor was it the puke pink Ronnie had suggested. Amy at-eased and began to focus on filling rooms of the Lady Bug Spa with bill paying clientele.

Lions Club attendance was mandatory duty,

because this well-connected cluster of men were influencers throughout the state. Amy knew that if she remained needy and demure, they'd work their contacts to drum up business for her spa. Amy assumed the status of mascot, far better looking than an African Lion and close enough to pat on the head. Their interest may have contained a prurient edge, a stroke of smarm, a carnivorous edge, but she'd handled men all of her life and these elderly gents were just that. Gents.

There was a new gent in the Lions Club midst today. And when he rose to introduce himself, she wanted to slide under the table.

However, she remained frozen, eyes glued to his face, his words thundering inside her head as he introduced himself more broadly than the initial intro of the Mayor. "Hello, my name is Travis Castro." He paused to toss a radiant smile around the room. "I've purchased the run down joke of the abandoned-by-owner bar in South Haven. I've named it TRAVIS' TRAVEL IN TWO, because I own a famous bar in Traverse City, upstate about two-and-a-half hours. As I looked around this esteemed group—"

Amy rejoiced when Travis' self-introduction lost its strut. He looked equally flummoxed. Surprise on both sides! In that instance, she abandoned her scheme for revenge.

Just as quickly, she re-ignited her vengeful intent. The Mayor and the upscale alcohol rehab (*what an irony*) manager, Phil Lactose, rose to save Travis' verbal skin. "Come on guys, you've all been to TRAVIS'

TRAVEL IN in Traverse City. He's got the best pool tables and best poker games in the best back rooms of any bar. You all don't just go to the casinos when you venture north, do you?"

Hands raised and the huzzahs began as men throughout the room clapped each other on the back... all except Pastor Wheems, naturally. His scowl mirrored Amy's. When their eyes met, Amy quickly turned her frown upside down. She beamed so as not to join his *shame agenda* yet avoided Travis' and Pastor's eyes.

"Furthermore," the Mayor continued, "Mr. Castro is going to spark the economy of the entire downtown. Let's give him a round of applause."

Amy wanted to plug her ears. She wanted to disappear into a hole in Miss Ellie's floor. Christ on a bicycle. Travis the troublemaker, in *her* town.

As the local hero, he'd be hard to undercut, eviscerate, and harm. Andrew Machinist was likely already providing protection services, and who knew who else, sliding cash into his pockets. The better to play poker at Travis' bars.

As the entire host rose to its feet and expanded its applause, Amy excused herself to the Ladies... she never looked back.

She loped to the Focus and crumpled into a ball. Her spirits lifted as she thought of potential, problem-solving allies. She climbed into her car, slammed the door, and texted Hernandez.

DO YOU DEPLOY DRONES?

WHATEVER ARE YOU SPEAKING OF, AMY?

Amy knew a 'stiff arm' tactic when she read one. Her parole officer would need a platoon of drones to supervise his numerous parolees. Plausible deniability was possible via text, but wait, just wait, until she looked him in the eye. His gallant-as-a-knight demeanor would crumble under her scrutiny. She, too, could read faces.

DO YOUR DRONES HAVE LONG DISTANCE FLAME-THROWERS? IF NOT, WHAT DARK WEBSITE DO I ACCESS?

DON'T DRIVE YOUR BUS OFF A CLIFF, AMY. USE CAUTION, FAVORITE PAROLEE. YOU HAVE BETTER USES FOR YOUR CASH.

Amy blinked. She blinked again. Tears of frustration, tears of joy, tears of...whatever fogged her sunglasses. *Christ on a bicycle, I wish I'd driven the Porsche.*

Amy jerked her car into gear and left MISS ELLIE'S parking lot, willing her tears to stop. She needed to get home before the Lions meeting got out and the glad-handing members smarmed the area, maybe carrying Travis aloft on their shoulders.

New town savior, my ass! I'm the Bad Ass! Travis will be the sorry ass for invading my turf!

Amy forced herself to slowly cruise South Haven's sole downtown street, the one that hugged the harbor, with motels on the lakeside and other service business across the street. It was a place she hadn't perused after all of the local business owners, plied her with monetary proposals, including Elvin as realtor and laundromat owner. Most of their prostrations embarrassed Amy. None were clever and/or worth it.

She didn't like having a target on her back and preferred her Lady Bug homestead. Amy hunkered there each day, though she had to admit she was bored and might benefit from Travis' presence. It would boost her business resolve to have an adversary. Her millionaire mindset needed a buffing and fluffing that a jolt of testosterone would deliver.

She'd make a dartboard out of his portrait. That would busy Andy at something. *If* she allowed him a turn at dart tossing.

Suddenly, there IT was, the signage already in place. It looked like a hollow shell of a business, impossible to have open by the Labor Day end of tourist season. A beehive of workers scurried, hauling wheelbarrows of sheet rock and ratchet lumber pieces to boxcar-sized dumpsters. Who'd given permits for all of this noise and dust? Somebody ought to karate chop his clipboard rather than allow this mess to go forward.

Amy stopped at the beauty shop for an impromptu mani-pedi. She'd think better while the woman worked her magic with a Brazilian Blowout.

Within the hour, Amy had ten new mental lists of to-do's and to-don't's, including a request for the manicurist and hairstylist to provide services in her Lady Bug guests one day each week. She sailed to Ronnie's log cabin home to kibbitz.

The need to drive safely, plus the luxurious look of her polished toes and fingernails, prevented Amy from slapping her own hands in contrition. How could she have allowed Travis to invade her space?

Ronnie was wide-eyed and bleary when Amy arrived at her cozy log cabin home. The air was purple-hazy inside the small space. Amy quickly retreated to clear her eyes and lungs. Ronnie's manic business ethic had seemed admirable on the Lady Bug Inn's behalf. Now Amy realized how and why.

Nevertheless, she longed for Ronnie's input. So, she plucked a scarf from her over-large purse, and tied it bandit-like as filter for the air she breathed into her nose.

"Don't pay the ransom! I escaped!" she exclaimed as she entered Ronnie's humble abode. She felt vague twinges of guilt that she lived in a palace while her best friend lived in a hovel but squashed them. This was a business call to her business manager.

Ronnie startled, but didn't dump her paperwork, though she did, Amy noticed, close out of an Excel program. "New face fashion, Amy? Are you ducking requests for your cash? If the rumors around town are true, you've been plied with every carney-business for miles around."

Amy's mood and facial expression plummeted. Ronnie's reminder of the on-going monetary assaults threatened to deepen her tailspin.

Ronnie noticed her friend's glum intenseness and winked. She picked up a notepad and pen. "What may I order for you today, future boffo spa owner?"

Then, she winked again and fluttered her eyelashes like a vamp.

"Gosh, I miss you, Ronnie. Sorry I've been scarce, and sorrier I didn't give you proper applause for trying to fix Andy's broken work ethic?"

"Whose wagon may I fix on your behalf today, my empress-of-the-lottery friend?"

"Travis Castro." Amy's voice only worked at half-power, so she whispered. *Perhaps I don't want to proclaim louder because I don't want to believe it's true.*

"What?" Ronnie strained to re-process what she didn't want to process in the first place. "The shyster who sent you to prison? Let me at him. I'll scar his sorry hide in all the visible places."

Amy began to shake and shiver and her scarf fell from her face. She didn't care. She inhaled, long and deep.

"Stop!" Ronnie cried. "We need our minds clear and our knives sharpened. Let's go to the Inn and hyper-snack our way through a movie. I'll bring this pad and pen with me, and we'll invent hundreds of ways to prank Travis out of this town. I'm stoked, so I'll drive!"

"Thanks, Buddy, I have a compulsion to out-do, out-smart, out-battle, out-connive, and out-last Travis. I know that's what got me into his mess, but I never figured prison would be part of my bargain with the devil. He did me more than wrong. I wish I could kick him in the gonads, but I do believe that he's about to kick mine."

"Thankfully, that's not possible," said Ronnie.

"But it will be our combined personal and epic goal to devastate his reputation. Agreed?"

"Agreed." Amy smiled for the first time in hours. "See these pretty nails? They're begging to scratch out Travis' eyes."

Ronnie looked, but nixed the idea. "We can do much, much better than that. Why muck an expensive manicure? We'll invent better—and better than that!"

By the time the vengeful ladies arrived at the Lady Bug, they'd planned a full opening day party for the spa, with a special invitation to each woman in South Haven. Ronnie would determine a means to collect all the names of men who'd lost money on TRAVIS' TRAVEL IN back room poker tables and consider whether or not to *out* them in front of their wives as a highlight of the festivities. With full use of Amy's cloud account, the event would be the talk of the town… and then some!

Chapter Thirty-Seven

A DOCTOR MAKES HOUSE CALLS

IN A LARGE house where everyone was bright-eyed and busy-tailed but the owner, another person may have been compelled to feel guilt. Not Amy. She'd spent too many hours doing other people's busy work, too many hours chained within, too many hours in relative poverty, too many hours obeying others' rules. She preferred delegating with dollars and following her own whimsy. A flush Amy enjoyed her millionaire mindset.

The spa took shape via her dependable staff, plus one oaf. The realization of the need to build clientele began to throw shade on Amy's attempts to relax and forget about Travis' threat.

Ronnie, her ever-wise confidant, advised, "Build

your own, better and faster," and did more than her fair share to support Amy.

Mr. Lactose, the manager of the long-term drunk tank, er, rehab facility on the edge of South Haven, pledged to slide many referrals Amy's way. Most of his inhabitants at the Country Club were men, but all had visitors, so he'd stock brochures prominently in the Country Club's spacious foyer. The Country Club wasn't a secret to anyone in the state, so word would spread. Drug-and-alcohol rehab was here to stay.

So was plastic surgery, Amy knew. Even inmates of the prison wanted to look prime, especially when a long sentence stole their youth. Or they simply wanted the next chapter of their lives as *out-mates* to look as well as feel different than the mistakes of their first chapter.

Most of the men wanted to score a hot mate, like the Playmate poster babes and the Sports Illustrated bathing suit models that covered their cell walls. Because she was blonde and six feet, Amy often suspected her presence in the prison library propelled some inmates to read, perpetually checking out the same book. It was a boon that prison garb was drab and decidedly not form-fitting and little make-up was allowed for imprisoned women.

The largely Boomer-aged Lions Club members reminded her of Steve Breeden, though these men treated her like a daughter or young cub. Not a lioness to be attacked, which is probably how Steve would react if/when he saw her now.

These men didn't letch as openly as the gnarly-hardened criminals, but lust glimmered often in their eyes. A few, Amy internally quipped, could use a chin lift and a bleph for under-eye bags. Because she'd heard Travis had abandoned his new tribe, Amy regularly attended meetings now, though she insisted that Ronnie accompany her. Both began to scrutinize everyone in town—even vendors who supplied the spa—with clairvoyant eyes as potential post-plastic surgery spa guests.

Amy had read of the Baby Boomer quest for perpetual youth in the womens' mags she and Ronnie perused when they did their nails. Together, avoiding the beauty salon in town. Fifty-seven magazines and online articles later, the need was affirmed. Now to gain access to the market and referrals.

As usual, Amy sought the counsel of Google. When she discovered eight large medical practices for plastic surgery within an easy drive of South Haven, she felt encouraged to proceed. But none of them, even the one lodged in the Grand Amway Plaza Hotel, had a residence in which to recline and heal privately. Shazam! How to gain credibility with that group?

Did she require a physician on staff? South Haven's pediatrician and sole internist wouldn't be able to help her on that score, each too busy with local families and the occasional tourist blunders to add another task to their roster of medical tasks. Neither professed to have time for Lions Club events when the president called them during the membership drive, a fact Phil stressed when he put the screws to her for membership.

Amy startled when her iPhone slipped from her hand. Daydreaming again. She needed to get control of her head. While she didn't need to work, she needed something to do and hobbies weren't in her repertoire.

She picked up her phone, jammed it into her yoga pants pockets, and strode the interior of her future dilettante spa. She text checked-in with Ronnie and Hernandez. She took a tour of her project, both floors. She barked orders and dispensed atta-boys, then looked at the time. Only forty minutes had passed.

And the humidity outside had caused a flop-sweat. She ran to her bathroom and soaked a plush wash-cloth to wipe her neck, face, and chest, allowing the film of water to evaporate in the air-conditioning. Her image in the mirror looked perplexed. How had a California girl, accustomed to ocean breezes and low humidity, gotten trapped in this locale?

Amy felt on the precipice of going to rot. Come on, brain, tick-tock-think.

Click-click, her brain complied. First, she ordered exercise equipment to be delivered and installed ensuite. In that matter, she'd sweat in air-conditioning.

Next, Amy decided that a millionaire ought to have a laptop and a desktop with several screens. Ronnie already had them for online ordering of supplies and soon there would be books for Amy to keep. She ordered personal supplies, including a camera and color printer for before/after photos with which to advertise the results of respite in her spa.

Staples accomplished, Amy cast about for someone sane to talk to. It was lonely out here in the woods.

Technology accomplished many things lickety-split, but not true companionship.

She grabbed a bottled water to rehydrate and Facetime with Woolworth Wilma. Amy missed her new mom.

"Hi, Amy! Nice to hear from you. How's things cracking?"

Amy smiled. How could anybody be angry at the world, or frustrated with spa problems, when one shared the phone screen with this unimpeachably good soul.

"Supplies are secured and my spa business is moving forward. I haven't had a date in five years. Otherwise, I've got nothing remarkable to report."

"You mean you haven't marched up to that Travis monster to knee-cap him or punch him in the nose yet? I was counting on you to settle the score. I'd expected that young idiot to have been pounded into the ground long ago! Back when I had a husband, he was unfaithful once and only once, God rest his dastardly soul."

Dastardly! What a dainty word for a bastard. Amy amused herself for a moment, trying to envision a dastard. She well knew what a bastard looked like. He was here, on *her* turf. He was front-and-center among her kaleidoscope of bastards crowding good men from memory.

Amy sat forward in her chair, anxious to hear battle tips, "What did you do to your errant husband, Wilma? Cut off his cojones?"

"No, I did worse. For a week, if he wanted dinner, I served it cold."

Amy suppressed a chuckle by drawing her bottled water to her lips and taking an extra-long drink. Wilma's self-satisfied cackle continued, morphing into hiccups, giggles, and fits.

In a few moments, Wilma pulled one of her embroidered linen handkerchiefs from a pocket and dabbed at her eyes. "Thanks for helping me recall one of my favorite revenges, Amy. I must say, I miss the dastard. He was the love of my life and a good provider. Some of the time."

"I'd not heard you mention a husband, Mom. What was his name? Did you lose him to war or something worse?" Amy felt inclined to be empathetic. For the first time in her life. She'd never had anyone die on her, though her schizophrenic mom had come close. In fact, she'd come so close so many times, Amy almost lost interest.

"Not exactly," said Wilma, winking broadly afterward. "He cleared out the cash drawer of our main Woolworth's store and took off with the clerk, never to be seen or heard from again." Rather than sad, Wilma's face projected mirth. "So much for happily ever after. As for his name, the only name I recall is David. The Dastard."

Amy didn't know where to go with this conversation, so she took it back to her needs. "Well, Mom, I'm pretty settled in South Haven, over on Lake Michigan. Have you been there?"

"David and I honeymooned there back in a year I

don't recall. I should have known that something was up because the honeymoon suite was dinky and drab and smelled of day-old fish. The scoundrel didn't even carry me over the threshold, and he only had three quarters to feed the massage machine on the bouncy double bed."

Amy drained her bottle of water with that tidbit. The definition of male bad behavior had shifted a bit in twenty-thirty-forty years. She wondered how old Wilma was, but didn't dare ask. That much politeness she had memorized.

"Did I share my dream scheme with you, Mom? I've bought a property and am building a resort hotel and spa. I've been befriended by the local Lions Club, whose members run the town. Things are going smoothly, but I have some man-power problems."

"Well, I'm surprised you don't have money problems, Amy. You were so down on your luck when we met. You know if you need any money, all you have to do is ask." Wilma practically extended her hand through the smart phone frame to prove that she'd help.

"No, no, my problems can't be fixed with money."

"You've got to be kidding, Amy. Did you try, honey? You have cache, allure, and good looks in a pert package and men can detect it a mile away. It's those pheromones and hormones. Men should be thronging to help. Didn't you mention a Lions Club? Why even if you act noxious and stuck up, someone as leggy as you can't repel men."

Wilma shook her head so vehemently throughout

her pronouncement, Amy feared it might fall off its pedestal. Now Mom's index finger joined the rhythm. "And I can't believe that dumb Travis hasn't come sniveling to your door, but I sure am glad you didn't trot those long legs of yours to him!"

I'm not ready to tell Mama Bear Wilma that Travis is here. Especially because she couldn't admit to her guardian angel that Travis had been the first person she sought, straight outta prison, before her life took a hard turn left.

The right turn, actually. Revenge was not necessary, though Amy doubted personal satisfaction would result without it. For now, Amy had a different type of man to attract. "I need a physician for my project."

"You do?!" Wilma shrilled and then hung her head. "My son's a doctor. Lives in your town, but he doesn't practice. He just fishes all day, says he's satisfied." Wilma paused, perhaps to snuffle back tears. "It's tough to admit when your one-and-only son is a loser."

Amy gripped the phone, so that it didn't fall to the floor. Did she have magnetic powers for men, as Wilma suggested? A physician was precisely what she needed to complete the roster of her spa. She hoped that Wilma's son wasn't a dentist or a veterinarian.

"You have a son? He's a doctor?" She knew she sounded silly, as her voice elevated an octave with every syllable said. "What's his specialty?"

"He says his specialty is scrapping scales off a fish, then frying it and eating it." Wilma huffed-and-puffed each word with vehemence. "We paid for ten years of medical school and another two of residency in Detroit. Missed him every minute and expected him to make us rich and satisfied. Instead, he quit the day he graduated cum laude. Said he was sick and tired of studying," she grumped and then dissolved into tears, her hanky in hand. She sobbed for a few minutes, then came up for air, "I'll make him work for you. That'd be the right penance for breaking his parents' hearts."

Amy felt helpless and thrilled at the same time.

"Wilma, I'm driving over there to console you, to give you a hug. We'll eat in the diner, sit in the same booth, have pineapple upside down cake again. But please, before I get on the road, tell me your son's medical specialty name?"

"His name is Bill Woolworth, and he's a plastic surgeon."

"I'll be there in an hour, Wilma. Is it safe to park a Porsche in the lot behind your store?"

CHAPTER THIRTY-EIGHT

THINGS ARE MOVING FAST

DR. WILLIAM WOOLWORTH was decidedly onboard. He smiled-and-filed voluminous paperwork to be rubber-stamped by his Medical Board pals, fast-tracked, and filed precisely, in case anyone needed to know. Anything at any time. All was copacetic. Time to fill the completed guest suites at the Lady Bug Inn.

Wiley Woolworth had a history of kerfuffles and affairs and had been invited to exit the many-partnered plastic surgery practice on Amy's hit list, but still retained a few friends state-wide, as well as throughout the entire Midwest. He even had a few contacts in Canada. He began to network full-time on behalf of the Inn, funded by Amy's Benjamin-a-week retainer, staring at his vanity wall of certificates and plaques and smiling. They were no longer mere tornado fodder to fly off the wall and conk him.

Woolly Bill contentedly lived with his mom in

Lansing, away from the humdrum and conundrums at the Lady Bug Inn, but only a text away if advice or treatments were needed. The only surgeries he performed were on crown beef roasts and turkeys on special feast days with his mom.

He'd be able to FaceTime Amy's staff to peel back bandages and proxy-disinfect wounds as needed. Woolly Bill figured he had it made in the shade. His rest-forever-days were assured.

Working the phones suited Woolly Bill's skill set and propped up his pride. By August, the Lady Bug Inn opened with two guests.

Phil Lactose tweaked his clientele to refer two women who had bundles and desired a hidden hotel. Visiting time was minimally allowed with their men in the lockdown wing of Phil's rehab establishment, though it was recommended daily to ensure recovery with sanity intact. The price of gas, coupled with privacy requirements, compelled them to Amy's place.

And they paid cash, upfront for a month. Amy stashed the cash in her lingerie drawer, as certain a place as any that Sticky-fingered Andy wouldn't plunder.

Perfect. All set. Because Dante and Tony yammered about their meager cash flows and the high cost of paint and supplies. Andy tried to request a salary, but Amy threatened to charge him room and board. With an enormous appetite and an invisible wallet, Andy was made to realize that he should never be the cause of anyone's bad day.

Especially not Amy, the queen of the cash.

Though Wooly Willy insisted he was working

his network and striving, Amy felt encumbered and raw in the world. The spa was getting *spendy*. Her extravagant taste, exacerbated by Ronnie's independent ordering of supplies, linens, and knick-knacks, caused her credit card balances to soar. Although each was paid automatically, so that she didn't have to feel the sting, Amy began to miss the play-with-money her small town bank VP days had afforded her.

With nothing to do, Amy felt like a voyeur of the millions. A guest in her own house. She felt beside the point rather than *the point*, as a money dominatrix was entitled to be.

Irrelevant and incompetent were the words Amy's mind contrived for herself. She couldn't even drive a nail… any more than Andy knew how to keep a pool. Did the siblings share a genetic defect?

So, Amy texted Hernandez and FaceTimed Wilma while she lounged by the pool. All, including Ronnie, were reliable and easy on her spirit—and the hundred idiots inside Amy's head shut their traps. There was much for a multi-millionaire to deal with and Amy climbed a long learning curve. She was not *steady as you go.*

Amy expanded her wardrobe with royal blue, purple, and gold tones that helped her masquerade as a full-fledged member to hang out with her Lions Pride guys. Each was a personality, an expert at something, and enjoyed her good listening. She was still not required to buy her lunch. No longer a newcomer, even the frosty hostess of Miss Elly's welcomed her presence. And Travis remained hidden and hurrying and hustling to grand open his bar by Labor Day, local Lions' Club scuttlebutt decreed.

Amy crossed her fingers, eyes, and toes that TRAVIS' TRAVEL IN TWO would never open.

The Mayor cornered Amy during the July Lions' Club membership drive. "You've been thriving on our hospitality for some time. Our group took you in when you were homeless and uncomfortable in this part of the state, but it's time for you to contribute to the Lions' welfare. Especially because we all agree that you're loaded. Our dues are $150/year."

The Mayor plopped himself in the chair next to Amy, as if he had all the time in the world to collect her cash. There was an aire of uncomfortable greatness about him, despite his ultra-drab wardrobe. He commanded authority, and Amy cowered despite her six-foot dominance of their shared air space.

Mayor Bradley had cultivated the lax linguistic habits of a *good old boy,* an acumen of local politicians who wanted to remain in office.

Like all Lions Club members, the Mayor was tenacious. Amy knew he wouldn't leave her side until she committed to dues. "If I pay next time, a full year for Ronnie and myself—in cash, would that do? My Master Card is maxxed, and I don't carry a checkbook."

"Sure, honey." The Mayor allowed himself an extra look at Amy's breasts and slowly swiveled a toothpick from his upper to his lower teeth. "Just write an I.O.U. to the Treasurer, Pastor Weems over there."

Amy pulled herself out of her chair and clomped

over to the Pastor, who always sat in the corner booth. He'd already plucked a white napkin from the restaurant's cheap aluminum dispenser and clicked open his Lions club pen. Amy wrote 2 X $150.00 and signed it. Within seconds the napkin nestled in the Pastor's inside pocket.

Amy's whispered request to never allow Travis Castro to join the Lions' Club was stuffed like earplugs in his ears with a hiss he'd never be able to unhear.

Elvin ushered her out of Miss Elly's and walked her to her car. He held her door after she unlocked her Focus, smiled, and whispered in her ear, "Thanks. My son's been clean-and-sober for six months now. Thanks for giving him a job." Then he shook her hand and walked away.

Clean and sober? Amy knew Dante had been foisted upon her, but she'd not known the why. She felt highly complimented, but still she had to rustle up $300.00 when she was functionally broke due to the Dante's lingering presence. Amy might have to bum cash from Ronnie, who topped her expense list. Not golden.

Amy sensed she was close to emotionally broke, too. Andy needed rehab, but he rebuffed her pursuit of the topic. A truth: her brother was a wretched sloth and crooked to the core. It caused regret of the very worst kind: all of her mothering could not change his genetic code. Andy seemed to have inherited Mom's schizzy tendencies.

It made Amy feel ultra-guilty that she'd enabled Elvin's son to become clean-and-sober, but she couldn't achieve the same for their mother's only son. Her talk with Phil Lactose, who'd offered a discount to enroll Andy in his nearby drug rehab facility, convinced her not to pursue the matter. He'd met Andy once, determining him to be a born liar and a malcontent. Amy should save her breath. Phil would do other favors for her, but not that one.

Blood was not thicker than commerce. Not today. Amy was on a mission to scrape up $300.00 for Lions' membership. It was difficult to feel like a millionaire with a money pit house which aspired to be a spa, including a *highway robbery* fee for an expedient medical consultant.

Ahhh. An idea sculpted itself in her brain. She'd submit spa phony charges directly to the online bank and request that the money be wired directly to her home, in stacks of small bills. FedEx was best. A plume of white dust filled the large window through which Amy gazed a few days later.

FedEx did not deliver the money. A Brinks truck did. And the bills were not small, spendable denominations. They were all hundred-dollar bills, banded together and stuffed into plain canvas bags. Amy had always had a problem with decimal points—did she misplace one again?

Two bags of money, stuffed full. Amy stashed them in her closet, behind her Barbie pink backpack, kept in fond remembrance of the day before she became a lottery winner and subsequently a multi-millionaire.

'Things' were passable for the next several days, but then Andy's benignly bad behavior became actively worse. He rose from a poolside lounge chair to swagger instructions to the construction crew. He derided every 'attaboy' Amy contributed, in her plan to be positive to further Elvin's positive ambitions for his son, as well as Hernandez' hopes for the twice recidivised felon.

"Various inspection objections from a skinny f*cker, who is long on opinions and short on facts," Dante gruffed in Amy's direction.

Time for Amy to get into Andy's face.

Interestingly, he was simultaneously stuffing several hotdogs, bulging his cheeks like a squirrel, so Amy was able to land twelve verbal punches before he could swallow. He mimed talking heads with the hand not holding the hotdogs, while his big sister spouted and tiraded and fumed.

Out of the corner of her eye, Amy spotted Dante applauding with paintbrushes, but that was the only rise she achieved for three lengthy minutes—until she'd run out of words. Silence extended, but then she tried one final sideswipe.

"Andy, why do I feel like we keep having the same conversation?"

To which he impertinently replied in-between mighty chews, "To me the. Conversation. Feels like a lecture." Andy paused for an audible gulp of a swallow. "My feelings are raw, having recently. Been a felon."

Amy gasped. Had Tony heard Andy say "felon"?

Had she heard blasted Andy right? Accusatory to the core? Amy was mildly flummoxed and about to flounder in guilt again, when he faked a downpour of tears. That did it! Amy shouted, "Get off my deck!"

Andy's head dipped, but before it nestled on his chest, she noted the look of betrayal in his eyes. His words sounded muffled as they echoed inside his three-days-dirty shirt. "I didn't believe you'd hurt me, Sis. Did you believe I intended to hurt you?"

When put in a box, how does one respond? Amy couldn't say "yes" to that nor could she say "no." So, she stalked off without a reply and pounded down the hall to hole up in her room.

"Equivocal" wasn't an option with another human being, especially one with the same blood circulating in his arteries and veins. Guilt ruled again, but Amy maintained her tug-of-war. Andy's presence was not golden. Nope, nope, nope.

She funneled Andy angst into her daydreams of Travis' downfall. Would it be too insidious to have Ronnie add an additional blanket to the spa linen order and infect it with flu virus before she gift-boxed the blanket and sent it, personal two-day delivery, to Travis as a bar-warming gift?

YAS-S-S or NO-NO?

What a randy-and-grand play! Better to get a drunken fool to ram the front door of TRAVIS' TRAVEL IN TWO.

Better to build your business up rather to tear someone else's down. Hernandez' admonition resounded in Amy's head.

Chapter Thirty-Nine

GOOD, BAD, AND WORSE

WITHIN DAYS THE Lady Bug Spa brochures were written, proof-read, and printed. The Lions Club den of men stuffed envelopes with a dozen brochures, along with a marketing letter formulated by the Mayor's press secretary, who had little else to do in small town South Haven, with his re-election established and the tourist season on the wind-down.

On the day of the Blueberry Festival, Amy stepped into place on Lions Club float.

She wore a demure tankini with a homemade sash and crown, declaring her the Queen of Lady Bugs. She ignored the glare of the Blueberry Festival Queen, who wore a proper sash and what looked like a purple balloon on her head. Amy knew she couldn't compete with the dumb of that giant blueberry look, so she threw her shoulders back, anchored her feet, and began to toss Lady Bug brochures into the crowds.

Dante and Ronnie and Andy skipped on the blacktop of the main drag, reaching into the crowds to kiss kids' cheeks and stuff a brochure in parents' hands. Ronnie tossed chocolate kisses with smiley face stickers on the bottom, which caused a near-stampede until people found that the chocolate melted in their sweaty, hot hands.

Looked out for Travis and then lofted Lady Bug Inn brochures from atop the float, occasionally tipple-turvying as the float lurched. Her heels were too high to carry this off on a less-than-sturdily built float, but volunteers couldn't be fired for their efforts.

Amy giggled as she observed women trying *not* to recognize Dante from his stripper nights, but their flushes gave them away. *Oh, my, how the Lady Bug Inn would flourish with him as spokesperson.* Amy smiled. It might not be so bad if the macho-man painted and over-painted for months.

As long as I can keep his crude mouth shut, and he doesn't spit his over-chewed tobacco on a client's back.

Jealousy sparked in Andy that day. He became more recalcitrant, more inflammatory, more unwieldy to manage. He caused many people's bad days. Amy loathed being the mediator/fixer between him and Dante. Or, God forbid, future spa guests.

Most of all, Amy was frightened that Andy would summon their schizophrenic mom from the vagrant streets of Long Beach. Life would go from bad to worse when the collect calls began. Amy would be hostage to her millions, hostage to the whims of the woman's craziness, just as she had been in her youth.

And, not that far away, Travis' lurked as a threat to her sanity. Amy's dread grew daily. There was much to fear by opening that Pandora's Box.

One day, when she could no longer watch paint dry or listen to the contractors hammer and yammer as they built out the floor below or manage Andy's feistiness, Amy went for a lakeside drive. In the quiet privacy of the Porsche interior, she called Woolworth Wilma about the non-productivity of her son.

Now the need for Wooly Willy had been bypassed because all licensing was secured, supplies piled in Ronnie's cottage and/or in place, and the two local physicians would tend to any guest needs or requests. The mass *air-mailing* of brochures from atop a float had brought spa occupancy to its max and a waiting list surfaced. While Amy had millions—and tons of interest surmounting the original lottery amount—a person who'd grown up hungry and poorly-clothed couldn't abide waste.

"Is this a good time, Mom?"

"Any time's a good time when you call me Mom." Amy could feel the true lady's smile through the phone. She could hear it, too, because Wilma's voice softened. "What can I do you for, Amy?"

Amy hemmed and hawed and hoped to think how not to offend her mentor with her desire to dump her one-and-only son.

"I don't like surprises, dear. When I was a child, I unwrapped all my Christmas presents so I'd know the facial expression to adopt when I opened them in front of my magnanimous relatives. Then I carefully re-wrapped each box and re-tied each bow with precision." Wilma paused. "Get my gist, Amy? I'm telling you not to compound my misery with news I'm not going to like. I hear wistfulness in your voice."

"I'm afraid I have to discontinue your son's contract to build the Lady Bug Inn business. I'm sorry to disappoint you, but I've got to cut him loose. He served his purpose well, but now he must be done-and-home." Amy winced and looked in the side mirror and surged the accelerator of the Porsche, as if running away from what she'd said.

"Honey, as a longtime business owner, I know the value of a nickel and the non-worth of my son. I concur with your decision. You have my permission to fire him." Then Wilma actually cackled. "Just promise me you won't buy his fish when you want to serve seafood in the spa dining room."

Several seconds passed. The only sounds inside the Porsche were the whine of the engine and the silence of Amy's tears. As she should have recalled, Woolworth Wilma had bred-in-bone beliefs. Amy hadn't lost her support by telling the truth. She'd even cracked a joke at Wiley Willy's expense.

"Did you hear me, Sweet Pea? I validate your business acumen. Over the years, I've always found that direct and incisive is best."

Amy wished the Blue-Tooth would answer for her. She could only manage a simple "thank you" before she broke the connection.

Relief in one phone call. More trust via a relationship with another. Not all family was bad.

That matter settled, Amy decided to let the Porsche open full-out on the untraveled two-lane roads of the county. She needed to wrest the temptation to seek Travis and carve him from her heart. Likewise with brother Andy, whom she longed to knife from her marrow.

The Porsche had only reached 65 m.p.h. when Hernandez' text bleeped:

PLEASE AVOID SPEED CITATIONS. WOULD RAISE INSURANCE RATES AND PUT YOU ON LOCAL COP'S RADAR. I DON'T NEED THE COMPETITION AND YOU DON'T NEED THE NOTORIETY.

To which Amy replied: YES, DAD. ALTHO NOTORIETY MIGHT FILL THE LADY BUG SPA. LORD KNOWS, I NEED THE INCOME.

Hernandez' reply text was a laughter emoji. HA-HA-HA!

Amy returned to her headquarters without a clue of how to handle the combustible threat of Travis. Or the increasingly propulsive threat of Andy.

Primary for now, how to finagle revenge on Travis without losing her soul. Amy knew she was incompetent when it came to man solutions, though man problems were her forte. Thong underwear, a push-up bra, and an unending supply of pizza and cash could finesse three workmen, but not the other entanglements.

Nothing handled Andy.

She hadn't resorted to prayer, as coached by the nuns. *If reverence were school, I'd have flunked. I'll never be the church lady type. So help me, God.*

Amy slowly cruised the pebbly drive of her huge home-based business, pinching her arm to assure that she truly saw the mansion she owned and not a mirage. She parked the Porsche in the garage and remained inside the vehicle for a while to mouth the requisite prayers.

The mortgage was real—and there was none other to rescue her. She'd try anything that might work.

Amy sighed, then stretched herself out of the racy car. She stashed the keys in her bra before she walked around the lower lever to inspect the build-out progress. On the way upstairs, she noticed a tiny black fleck on the doorframe.

Disgusted with life in general, she whisked it off. The fleck twerked—trying to fly?—then flopped into the nearby flower bed. Belatedly, Amy realized a lady bug had mired itself in the fresh paint. She gasped, tapped her heart, and then formed a cross. She almost cried at the symbology. She'd wiped hope away like a wasp.

Was that the universe's answer? No hope, no money or man, to make her feel whole and unburdened. With whom could she share secrets, lies, and/or problems? Alone had been her true grit for a while, but she ached for more than Dad Hernandez. She craved muscles in bed and hugs. Someone's touch. Someone to bolster her backbone, literally and figuratively.

If I kill innocent lady bugs for spite, what else would

I kill with my moods? Money equals power. Have I let it go to my head?

Amy nearly collapsed when she realized that she'd enacted her pet peeve of brother Andy's behavior. She'd been the cause of somebody else's bad day, albeit a bug.

Secrets and lies and perpetual self-hatred surged. Amy longed to open up, like the Porsche when she'd pushed the pedal toward the floor. She feared if she told anyone her pasts' totality, the facts would morph into pieces of flying debris in an already dangerous storm: her head.

Could she relent and trust Dad Hernandez? Probably not. While he had a badge and a precise moral compass, he already knew much about her and more might slash him from her side. Not worth the risk.

Ronnie was a definite no. That woman swished and swashed and sided with whomever would cover her butt in the long term. She was loyal, no doubt, but loyal to what? And for how long?

Travis? Not even in the ballpark of integrity and trust. Fast forward, please. With or without revenge, Travis was fading in relevance. Hit delete. He'd sell his own mom to make a buck.

Woolworth Wilma? Maybe. With her embroidered handkerchiefs and a willingness to hold Amy's hand in the short term, she was a safe bet. But the truth, the whole truth, and nothing but would toss her over the moral cliff, too. Amy felt she'd survived a hailstorm after giving *Worthless Bill* the axe.

Wilma already owned one burden—her brilliant

but wastrel son. Amy was determined to be the *good child* and not ask for more. She'd be self-reliant, something at which she was skilled.

Chapter Forty

UNSTASH THE CASH

AMY RAN DOWN the long hall and threw herself on her bed. After a pause, she scrambled up and slammed the door. Rather than cry, she rolled onto her back and snoozed. She awoke with a jolt and stared at her closet. The answer to prayer was hiding in plain sight.

She sped to the door and stepped inside. She bent to fumble through her shoe boxes, soon fondling her two big bags of cash. All smiles, no secret alliances needed. Money was on her side.

She set her phone on silent. Let the housekeeper or cook handle any guest problems. She'd be up to her elbows in cash for a while.

The bags were so heavy, Amy sat on the floor. In the closet. She tugged at the clasp and soon each bag yawed. Amy peeked inside and almost shrieked.

She slipped off her favorite sandals to go to jump on the bed.

Back in the closet, she began to do the highest math she'd done in her life. Soon, she stretched her cramped legs, so she scooped up all of her shoeboxes and dumped the contents on the closet floor. Then she packed each shoebox with bills, methodically, evenly, counting stacks as she went. Cha-ching, cha-ching. Now she saw *and* felt her wealth.

She also felt stupid. Why had she allowed Elvin and the banker to dupe her into a mortgage on the manse? She felt foolish because she'd been the one to set herself up as the money madam each business would seek. She wasted all of her steel-spined resolve—when she could've/should've paid cash for the $4,000,000.00 house.

Of course, word would have been flung around, but there'd be rumors without proof because the deed would be in her safe.

She could have cash-paid all of the workers, including pal Ronnie. There'd be no paper trail for the IRS or worker's comp. Ronnie could have ordered all of the needed supplies, C.O.D. It all could have been simple and direct.

Rather than wasting time on self-chastisement, Amy re-shelved the shoeboxes. She hummed as she stuffed the Barbie pink backpack with the remaining money stacks. She had enough in the boxes to pay off the house and would do that pronto, perhaps commanding the bank President to come to her home for a personal audience, the house deed in his briefcase, ready-set for transfer. She thrilled in advance at the eye pop he would attempt to cover up when he was made aware of his initial *mistake.* He'd feel the screws—and his sole witness to the transaction would stop gossip in its tracks.

Amy skipped down the hall and ran splat into Ronnie.

"Thank goodness, you're home," Ronnie said, blunt as ever. "Where have you been? We have a new guest in the fourth guest room. More are booking via the website, and I'm wondering when the lower floor's suites will be done?"

Did Ronnie will herself to be confrontational and make demands of the boss?

How impertinent. Though Ronnie was the salaried manager and Amy the mega-millionaire, Amy felt like the slog-horse of the Lady Bug Inn.

"I don't know how to answer that, Ronnie. I honestly don't." She wiggled her eyebrows. "May we sit and munch one of the sandwiches I hope you've made?" *Let Ronnie feel like the slave.*

Ronnie scowled and tromped to the frig.

Just then, lanky-and-famished Andy strolled in. "I see that we have a new guest, Ronnie. The drapes are drawn, so I can't peep in the room. If there was a slider, I'd let myself in to reconnoiter."

"Don't you interlope on our guests!" Amy reinforced the order by shaking a finger in Andy's face. "Our policy is their privacy. Stand down. Or, better yet, do something useful, you pipsqueak."

"Make me, Ms. I'm-never-here-and-even-if-I-am-

I-don't-contribute." Andy chest-bumped. "By the way, Ms. High-and-Mighty Owner, you need to put a Keurig and complimentary coffee in each suite. I'm tired of being the errand boy for your guests, literally on call for their every whim, including multiple cups of coffee in the morning."

"You have a phone? The ladies call you? How did they get your number?" Amy sounded so aghast, her voice came out pitched like a dog's squeak toy. She could tell by Ronnie's wince.

"I gave it to them gratis," Andy said off-handedly, grabbing at the tray of sandwiches Ronnie ferried to the table. "Or, another way to think about the situation is, the ladies are basically gnats drawn to the light that is me."

"Order fifteen Keurigs, Ronnie," Amy ordered to divert attention and gain the upper hand. Inconceivable. Andy's presence was worse than she'd thought. She could feel a migraine coming on.

"Order Willie Nelson's Remedy Coffee, too!" Amy wheeled her head around and glared at her brother. Where did he get off commanding *her* staff?

She whipped her head back to face Ronnie, who'd seated herself and was now into her second bite of a tuna salad sandwich. Amy watched her chew and near-gasped after Ronnie swallowed and said, "Already did," and then picked up a bottled water to guzzle nearly half of it in a single gulp. "Also hired a cook to make breakfast, lunch and dinner." Ronnie then returned to munching.

Who was running this show? Not I, said the multi-millionaire red hen.

Amy turned her eyes to the plate in the middle of the table. There was a single sandwich left. She'd better grab it before she was left out of everything.

Amy kept her head down to her plate, chewed slowly. While she realized she was emulating dairy cows in a pasture, she felt it better to not retort—or else Ronnie might quit. Then, she'd be deciding, ordering, and running the business, whereas now she merely had the paying part.

Amy wished Andy would quit. How to accomplish that was her rumination for the rest of the day. Chew to chase the migraine away, as well as the cheeky, entitled kid.

The encounter with the banker occurred the next day. An orgasmic event.

The path was cleared for Amy to solve her double man problem: how to get rid of Andy and Travis. Neither would be as easy as getting rid of a mortgage, but if she needed to flash cash, she would make a simple withdrawal from her closet.

She hadn't felt this giddy in months.

Chapter Forty-One

PATIENT-AND-PORSCHE SHENANIGANS

A FEW WEEKS later, the Lady Bug build-out was complete, yet Amy felt squeezed. Though she had a dozen spa guests, only eleven of them paid. She had money in a backpack in the bottom of her closet, she considered that emergency cash.

Besides, the free-loader was her brother who lived in a cabana the contractors had installed around the pool, at the end opposite the diving board. Not-dandy Andy hung his pool-washed clothing—two pair of cargo shorts and two shirts—on the exterior of his assigned cabana, signalling that he slept in the nude and could be had.

Each day Amy renewed her pledge to ignore Andy, although she doubted it could be done. The more she ignored his ignoramus endeavors and outlandish cursing, the more Andy escalated his antics.

Because she employed a cook, a manager, a pool cleaner and gardener, as well as several house cleaners, Amy had little to do. She also seemed to have perma-employed a painter. Though the entire Lady Bug Inn perimeter and all interior rooms were done, Dante seemed disinclined to leave. So, she wondered if he was a spy under Hernandez' employ. That could account for the uncanny alertness Hernandez possessed to know the entirety of Amy moves and non-moves.

Because she missed her prison-exercise-yard tan, despite the humidity-amped heat, Amy sunbathed by her pool. She enjoyed reclining on the deck chairs, casually mingling and chatting with the spa guests and snapping her fingers for peach daquiris or dirty martinis, the specialties of the house.

Amy understood that, due to the inherent perversity of her nature, she was showing off her non-surgery-enhanced body and face to the women. Not to foster envy, but to facilitate recidivism. *The reward for more work was more money.* She struck a deal struck with one of the plastic surgeons: if Amy's former Lady Bug Inn clients returned to him for plastic surgery, she would receive a kickback.

The morality of her Catholic youth and the ethics of Michigan State, reinforced by the cloister of prison life, continued to slip-slide away. Amy felt more of her perdition bound self emerging each day, massaged by diabolic plots against Travis.

Perhaps she shouldn't have been surprised when one of her poolside-reclining clients casually unleashed her bikini top after she'd secured her position on her towel-draped chair.

But she was. Shocked, in fact. Amy had anticipated mature and demure surgery-seekers.

The what's-her-name, fifty-something's eyes were visible over the tops of her cat eye sunglasses, so Amy watched the lightly-bandaged woman's calculating gaze of Andy's flip-flopping walk. It was clear he'd awakened not long ago—and maybe not alone—because the look Andy returned to the woman was more personal than warranted.

Andy clearly had ambition: for *effect* and *sex.* No wonder he was no longer restive and no longer bickered with Dante, conditions that Amy good-riddanced.

She was cool with the détente but playing the cock among the hens was not cool.

The shocks to Amy's sense of propriety didn't end. Andy swaggered to the diving board, jumped a few jumps on its tip, perhaps as a test of its limberness, and then cannonballed into the pool! Amy added *show-off* to Andy's three strikes.

Amy slid on her Dolce & Gabbana sunglasses and began to scan the pool perimeter. All clientele eyes were on the surface of the pool, waiting for Andy to surface… and then, the entire group squealed in delight! Un*king believable! When Andy smacked the surface of the pool, more squeals erupted. Seriously, these women didn't mind getting wet.

Oh, the one who had abandoned her bikini top

minded… when she sat up swiftly due to the cold-water splash, her newly-implanted breasts exposed as plump double-Ds. Andy's eyes may have popped in response.

Didn't freshly-incisioned women have stitches to protect? Didn't they have husbands at home who expected to see the results of the surgery, roosters who paid the bill for the work? One didn't consider the possibility of these mature females having to protect their virginity, so no lawsuits could ensue, yet Amy wondered about the hanky-panky her brother's presence encouraged.

And he was unkempt, not cute. Neither debonair, nonchalant, nor gallant in attitude.

Was Andy an unselective lover boy? *Four Strikes.*

Her eleven lounging ladies returned their heads to their respective beach reads.

Amy was amused, not annoyed that the ladies were dedicated to their non-notice of her, the spa owner. She had Hernandez, Woolworth Wilma, and Ronnie on speed-dial, with intermittent acknowledgement from Charlene Braghorn, an old friend from her former 'hood, who sauntered in as the spa's first plastic surgery recoveree. Amy had felt blessed and nearly wept that the woman came to her place, a Godsend to pay bills and refer others. Her recovery cycle almost complete, Charlene now spent her free time with Judge.

Sigh. Soon, Charlene would be gone. Amy crossed her fingers, eyes, and toes that replacements would arrive soon. Amy had a circle of friends as family, so she felt set there. She'd accept any body that bled cash to keep the Lady Bug Inn at full occupancy.

Now a new income stream notion popped: she'd stock a library of romance novels for sale. Amy made a note for Ronnie to contact Harlequin and purchase copies of the top ten all-time best-selling bodice rippers. Her ladies-in-repost needed to pass their hours of recovery and would be righteously pissed if Andy splashed on their paperbacks. The sex he delivered couldn't be as good as that suggested in novels by Christina Alexander or Chris Lentz.

Amy wondered if Andy accepted cash only for his services. She wondered if he'd tire of the steady influx of female guests. She knew she wouldn't tire of the cash cows, but Andy was a question mark. Five strikes were possible, and he'd be on his way O-U-T.

On Thursday, Andy stole the Porsche. Well, he didn't exactly steal it, he later confessed. He merely borrowed it. For a joy ride.

It was impossible to not hear the Porsche depart, especially when Andy vroomed the engine. He did not ease it out of the garage. He did floor the gas pedal—for a highly discernable second—dust and gravel flying about. Gr-r-r-r, Amy gritted her teeth. *Five, nay six strikes. Vroom-vroom.*

Amy watched grimly as the brat rooster-tailed the lane. The cost of the Porsche's up-keep just rose. More zeroes to the cost of Andy's upkeep. Amy was beginning to feel unsafe in her own house. Her over-burdened bank account was in jeopardy, too, if this kept up much longer. Sigh.

After several hours, Amy was about to call Andy's sorry red ass, when her iPhone rang. Its caller ID warned her that it was Andy.

Amy was already worn out from Andy's six strikes and now this bad news could be seven. Soon she'd have to put hash marks on his cabana door to keep track. Her ravaged soul suspected that this call could go nowhere but down.

"What the hell were you thinking, Sis? Leaving a Porsche 911 in the garage with only a half a tank of gas!"

Oh. Andy must be from the camp of *the best defense was a formidable offense*, something that Brandon, the star football player, had taught Amy. Did all men know the gambit?

"Where are you, Andy? Did you get arrested?"

"I'm in Traverse City. And no, I didn't get arrested. Duh, I'm a felon on the lam, too."

He certainly had a quirky way of saying "I love you" and aligning with Amy. She ought to make this set of actions, with his accompanying remarks, three more strikes.

Equals ten.

"Why'd you head to Traverse City, Andy?" she asked, attempting to keep her voice benign.

"I'm twenty-two years old and bored, Sister. I overheard some of your ladies talking about Traverse City casinos. You let me drive the Porsche once, and I hungered for another drive. I thought I heard it calling my name. *Take me to Traverse City, and I'll show you some action.*" Andy paused to return to his own weaselly voice after the growl he'd used to emulate a Porsche. "The shiny red thing practically pleaded with me."

"But Traverse City is two hundred miles from here. You got yourself there, and you can't get back? What's your plan, man-child?"

"I figured you'd come and get me, we'd gamble a bit and take in the sights, like we truly were siblings, you know. Build some memories, start a riot, and other quiet shit."

"Gamble with what money, Andy?" Amy shouted at her cell. "How did you plan to buy poker chips?"

"Well, I wasn't in need of a stake of your cash, if that's what you are implying. I have my own stash. It's a bit meager, but with my gambling skills, it will grow into a mountain."

Amy's suspicions of Andy boffing her guests now officially confirmed, her anger sky-rocketed. Another strike was mentally hash-tagged above his cabana's door.

"Here's what's going to happen, Andy. Sit your ass outside the car. I don't want to find you in it when I get there. A Focus has fewer rpms than a Porsche 911, so it may take a couple-three hours. Amuse yourself with games on your phone."

"What if I gotta pee?" Andy whined.

"Go in your pants, for all I care, but I'll kill you if you pee in the Porsche."

"Ha, maybe I'll just wee on a back tire."

Amy could see Andy's smirk through the phone. She didn't need FaceTime for that. "I'm hungry, so hurry."

F*CK! The kid just didn't know when to back off or let up. Maybe she would grab Dante to drive her to Traverse City to fetch her feeble-planned brother. *Yeah. All good.* She'd let Dante punch Andy's lights out rather than her. She'd let Dante strip the twerp of his unearned pride.

"Okay, Andy. You've got to agree to my constraints, or I won't rescue your bony ass."

"Don't you care about the Porsche? It'll be stripped within hours if we leave it alone?"

"It's not in your wheelhouse to solve the problem of the Porsche," Amy declared. "And, while we are *chatting*, let's be clear on another item." She crooked her neck to slide the phone into its clench, so that she was hands-free to make fists. "You are grounded."

"You aren't the boss of me!"

"While you are under my roof, I am. I'm going to click off this call and get on the road. See you in a few hours."

But Andy meant it when he said Amy wasn't the boss of him. He didn't remain in place, nor did he play games on his phone. He had to pee awesome bad, so he hitched a ride to a Traverse City casino.

The driver was an accommodating dude, who happened to mention he owned a bar before he dropped Andy by the most infamous casino.

In his defense later, Andy would state that he'd relieved himself properly and planned to exit the casino, when the enormous roulette wheel near the entrance caught his eye. He'd taken the free spin that was offered—and he won!

In deference to his fervor for the arrest-me-red Porsche 911, Andy returned to stand guard by its side. He couldn't abide it being stolen. He hoped he could wheedle Amy into allowing him to drive it again.

Andy traded his instant win of ten to further turns at the wheel.

He was golden. He was on fire. He was a star.

He was an addict. He'd return to Traverse City again—he'd hitch if he had to—to gamble and become a high-rolling talent, known and admired everywhere.

It was his destiny.

CHAPTER FORTY-TWO

PEACE MORE-OR-LESS

THE RETURN OF her attention to the Lady Bug Inn was complete, Andy's boundaries set. Amy buried herself in guest attentiveness the rest of the afternoon. Kind, tender, yet walled-off, she mingled, trying not to lose her lunch because many women had removed bandages to fully reveal their purple, yellow, and blue mottled foreheads and necks and breasts. Ick!

There was the Chicago Gold Coast aristocrat, who wore body piercings of Tiffany diamonds and *Fort Knox worthy* gold. The surprised look of an overdone forehead lift, the tuck of tummy without the coordinate thigh work, which must have been phase two.

It was all mildly sordid and disgraceful, the open display of self-despise. Amy began to wonder about her Inn and its partnership with body-shaming, the rampant sub-culture that dehumanized women, failing to elevate their best contribution to society: birthing the next generation and keeping culture and humanity alive.

Yup, Amy felt culpable, more or less, in the crazed carving of bodies to ideal. One of Hernandez' coaching-the-parolee lines came to mind, "Everybody thinks of changing humanity, but nobody thinks of changing themselves." A quote from Tolstoy, he'd said. She'd had to make him repeat the name twice because she'd first heard 'Toy Story.' She didn't recall Buzz Light Year or Woody making such a pithy remark.

"Well, arguably, not everyone," he'd admitted when Amy stared him down in full wonder as she contemplated the parameters of his remark.

"Do you want me to change myself, Dad?" she'd asked. "Do you care about one parolee that much?"

"Yes," Hernandez replied, "and you can start with shedding your scuzzy faced and assed brother."

Amy swiveled her head so swiftly that, if she'd been one of her plastic surgery guests, she'd have popped stitches. Hernandez had felled her with that recommendation. Amy felt like she'd been hit by a stun gun.

"Yes. I said that. Amy, everyone is enrolled in your personal rehab program except that punk. I know he's your blood brother, and you are bound by some sort of guilt. I'm aware there's so much unspoken backstory in your mutual past, the Jaws of Life would be necessary to pry you apart. Maybe there's a parent or non-parent lurking as a deadly underground force."

Amy's skin sizzled with embarrassment as Hernandez drove his points home. Her heart felt staked. It plummeted to her toes. Her stomach tanked. She felt on the verge of throwing up. She flailed at the air, the ground, and at Hernandez' stoic face.

Though Amy was seated, her body felt engulfed by marathon sweat. A lengthy pause ensued. Either Hernandez was allowing her to absorb and understand his take-or-leave-it stand, or he wanted her to recover her equilibrium for more to come. She looked at him. "If you've got any more punches, you ought to get them over with."

Hernandez' face softened, and he reached to hold hers in his fingertips. "Your allegiance is misplaced, and your thinking is choppy, Parolee-of mine."

Amy felt like choking as she attempted to reply. Hernandez had been the one constant in her after-prison life. They broke the mold after they made him. How would she refute what he said?

"The next time Andy parades around the pool in his shorts, enticing and laughing at your clients, not with them, I'd like permission to handcuff-and-march him off the property."

Amy wondered if she'd be able to do that. She flung her head into her palms.

"Amy, face your shame and conquer it."

"Shame?" Amy cried, incredulous that reliable Hernandez would say such a thing.

"You don't need success or money or fame—or infamy—to be great. You don't need to be brought down by some skank, brother or not. Everybody is pulling for your success except Andy. The Lions, your clients, your friend Ronnie—more or less."

Now Hernandez gripped one of Amy's wrists. She forced herself to look him in the eye. "Cut Andy loose," he said.

Chapter Forty-Three

GAMBLING DEBT

ANDY CUT HIMSELF loose the next day, albeit with the intent of the single score that could fund Departure from under Bitchy Amy's thumb. He thumbed to Traverse City and strolled the Casino corridor. His first intent was to scrounge free coffee and doughnuts.

He needed to fuel his foray.

Travis and Andy recognized each other simultaneously, as if their meet was ordained by a stimulant seekers' god. This morning's order was coffee—and lots of it—for both. Both were squinty-eyed and draggy-assed and needed to boost to meet the day head-on.

"Bro," they said simultaneously. And then said it again. It was obvious neither remembered the other's name, and they didn't know whether to fist bump or bro hug. Finally, Travis broke the awkwardness in half and extended his hand for a shake.

I've got a bar nearby. It's called TRAVIS' TRAVEL IN. I can make us some coffee. I sense we are going to have a relationship, so let's start it right."

"I think you was the dude who picked me up when my Porsche ran out of gas the other day."

"That your 911? I hope it was okay when you returned. Here's my bar. Let's chat while the coffee makes itself." Andy looked at Travis oddly. "I prepped the bar's coffee maker at 1:00 a.m. when I closed down the bar. All I have to do this morning is punch a button."

"Wouldn't it be great if every morning was that easy. Just punch a button and your quest is done," Andy ventured.

"Speaking of quest. What brings you to Traverse City? And, why are you walking the streets? Where's your Porsche parked?"

"Not my Porsche. It's my sister, Amy's. She's got a gigantic house down the coast. Got a lot of women slithering around in post-plastic surgery bandages. I've made some gains among the hens in the house, but I'm not sure it's worth it. I'm basically grounded for life amidst a gaggle of giggling and grousing women. I need some cock talk-and-walk, if you know what I mean. Someone who can give and take an off color joke."

"How'd your sister—Amy, is it—come by a big house and a Porsche?"

"Don't know. It's a secret source, but it does seem to be endless."

The Bunn made its final burbling announcement that the coffee was ready. Travis poured Andy a to-go cup and then rubbed Andy's soul-patched chin. "Come by the bar tonight about 9:00. There's a low stakes poker game in the bar's backroom. Iif you have a Benjamin, we'll help you be as rich as your sister. Sound good?"

"Yes, but what's a Benjamin? I've got no friends in town, no friends at all because my damn sister keeps me couped up in the country," Andy groused.

That was when Travis knew he'd found the right yokel for tonight's game. He'd lassoed the innocent. Now to tighten the noose.

"Hey, before you go on your walk-about-town, grab yourself a couple of pickled hard-boiled eggs. Stop by for lunch and supper grub, too. You've got to keep your brain buff to beat the locals at poker."

Andy actually waved as he departed. He fairly skipped to the gaudy casino where he intended to win a car in one of his ten free spins. Hot Damn! It was going to happen for him, something bigger and better than what had happened for her.

It took all of ten minutes for Andy to gain exactly nothing with his ten spins with the fancy giant roulette winner. While he enjoyed his near-celebrity status as a crowd gathered to voyeur his brush with greatness and to chant "Andy! Andy! Andy!" their loud clapping obscured the shouted words.

The crowd evaporated more quickly than it had

amassed. When a leggy barmaid tried to maneuver Andy to the bar to drown his early a.m. sorrows, Andy waved her off.

He'd made a fool of himself, probably inevitable. He felt consigned to a screw-up life. Maybe second fiddle was his permanent perch.

Besides, Travis had reserved a place for him at the TRAVIS' TRAVEL IN, complete with a free lunch, nap zone, and supper.

So, Andy ambled back, drawn by the magnet of affinity hood, though he wasn't certain of the source of that yet.

"Ready for lunch?" Travis hailed Andy as if he were a regular. "Here's our bar menu. Pick any item you'd like."

"What's steak tartar?"

"It's the perfect lunch for a dupe, er, a dude like you, my man." Travis leaned over the bar to clap Andy on the back. "And, I see you noting the price…forget about it. Lunch tab is on me!"

Travis inwardly smiled at the symmetry of the situation. Not that long ago, he'd met Amy over lunch. She'd disappeared—or else there'd have been further interaction. Andy seemed like a second chance.

"What's your most expensive beer?" Andy asked. "I'll have whatever it is, with another behind it to chase that one down. Please, don't card me, Travis. I left California in a hurried mess, and haven't had time to apply for a Michigan license."

"You hound!" Travis put out his fist for a bump. "You drove a Porsche without a license!?! You da man." He drew the beer to the top of its glass, and served the steak tartare pronto. Travis bolted to the backroom to text his coven of players about the whale who was eating tartare.

Besides, he didn't want to see expensive tartare puked with his most expensive IPA beer. Let the barmaid earn her pay for the day.

After midnight, it all came down. Down to Andy's last card and his last pile of chips, shoved *all-in*, with five other mens' chip mountains. He didn't know the game was rigged. He didn't know he was the mark. Andy wouldn't recognize a poker shark if he met one—and he'd met five.

He hadn't noticed Travis' wink to the last hand's card dealer. Travis was about to rake. Travis was about to own Andy's hide.

Andy face-planted when the last card was shown, so he didn't see the quartet that sidled out, leaving him alone with his new owner, Travis.

Andy lifted his head to Travis' intent stare. He suddenly felt insecure, like he needed a life raft to depart the bar.

"What we have is a *situation,*" Travis began and then paused for effect. "You seem to owe me a righteous amount of money."

Travis winked, but Andy didn't return it. He was

too numb to even ask what the amount was, because he knew he couldn't pay.

"I have a business proposition, Andy. You may repay your awkward amount of indebtedness, enough to melt your hide by the way, by becoming a mule for dime bags to the hotels, motels, and casinos in Traverse and its surrounds. It's a good deal for both of us." Travis looked away, a sort of signal for Andy to give the deal serious thought.

The serious thought that Andy, indeed, had no choice.

"I can't. I'm an ex-con."

Travis grinned. "So what?"

"Besides, I don't have wheels."

"Whose can you borrow? A car like a Porsche has plenty of horses for deliveries."

"I've got no driver's license, remember?"

"That can be fixed, my man." Travis leaned in. "What's it going to be, Puke?" Andy reeled back into his chair. "Yes, I still see the puke on your collar, punk. I wasted a ton of tartare and two tankards of good beer on you. You slept the afternoon away in my back office and supped at my place. Shall I add those items to your tab?"

"Well, my sister who has two cars: a black Focus and a red Porsche 911, the one which ran out of gas. She can probably pay." After he offered this notion, Andy hung his head and stared at his hands. "But Amy's an ex-con and likely no more trustworthy than I am."

Travis almost bolted from his chair at the mention

of Amy's name. Instead, he grabbed one of Andy's hands and guided him back to the bar, which was now closed for the night. No witnesses for his next move, which didn't matter because Travis owned the bar—and most of its regulars. It was his ambition to become mayor of Traverse City, as well as its richest citizen. His new venture in South Haven would ensure that.

Travis opened a beer and slid across the bar top, directly in front of Andy. He raised another opened beer and proposed a toast. "Here's to ex-cons." Each drained the beer, contemplating his own inner demons.

"Let's go for a ride," Travis said. "I'll show you the long-distance route, down to South Haven and over to Holland, and then back."

"My sister owns a country home near South Haven."

"Let's go visit while we deliver the weed. What's the name and does it have a website?"

Yes, there was a website… with GPS coordinates for its obscure P.O. Box address. Easy to locate on Google Maps. Wowzer!

Now, Travis Zillowed the property. Wowzer more and more. How had Amy acquired such a property? Perhaps, thought Travis, I have a new and better mark.

Now Travis was eager to see Amy's place. He was absolutely hasty. Lusty, in fact.

"Mind if we drive sleepless?"

"Well, I ain't driving, so suit yourself. Mind if I nap while you deliver?"

"Yes, I mind, numb skull. I'm about to model how you are going to repay your debt… besides, you had a nap!"

Several hours later, near dawn, Andy and Travis arrived at the end of Pinnacle Lane.

Travis nudged Andy, who had fallen asleep. "Can you walk from here? I want to remain unknown in these parts. I have a reputation to uphold." He near-pushed Andy off his bike. "Don't forget your debt, Punk. I'll expect your expedient return to duty or tons of cash in its place."

Andy gave Travis a weird look, shrugged his shoulders and removed himself from Travis' sight. He was not the power in this situation. He was the supplicant, subrogated to his gambling debt.

Travis zoom-zoomed off without a wave.

Chapter Forty-Four

HANDFUL FOR RANSOM

ANDY WALKED TO the house, arriving in a mild sweat, dirty underwear, multiply-ripped jeans, and a TRAVEL IN shirt. He immediately stepped out of the motley garb and cannonballed into the pool. "Did you miss me, Sis?" he said after he surfaced, sporting a wicked sideways grin.

Though she lounged on a patio chair, slathered in #30 sunscreen, Amy looked up to acknowledge Andy's trepass—after a peek at her Apple watch confirmed that it was 7:00 a.m. "No, I didn't miss you, Andy. Why would I? I own a business that runs on decorum. Your presence is fractious to the guests. Your antics are disruptive when you are here. When you're gone, peace rules. My guests need a calm environment to heal."

Grumpy that Amy hadn't missed his presence in the poolside cabana, Andy ambled to his *room*, dripping a path on the pool deck. He felt as unimportant as hell. He considered keying the Porsche but stopped… he intended to own that sweet ride—or one like it—after he paid off his debt to Travis.

He lurched inside, plopped on the chaise, and then realized he had to pee. It'd been a long, ball-jarring ride, and he was sore as hell. In more ways than one. Grumble, grump, harrumph. His true desire was to slobber every square inch of the high gloss red Porsche with his tongue. In the interim he galumphed to the nearest bathroom.

"Mind the house, would you?" Amy called after him as Andy slammed the bathroom door. "I have to dash to a mani-pedi appointment. I'm taking one of the guests, so I'll have the Porsche."

Dang, thought Andy on the other side of the door. *Opportunity doesn't strike twice.*

He did his business—and then went onto better business, almost salivating at the opportunity before him. *While the cat was away, the mousey brother would play… the bitch would pay.*

His Travis debt.

Andy looked one way. He squinted to look the other way. He cocked his head to listen. Then, he tiptoed down the hall. He didn't bother to knock on his sister's door. He entered, wondering why he was tiptoeing. Was he ashamed of what he was about to do? Which was… to burgle his own sister.

He stepped to her dressers and rifled every drawer. As if fingering his sister's lingerie was an everyday thing. Normal mode for Andy—and any thief.

Aware that guests might be holed up in their rooms

of recovery. He paused to listen for a TV or music. He heard no sound, not even of pages turning in a book.

Andy stepped away from Amy's drawers, where he'd discovered ten bucks in a pair of panties. Stuffed the cash in his pocket and left the panties, idly wondering why she'd stashed the money there. He glanced around the room. He looked under the bed, fluffed the pillows, and patted the coverlet down. He swashbuckled the drapes, as if there were another person hiding there. One with deep pockets of cash.

Then he spied the monster closet. There!

The Barbie pink backpack was easy to spot, no matter that it was hidden among Amy's boots and burgeoning amount of shoes. Andy zipped to the backpack, bent, and easily tugged it open, though the backpack had fallen to its side. It seemed to be stuffed.

With Benjamins. Now, he knew what a Benjamin was— and there were hundreds and hundreds of the hundred-dollar bills, banded together in packs. Amy had stiffed him. Travis had used him. This cache deserved to be stolen and put to better use than hiding away in a closet. Andy was about to end his indentured servitude.

Andy texted Travis: GOT THE DOUGH.

Travis reply-texted: WHERE THE H R U?

Andy replied: COMING SOON. WITH LUNCH.

Travis, halfway to Traverse City on the back of his bike, didn't reply. He merely slowed and turned his bike around, fast on the gas to return to Pinnacle Lane.

Meanwhile back at the Lady Bug Inn, Andy stuffed

sandwiches, celery sticks, and string cheese, the entire contents of the frig, scuttling out of the kitchen just prior to one of the guests' arrival.

"Wait, you took all the lunches!" a guest cried at his back.

"Eat chips!" Andy shouted. He ran down the lane as fast as the weight of the backpack and his unhealthy self would allow.

He huffed and puffed more than ever. He shoulda stolen the Focus, since the Porsche was gone. It would be tough to take the ribbing he'd get as a hitchhiker with a pink backpack. But it was worth it.

Especially when Travis arrived at the end of Pinnacle Lane. Andy attached the backpack with a bungee cord on the ass-end of the bike and clambered on, ignoring the scowl on Travis' face. He knew his debtmaster would be smiling. Soon. In two hours of soon.

And then some. Woot!

Two hours and twenty minutes later, Travis drew two beers and then settled beside Andy in a booth in the back of the TRAVEL IN. Andy was already hunkered with the pink backpack scrunched between his legs.

Andy boldly proposed a toast. "To wealth and health!" Deferentially, he allowed Travis to take the first sip. After all, it was the dude's bar.

"Take 'em out slowly, one at a time," Travis commanded.

Andy remained polite and compliant. He brought up a stack. And, another. Then, another. He could see

Travis' mind rolling the numbers, actively calculating the total as the hundred-dollar bills appeared.

Another stack. One more. Then, another. And then the stacking was done.

Andy held his breath and, uncharacteristically, his tongue.

As slowly as the stacks mounted, pausing to drain his beer, Travis level-eyed Andy. "Twerp. While I might be inclined to commiserate, seeing as how you were one of our best marks, er, poker partners, this money ain't enough to buy your debt. You, my little brother friend, have got yourself a plight."

"How much exactly do I owe you, sir?" Andy tried, but he couldn't keep the whine from his voice.

Silence. Andy saw more calculating behind Travis' high forehead, as if the math gears in Travis' brain needed more juice.

"May I pull you another beer from your tap?" Andy jumped up before his debt owner could respond.

Travis grabbed Andy's wrist and pulled him back into the booth. "First, replace the money and slide the backpack to me, under the table."

Andy did, while Travis slurped.

"Now get out your phone and call your sister."

Andy raised his eyebrows.

"Don't. Text." Travis clipped each word as if using scissors.

Andy shivered. The undercurrent was clear. If he didn't do as told, more clipping would occur and all of his hair might be gone, gone, gone. Next, his life cut short. And for what? A little money? His cold bitch of a sister apparently had lots of money. She owed him. She'd cough up money in trade for her baby brother, he felt sure.

"Dial her number and then give me the phone." Then, Travis smiled. Well, actually it was a leer, as if he had *Amy* by the balls. What could that mean? Andy worried. Was there history between Travis and Amy? A different history than he shared with his sister?

Travis' cunning became clear when Amy answered. "Hello, what the heck do you want? I'm in the middle of a pedicure. Make it snappy."

"I'm afraid there's been a little adjustment to your brother's circumstances, Amy."

Andy could almost see Amy's recoil at the snarled remark—in part because Travis leaned into the call, with little pause for Amy to respond. Dude was in control and he asserted. "I know where you live, Amy. I can come and get you anytime I want."

The menace in Travis' voice was unmistakable. Andy now knew that there was history—and that Travis felt he had the upper hand. He held his breath, wondering what the heck would happen in this duel/disaster… a potential disaster for him and his cash cow sister… and it finally dawned on him that he cared. Not just for his own skin, but for Amy's.

"Your puny brother ran up a little gambling debt at a backroom poker game at my bar. You know where it is, don't you, Amy? You came here to visit me, early out of your ten-year prison sentence…"

"You scoundrel. Give me back my brother!" Andy could hear Amy shout and he felt proud. She loved him.

"I'll give him back to you *after* you pay a ransom of thirty thousand bucks."

There was a long, unearthly pause. Andy finally had to take a breath. He coiled his body, hunched to protect his heart, then worried that his neck was exposed to a sword. Andy crossed his fingers and hoped not to die.

"Ten strikes, Andy's out!" came the cry. "You keep him, Trav. I don't want the rascal back. He's a disappointing family member and a peccable ex-con!"

Andy recoiled at the vehemence in Amy's voice. His head snapped back and his heart sank. This entire discourse was going badly for him. He felt eyes on him. As intent as an eagle on a prairie dog.

"Well, the pecker does look mighty slim. He must be underfed, not doing well in your care in your ginormous palace, Amy. Let me remind you that you are an ex-con, like your brother—and I am not. We ain't done yet."

Travis hung up and jammed the phone into his jeans—just as a silver tray with a single folded note appeared, as if on a hidden conveyor belt, before its deliverer slunk away. Travis snatched the note from the tray, read it quickly, and blanched. Andy thought he looked like a bomb had gone off in his face.

Travis dropped the pink backpack and stalked out of the room. Andy heard a backroom door slam, but he was too frightened to move.

Amy may have been a bitch, but she was his bitch. He wondered what to do but was frozen to the spot. Andy felt like a ghost.

CHAPTER FORTY-FIVE

ABANDON HOPE, KEEP THE FAITH

AMY NEEDED SOMEONE to talk to about the dilemma with Andy. And Travis, a threat to her success and now a threat to her brother.

Not Ronnie, unfortunately. That former closer-than-close, risk-taking friend still pouted because Dumped her weed it up often enough to seem like a nag.

Perhaps the owner-manager relationship warranted more distance than separate abodes. Perhaps, it was the complaint that Amy looked over her manager's shoulder to question purchases, the excesses the *blank check* mandate Veronica had bargained into their unwritten contract had decreed. Ronnie had once verbally slapped Amy full in the face. "You're no longer my vibrant, kick-ass friend. What stole you from yourself?"

"Debt," Amy slapped back. But as she walked away, full realization swelled and her cheeks got wet. Started and throttled by truth evoked tears—and not the alligator type that she'd sometimes accompanied with flashes of lashes, when her full height hadn't helped get her way. Crap! She had a closet filled with acres of clothes, so Amy sobbed with abandon.

All time to thoroughly reflect and absorb the bottomless truth. Before spa-building had been a prison sentence, cut in half for good behavior, to cement the shame and bold hinderance to all of her life goals. Money—and a lotto money—didn't fill the crater in her self-respect. The debt of a hard scrabble youth underpinning it all.

So, Ronnie was scarce, had a divergent set of friends, and not fully missed. Amy was now convinced Ronnie had never been an amenable-to-solution ear. She was crazy for good times—and a decent manager for a former WalMart clerk whose ambition was to be the best wedding cake baker in Hiawassee County—and shallow, small times. Amy knew Ronnie was not the resilient kind of crazy Amy herself was.

She knew Woolworth Wilma to be among the most resilient souls she'd ever met, along with Jackie Breeden, her ex-mother-in-law. Since she wasn't calling Jackie any time soon, Amy called Wilma, who'd qualified as Amy's supporter for life with a few kind words and supplies.

"Hi there! Things must be going well. Haven't heard from you in a while." Wilma began.

Amy winced. "Not exactly."

"Is that why you didn't FaceTime, sweet girl?" Wilma's voice intuitively softened and she paused.

Amy started to hiccup. "Let me get somewhere private," she said between "hic" and "up."

Amy hung up and bolted down the long hall to her room, praying that none of the guests would step into the hall. It would be a major embarrassment if she bowled over one of her paying clients. She reached the door, slammed it open, and then slammed it shut.

Surprisingly, that action proved to be a hiccup cure.

As if to replace the hiccups, tears surged. Amy deferred a FaceTime redial, trudged to her luxo sink, splashed her face, and then plunged her head under the faucet. She massaged her scalp and reached for a large towel, not caring how much water dripped onto the floor. Her hair near-dry in seconds, she felt refreshed.

She reached into her vanity drawers and drew out a plush brush. She gave it a whirl through her short blonde locks, and then grimaced at her image in the luxo mirror.

She needed a haircut. Her hair needed a millionaire-worthy shaping and a small-town establishment wouldn't do. Amy didn't need another small business owner to hit her up for cash. Or to gossip about whether the color of her hair was real or the size of her tip or anything else that would please a stylist while Amy was held captive in her Naugahyde chair.

Maybe Wilma knew a stylist in Lansing. She FaceTimed Wilma to request info and to make an appointment. Pronto! Wilma agreed to lunch afterward and to listen to Amy's tales, troubles, and woes. Wilma said that she couldn't imagine any.

"Just you wait," Amy replied.

Amy jumped into the Porsche without a word to the housekeepers or cook. She zoom-zoomed to Lansing with the radio volume up and the convertible top down. The top would be up on the return trip, the better to preserve her millionaire locks. Music would infuse the 90 m.p.h.ride.

Amy didn't talk during the stylist appointment. The male stylist didn't require it either. He seemed focused on his dancing and prancing and circling the pumped-up chair. He was busy-tailed and not in a hurry as he clipped and styled. Occasionally, he shook his head, as if in wonder how she'd survived without his hair influence.

Amy noticed he spent as much mirror-time, scanning himself as he did scanning her hair. Clippety-clip-clip, he whirled and twirled with his magic scissors… and voila! Amy almost applauded. Ya-asss. She looked like the high-dollar broad that she was. Star! She handed the dancing dude her credit card, not bothering to look at the amount as she signed.

She stepped out in the mirror-ball world, her problems already halved.

Still, as she lunched with Wilma, it all came back. Amplified and detailed and more painful with the report…all of Andy's ten unlucky strikes exposed and layered with nuances and hurts. All the way back to their hardscrabble childhood Amy disgorged details, gushing with total recall, past years of repression and papering over gaffs.

It was a small miracle Amy's eats remained in her stomach. Perhaps she had more space for food, now that all secrets divulged. Nothing held back, nothing diverted, no valley of shame not unearthed.

Amy surprised herself, but not Wilma. She, too, had grown up with kin.

When the pineapple upside-down cake was served, Amy chuckled nervously. "I hope that you still like me, Wilma, now that I've spilled the upside-down nature of my life."

Wilma reached across the table with another of her signature handkerchiefs. "I suspect that you're not yet teared out, my dear. You've shared some of your backstory, but you haven't brought me up to speed on your present."

Amy palmed the handkerchief and hung her head. She waited until, out of the corner of her eye, she saw the waitress return with a can of whipping cream to smother the large slab of cake with three inches of towering white. Only then did she lift her head to look Wilma in the eye. "Ready, set, go?"

When Wilma nodded, Amy let loose the Hernandez end of her tale, what had driven her to visit for counsel. She was heartened by Wilma's willingness to listen to her millionaire burdens ("I'm a land-rich millionaire myself, my dear"), and even more heartened by the sincere words that Amy had a certain *boomerang appeal*, so that Wilma was happy Amy had reappeared in her store, a success story, if you will.

Amy felt safe. She recounted Hernandez' tough-love advice. "Can't abandon Andy, can't give up hope. Hope pulled me through 2000 days of prison." She cupped her hands over her eyes, trying to stem the flood of tears.

"Yes, you can, Amy. You must." Wilma followed her strong affirmations with the Tolstoy line. It was the second time Amy had heard the wise guy mentioned, and from independent sources, so must it must be the truth. "You must abandon all hope. You may not be able to save Andy, but you can save yourself. I have faith."

Amy balked, not feeling safe to carry forward by herself. Wilma reminded her that she had Amy's back "For as long as you need, Missy. You've got to learn to trust somebody and that somebody should be me."

Wilma's next remark shocked Amy. The elderly woman's 'sweetness and light' sincerity partnered with her flinty resolve. She leaned forward in the booth and appeared to plant her feet firmly on the linoleum floor. She grabbed both of Amy's hands, knocking the embroidered handkerchief aside. Her grip was iron, and Amy stiffened in response.

"As proof of how far I'll go to protect and serve

you, let me say this." A shiver rippled through Amy's body. This skeletal dearheart with the steel colored hair and deeply lined face forced eye contact upon her.

"I know they say that blood is thicker than water, but what the heck do *they* know. *They* don't know me."

Amy realized that if Wilma had had a chaw, like Dante's perpetual cheek filler, she'd have paused to spit on the floor. "If I need to get my hands on that skunk of a brother Andy has repeatedly proven himself to be." Wilma leaned back for effect, but she didn't let go of Amy's hands, "I'll drown him in a tub of water myself."

Amy recoiled. Was murder on her sweet Wilma's mind?

As if she'd expected the effect of that scald-to-the-soul comment would shock Amy, Wilma smiled. Her eyes crinkled and twinkled again. "Actually, dear Amy, I've found that God and Karma are more talented and powerful at exacting revenge, so I sit back and allow their recompense for harm done."

Amy's shoulders relaxed when Wilma bent in to kiss her on the cheek. "And, if you're lucky, when a bad guy's time comes, God will let you watch." Wilma's wink urged Amy to wink back. "That, my dear, is the very best kind of revenge—when God is on your side."

Amy drove home in peace, maybe even joy, certain about God and faith and Wilma. She wondered what was in God or Karma's plan for Travis? It might be a very good show. And Amy would have a front row seat.

Chapter Forty-Six

A MOB BOSS WALKS IN THE DOOR

THE KNOCK ON the front door sent a jolt of electricity through Amy's body. Perhaps an unexpected Prince Charming. Certainly not Andy, who was doomed to be scarce.

Amy hoped that Andy and Travis enjoyed each other, two bad apples in the same barrel at the TRAVIS' TRAVEL IN. Amy idly wondered if TRAVIS TWO was a go, hoping not because it was too close to her Lady Bug Inn.

Enough of crap thoughts. I need some twenty-four-carat fun, and the source might be at the door.

Amy quickly rose and ran to a mirror, fluffed her hair, and checked her shirt for mid-chest stains. When she approved her look, she skipped to the front door and flung it open.

The bulked-up dude at the door was swarthy. He pushed Amy aside, a bully with a walker. Even his pause in the entry contained swagger. A grandly intimidating man, Amy's chest squeezed—and a wave of paranoia slithered up her spine.

"Name's Guido," he announced to no one in particular. Even the air fell to its knees to embrace his entrance.

Behind Guido, Ronnie lifted her eyebrows to her widow's peak, probably miming the questions that squeezed Amy's forehead into fear. It was a moment of flux for both. Who was in charge here?

Clearly, neither of them at that moment. A fly took advantage of the open door and zzzd toward the kitchen. The germaphobe within Amy shuddered, but she couldn't take her eyes off Guido. Had this man of Italian Mafia descent come here to knee-cap her?

"I like whatcha done to da place," the mildly gimpy guy boomed. He was a ruddy-hued beef. Already Guido's persona commanded the space. Amy felt flattened…and then noticed that she was up against the wall. She'd spread-eagled, as if ready to be searched. Was she, one of the richest people in Michigan, succumbing to intimidation by a man?

It was an event, a feeling of loss and astonishment, which Amy had never experienced. *Up against the wall?* Never in prison or elsewhere. She'd flabbergasted herself.

A huge mitt burst over the top of the walker, grabbed Amy's hand, and nearly shook her shoulder out of its socket. Then, Guido thrust aside the walker and bear-hugged Amy.

Imprisoned in the entry hall of her home! In her destiny spa?! In, in, in.... Amy gasped to catch her breath, willing her inhaler to pop out of her pocket, and clang to the floor. She willed Ronnie to pick it up, shake it, and clamp it to her mouth.

Or else, to tap this beef of a man on the shoulder so that he'd let loose.

As abruptly as his bear hug began, Guido released her. He was already striding down the hall and looking into each room—an imposition that elicited some shrieks. Behind him, Amy and Ronnie straggled, helpless to regain control. Who had visited this bad drama on the Lady Bug Inn?

Guido clomped to the end of the hall, loud with three steps/per move due to the walker. *At least the dude has tennis balls on the back legs of the walker, so that it doesn't harm the mahogany floors.*

When he came to the room at the end, Guido walked in like he owned it. He moved his walker to the middle and wheeled his head around and then clomped into the bathroom. He smiled and turned to his inadvertent entourage. "I'll take it!"

What? Amy's eyes flicked to Ronnie's face, searching for clues to this farce. Amy too frightened to speak, couldn't admit she hadn't received the playbook for this apparent move-in. Perhaps she wasn't really in charge of her destiny? This hulk looked capable of anything.

Ronnie blinked, apparently attempting Morse code. Amy shrugged.

"What?" Ronnie said with very contained gestures. "Uhm, Mr. Guido is our new post-plastic surgery guest. He apparently registered online. A check with his physician's office verified his surgery and subsequent referral to the Lady Bug Inn."

"Had my love handles removed, if you know what I mean," Guido interjected with a salaciously salacious wink. "Dey was from de gal I divorced, and my new gal don't like 'em."

There seemed little to say, so Amy continued to gape.

Ronnie stage-whispered, "Mr. Guido's pre-paid six weeks."

Amy knew what that meant. The credit accounts were maxed again, so Ronnie had allowed an additional guest… when the dozen guest rooms were full. An epic mistake had just been compounded. What else would blow up in Amy's face?

"I can see that our last guest left the room unkempt," Amy said, thinking of her underwear soaking in the sink with the spa's specially formulated shampoo. Her closet overflowed with her clothing and boots and sandals and hats… and, oh my god, the backpack stuffed with bundled Benjamins! "If you'd join me for tea or limoncello in the living room, I'll get housekeeping right on it. Do you require a valet for your luggage?"

"Uhm, Mr. Guido arrived by limousine," Ronnie

said. "I believe that, if he gives the signal, his driver can deliver the bags. Am I right, Mr. Guido?"

"You guessed it, girlie. My man's also trained in judo, if you get my drift? You got any place to garage my town car? I gotta keep this visit under wraps. Don't need da press, capeesh?"

Amy stared at Guido as if he had a smoking cigar in one hand and the ash at the end was about to fall. This man spoke in riddles around her blonde hair. She could barely keep up, still back on the page she'd imagined in which she and Prince Charming were in bed.

"The Inn has a three-car garage, Sir." Amy shot a furtive glance at Ronnie. "My assistant will walk your man around to the half-hidden garage, Mr. Guido. I think you'll be pleased."

Ronnie peeled off to attend to that task. Amy felt jealous for her opportunity to escape.

"Now, may we restart, Mr. Guido. My name is Amy, and I am the proprietor of the Lady Bug Inn. Please join me for tea in the living room while we prepare your room for your stay. Will your driver require a room? Do you have any special requirements or dietary needs?"

"First off, I need the limoncello, Missy. We'll figure out the rest of the stuff later, 'cause we gotta hurry. I'm in pain and you don't want a Guido off his meds."

I'm sure we don't. Now, I can occupy the cabana built for Andy, because he's scarce. But, what the heck to do with my clothing and accoutrements, the backpack of cash?

And where will the chauffeur bunk? Christ on a bicycle. Being an innkeeper gets more complicated all the time.

Within fifteen minutes Guido calmed into a pain-free zone and no longer presented the symptoms of an edgy prize fighter. Luggage amassed. The driver stood at attention by the door from the underground garage. Ronnie slid her arm around the man, and Amy winked. She knew Ronnie had settled the problem of where to bunk the chauffeur.

"Bartley, what's the shape of the Porsche? Did you check the odometer?"

Amy's conscience and subconscious did a tango in her throat. Something untoward wiggled and waggled her innards. She felt faint. Was this the one-and-only, down-due-to-debt Chicago mobster, who fire-saled his house to, to, to her via Elvin Goodrich, her realtor? Had he come to reclaim his summer house? Was she about to go down before she'd begun? What if, what if, what if…

"I seen dat look on your face, Ms. Proprietor." Guido sounded hoarse, like his throat had been lasered along with his belly fat. "You're wondering if I came to repossess the Porsche."

Amy shook her head, slowly, as if she were underwater. She needed to plausibly deny her thoughts, lest Guido's driver drop her with a judo kick. Amy looked around, didn't spot the liveried-man, and let out a long sigh of relief. "No," she mouthed the word along with a fervent head shake.

Her nay-nay failed. "Don't you go denying me,

Ms. Amy, I'm-too-tall-for-you-fool. I'm a mind reader. That's how I stay ahead in my business, so nod "yes."

Amy complied. What else could she do? Guido had her under house arrest.

"Now, let's get to the real reasons the Lady Bug Inn was chosen for my, uhm, recovery: 1. You gots the privacy factor covered; 2. You're beholden to a parole officer that I just happen to know, though you can't ask me how; 3. Your place, with which I am highly familiar, is a mere two hours from Traverse City, where my organization just happens to have a high-dollar debtor." Guido paused, as if he were allowing Amy something to say, which, of course, Amy knew she couldn't, she shouldn't, she wouldn't.

"We knew you might allow my driver to borrow the Porsche to make a quick visit to Traverse to deliver a personal note. My debtor is trying to siphon profits from his business there to open a new bar here. It ain't gonna fly. Dat's why I came to dis town."

This man is not only presumptive. He's also a dangerous crook… can I trust him?

Guido's eyebrow twitched. Amy knew he was enjoying every twist of his verbal knife, but she willed her body to be still—and her mouth to not quip. She knew Guido heard her "Yes, Sir" whether she uttered it or not. He assumed.

"Ever heard of TRAVIS' TRAVEL IN, Missy?"

Amy began to tremble. Could it be that the same Travis to whom Andy was indebted—was indebted to this bigger kettle of fish?

Amy felt she'd been handed a key. But she didn't

know which of three doors it fit. This wasn't a game show.

Amy's phone buzzed with a text. She bravely chanced a glance at the screen.

GOT YOUR BACKPACK OF CASH. WILL EXPLAIN LATER. CAN YOU COME GET ME AT TRAVIS' TRAVEL IN?

Coolly, deliberately, Amy jammed the phone back into her yoga pant waistband slit and perked a smile at Guido. "I'll happily loan your man my Porsche, if he's willing to return with a passenger."

Guido grumped. "Describe passenger," he blurted.

Amy showed her cell phone picture of Andy to Guido and his man, a double mission to be accomplished within hours. Win-win, bad-da-bing.

Chapter Forty-Seven

BACKPACK AND REVENGE

FIVE HOURS LATER—BADA-BING, bada-boom—Andy lunged into the house, backpack strapped backwards so that it hugged to his chest. Since the pack was pink, he looked like a Dolly Parton imitation, though his big sister bit her tongue on that remark. Amy knew he wouldn't be thrilled by the comparison. Any mention of Dolly might be taken as a slur on some guest's boob jobs, if one of them overheard.

Andy's arms were drained of blood, as if he'd held the backpack within an inch of his life. He scrambled faster than Amy'd ever seen him move and thrust the fat pink pack at her before he plummeted to the mahogany floor.

His chest heaved for several minutes. Amy wondered if she should offer him water, but she was afraid that, if she opened her mouth, her words would be pissy. His sweat drenched the wood floors.

"Christ on a bicycle, Andy!" came out in a blurt when Amy found her voice. "What the hell happened to you?" A glance at her Apple watch told her that she'd held her tongue for six seconds.

Andy lurched onto his forearms, but his legs seemed unable to move. "Yes, yes, I need water." Then he sat upright and smiled. "Don't pay the ransom—"

"I didn't!" Amy snapped. "I also happen to know that you didn't walk or run from Traverse City because I arranged a ride." Amy thrust the backpack behind her, so that her body was a shield if Andy got *tweaky* again. "Cut the cute act for sympathy, so you can explain why you handed me my heavy backpack." When Amy set the pack on the floor, a suspicion filled her head. "You didn't lighten it by several stacks of cash, did you?"

"Remember that I'm your brother and you are supposed to love me—" bleated Andy.

"And so. That entitles you to exactly what?" Amy couldn't refrain from a sneer.

"You've had ten strikes, you little monster, and I don't want you back. You are my boomerang burden and not exactly the brother I want."

"But I'm the brother you've got," tweedled-deedled Andy.

Before Amy was compelled to reply, Ronnie interjected, "Are you done with the driver, my date for the night?"

Amy startled. She'd been so frustrated with Andy's

presence, improbably adorned with a backpack filled with money, she'd failed to hear Ronnie slide into the room.

"If you handled the housekeeping so that Guido and all of our guests are comfortable, you can do whatever, Sis." When Ronnie took a step back at that inclusive, yet commanding remark, Amy hugged her to whisper in her ear, "You can wrangle all the mayhem you want from that man, because I've got my hands full with a lump of instability and mayhem here."

Ronnie smiled when Amy released her.

Amy turned before she could change her mind and squinted down at Andy, whose height was slighter than hers. She fisted her hands behind her back so she wouldn't punch him or shake a finger in his face. "You're lucky my brain has a shit-ton of compartmentalization, baby brother. But your duplicitous act will not be forgiven easily. Whatever the hell it was!"

"You wants I should break his legs," Guido said. "He should be punished for carrying a pink backpack. It's not manly." He winked at Amy. "I got a passle of guys who specialize in hits of any kind. Been thinking about laying a hit on a dude already, so I could give you a two-fer rather than the big rent on my suite."

"Thank you. No, sir. Not at this time. I don't know what you charge to, uhm, 'hit' a guy, but right now I'm thinking he's not worth it."

Amy avoided direct eye contact with Guido. The fact was that she was feeling alarmed. She allowed the mobster to sneak up on her—when she had a shit-ton of money, hastily shoved into the pink backpack that she'd thrust behind her. How easy it would have been for him to purloin the pack out from under her shoulder blades!

Yikes, and Christ on a bicycle! She should be thanking her ne-er-do-well brother instead of verbally spanking him. Andy had stolen her cash before Guido could! The backpack had not been in the bottom of the closet when Guido co-opted her suite.

*Whew! Saved from one f*cker by another one.*

However, Andy as hero didn't sit. Amy yanked him up, pulled him out of the house, and marched him to the cabana. With a backpack and a brother tethered to each of her arms, Amy's parade must have looked odd to her spa guests. Though Ronnie whistled shrilly before she left with the driver, only Amy paid heed. All potentially roving guest-eyes were glued to their books.

Amy pushed Andy into the cabana with all the force she felt like, which was a lot.

The skin on his shins scraped noisily, and Andy howled like a lackluster punk. "I'm going to get blood stains on my cargo shorts."

With that remark, Amy lost it. She took off one of Andy's flip flops and flogged him, ten quick lashes on his skinny, unplump butt.

"What was that for? I returned your backpack stash. You should be applauding me, not punishing me," Andy whined.

Amy's cellphone buzzed. After a quick look at the caller ID, she pointed to the broad couch in the cabana and mouthed, "Stay!"

Andy did.

Amy answered the phone.

"Your brother owes me thirty big ones," Travis said with a bold note of triumph in his voice.

Amy clenched her jaw. The disrespect in Travis' voice was the narrative of her life, the outline inside of which Amy had lived. Emphasis on *had.* This man had done her wrong, a great, great wrong. Amy was not going to shirk herself this time.

"I'm angry, Travis. Why didn't you keep him when I said I wouldn't pay the ransom."

"You've got no leverage, Amy. I hold the cards. Your brother's a great mark, but a bad poker player. He's a tool unworthy of both of us, but he's your kin, not mine."

"There's no room for him at the Lady Bug Inn."

"That's quite a place you've got there, Amy."

"You saw it? When?" Seeing Travis—only once, thank God—at the Lions Club had creeped her out, but the thought of him on her property made her want to thrust a dagger in his neck.

Travis may have sensed it, over the airways, because he hung up. Amy returned her full fury to her brother.

"Andy, I'll bet if you peed in a cup right now, you'd be brought up on drug charges. The only question could be which one? Alcohol, coke, or weed? Horse or Oxy or something else?"

"I'm high on the love of my sister, she of the backpack with thousands stashed within."

"Well, I may just have to empty it out, give the

pack to you for your clothing and sundries, because you can't stay here."

"What?"

"The Lady Bug Inn is at full occupancy. Overfull. In fact. This is my room now."

Before Andy could respond, a gruff voice spoke behind the canvas cover of the cabana, "Is somebody bothering you, sweet Angel Amy of the Cabana? Remember my crew specializes in whacks. Sounds like the score in there ain't going your way."

Amy signaled 'sh-h-h' to Andy.

"Thanks, Mr. Guido. I appreciate the offer, but you are my guest. You need to rest and recover from your wounds. Has my staff checked your bandages lately, given you cold compresses, and a beverage? Offered you turndown service? You'll find that the sheets are Thai silk."

Amy hoped she wasn't too loud as she projected her voice through the sun-resistant cloth. She knew her words and volume walked a fine line between shouty and desperate, timid and adamant. She had to be tough, but at your service sweet to thwart Guido's repeated murderous offers.

"Youse know where to find me if you need me. I want you to keep your pretty nose clean, Doll, so's I can get my proper rest."

"Good idea, Mr. Guido. I'm going to take a nap now. You should, too."

Amy stuffed her fist against Andy's mouth until she heard Guido shuffle off. It was clear the swarthy man was unused to spa flip-flops and/or being quiet when stealth would be prized.

Somehow, Andy got his mouth skewed past her fist. "He's got a good plan. You ought to take him up on it. Travis is a serious lout."

"Do you even know what a lout is, Andy?"

Andy shrank back into the abundant pillows on the chaise, so that a small pillow now seemed self-stuffed in his mouth.

"I'll take that for a 'no'," Amy hissed. "In fact, I would have chosen that word to describe you. So, button that lip while I think."

Chapter Forty-Eight

REVENGE AS A THREE COURSE FEAST

IT DIDN'T TAKE long for Amy to cotton to a semi-revised version of Guido's offer. It took twenty-four hours. Andy's negative stamp continued to loom over the calm of the Lady Bug Inn. The cabana was not enough space for the siblings to share, especially when Andy was twitchy—and tiresome.

"Guido, want to go for a ride in a red, hot Porsche?"

"The temperature is red hot today. Think we can outrun it, Ms. Angel Amy?"

"It's worth a try, rather than sitting around here, like roasting pigs on a spit."

Guido's laugh was as coarse as the gravel embedded in Amy's long lane. His laughter was enthused and hardy and dared Amy to join in the unseen joke. She laughed and laughed, in spite of herself and almost incited an asthma attack.

When Guido smacked her on the back, the action gave her a jolt. Dude packed a wallop, but Amy had to admit she was all clear. She hadn't felt this certain in days.

Amy grabbed the keys and crooked her finger, something she'd never done to a man before. It gave her a small thrill to be the leader of this pack.

"Wait! Ain't you forgetting something, Ms. Amy the Proprietor? Shouldn't we sandbag your nutty rascal of a brother, maybe stuff him in the trunk of my limo or chain him to a pool chair?"

"Now you see my problem, Guido. No harm can come to him, because I'm kind of his legal guardian, but no good comes from him, either." Amy and Guido shook their heads in unison, a chorus of doom.

"Wait!" perked Amy.

Guido looked as proud as punch, as if he had injected a solution into the frey.

Amy whipped out her phone and texted Dad Hernandez: YOU STILL BABY-SITTING MY HOME? GOT EYES ON THE PREMISES?

Amy tapped her toes nervously. Guido chomped at the bit. His horses were as ready to go as the Porsche in the garage below.

Hernandez' text arrived a few minutes later: OF COURSE. NOTHING ESCAPES YOUR DAD.

PLEASE LOCK YOUR COORDINATES ON MY BROTHER, ANDY.

IS HE STILL CROWDING YOUR HOUSE?

YES. PLEASE WATCH HIM FOR A COUPLE OF HOURS.

YOUR WISH IS MY COMMAND, MY FAVORITE PAROLEE. BUT WHO'S THE NEW DUDE AND WHERE ARE YOU GOING?

OUT, DAD. I KNOW YOU'LL HAVE ME UNDER SURVEILLANCE, TOO, SO THERE'S NO NEED TO WORRY. THANKS, BTW.

Amy drove like a bat. Guido hung on for dear life, wearing racing gloves and a delicious grin. It was obvious he had a need for speed… but there was no way Amy was going to let him drive *her* car. She didn't even allow him to question their destination and, to Guido's credit, he didn't ask.

Within thirty minutes, she'd parked at the public lakeside park, the first place she and Ronnie visited when they moved to South Haven.

"Don't you want to cruise by my debtor's bar?" Guido said.

"Not until I give you my three-course plan." Amy said. "I don't want to be influenced any more than I have been." She didn't want to explain more, so she didn't. She led Guido silently to a picnic table with a small children's playground nearby.

The fact that he followed her told Amy much and, yet, nothing. Why was a mob boss being so obedient? What was his skin in the game?

Is he eager to consummate revenge on my behalf? How did I gain his allegiance? And what will he expect in return?

Amy seated herself at the picnic table and invited Guido to join her. He limbered his legs through the notch, which was no easy feat. Perhaps she hadn't chosen wisely for the place of their meeting, but the symbology of her three-course feast of revenge was unmistakable to her. Besides, if Guido was seated, he'd listen more closely, and she wouldn't feel threatened by his incredible hulk.

Guido sank heavily to his side of the table, the seat board creaking like a boat that had spent too many days in drydock. He clasped his hands in an imitation of prayer and set them on the table top. "So why you bring me here, away from my comfortable room? What if my stitches pop after I hear your news or requests?"

She wanted to quip, "Well, you could go jump in the lake," but realizing the poor taste of that, as well as Guido's tendency to take things literally, she kept her mouth shut.

Besides, Lake Michigan is fresh water, not salt water, her college graduate self chided her, *there are no curative powers inherent in that murky water.*

Rather than speak, Amy pulled a folded piece of paper from the pocket of her jeans and spent several moments flattening its curled corners and creased-into-quarters surface. She was gathering more nerve and soothing her spirit with each swipe.

Then she wordlessly pushed the paper to Guido, making sure he had it firmly in hand before she let go. No winds would whip her plan from his hopefully complicit hands. She righted the paper with its bullet-pointed list so that Guido could read.

He shielded his eyes from the sun, now in the western

sky, mouthing the words as he silently read. Other than his lips, no facial muscles moved to convey an attitude about what he read. To Amy it seemed like he read for hours and days and centuries. Her stomach had twist-tied itself, then untwirled and twisted again. It wasn't the best way to digest food.

Guido looked from the paper into Amy's eyes. One palm still shaded his eyes, with the other held the list flat to the table, as if to disallow anyone from cribbing Amy's notes. "First, I got an important question, Ms. Blue-eyed Fair Beauty. Why you want to cut the nuts off this man?"

Amy put up a single finger salute to answer the question. "Because the f*cker sent me to prison for crimes we committed. I paid the freight and he got off scot-free."

"You seem pretty crafty, fair miss. How'd a dude pull wool over your eyes?"

Amy felt as if Guido was boring a hole through her soul as he continued to stare. He seemed never to blink, despite the flies flitting about their heads. She knew this aspect was her deepest shame, that she'd allowed herself to trust Travis—hell, she'd been in love, but he had only been in lust. He'd allowed her to be incarcerated. For ten years.

He'd not attended her trial. Amy had to rely on a public defender. Travis ignored the subpoena for his testimony. He'd not visited her once in prison. Nor called her or sent a missive of love. She had not been valuable to him—except as a fall guy for *their* felony.

Amy didn't say a word but found that she didn't have to. Guido understood and he reached over to hold her hand. Then he folded the list into his shirt pocket.

"Here's da plan, Ms. Amy, the Lady Bug."

Amy allowed herself to hope.

"First, we gonna ruin da dude's bar reputation. It's his golden goose and de goose will be cooked by Thanksgiving, providing you a tasty get-even feast. When the crowds no longer clamor, his profits will plummet and you're gonna buy da bar at a fire-sale price."

Amy perked up. "After I buy the bar, I could give Andy a job as the bartender."

"Not such a hot plan from what I've seen of that dumb-ass," Guido said. His head shook violently "no", an action he punctuated with a finger stab on the table top. "Listen and don't butt in, Missy. I'm a master at revenge."

Amy sat on her hands to protect them—and as a reminder to not open her mouth. She took a deep breath, inhaling trust, vowing to never let it go.

"Trust me, Doll, Travis will trade Andy's gambling debt for something good, like his right arm to keep the South Haven bar and its books. You want da dude to make a success of *his* bar, so you can make great profits. He will be your indentured servant."

Amy began to giggle, but suppressed big guffaws because Guido was still staring at her, though unseeing just now because he was deep in thought. Amy fought off nerves to remain calm and in tune. Something great, more and more, was bubbling into Guido's head. Images rolled through her mind, like Travis, dressed in an orange jumpsuit and shrouded in chains.

"Now, if you wants, we can build out TRAVEL IN TWO, the bar Travis and his investor were going to build in South Haven and install Andy as the bartender there. That way we can keep him close, directly under our surveillance." Guido winked broadly.

"I'm not certain I understand, Guido. Are you telling me that you are Travis' construction loan holder?"

"I was." Guido beamed. "But if a pretty lady could come up with a huge chunk of change, she could be part-owner of TRAVIS' TRAVEL IN TWO… you dig?"

Amy lay her head in her hands atop the table. If she hadn't, it might have spun off like a top and/or sailed like a Frisbee into the lake.

"How do you know I might be able to come up with the money?" she squeaked when she lifted her head. She dared not look Guido in the eye, but she had to come up for air. She felt as if she might suffocate from the possibilities of what he knew.

"Guido the Godfather knows everything, sweetheart. The local bank is owned by yours truly, and the President called me not long ago. Something about you bringing in shoeboxes of cash—that his entire staff had to help you carry into his vault—to the tune of four million bucks to pay off the Lady Bug Inn. Now, I ain't gonna question you about the source of that cash, Emelda Marcos, but I am going to ask you where you stashed a hundred pairs of shoes."

Guido threw back his head and laughed, loud and long.

CHAPTER FORTY-NINE

THREE-COURSE RELENT?

AMY LOWERED HER head to her hands, embarrassed. She knew she was sunk. Maybe she'd take a nap, right here and now. Maybe she'd pray for the skies to open up and take her away. Whatever. She wondered what Guido's next move might be? Christ on a bicycle, she wanted Travis broken. Not his death. Neither did she wish to die for her unwitting wrong-doing.

She didn't wonder long because Guido ended his roaring laughter. "Youse did know it's illegal for a bank to deposit any more than $10,000.00 cash from anyone at one time, didn't youse, since you worked a small-town bank similar to this one in South Haven."

Amy kept her head down, whispering a muffled, "Yes."

"I didn't hear you, Doll, and I want to be certain. Did you say 'yes'?"

Amy lifted her head, aiming her chin at Guido's nose. "Yes! So, what's the ante for me, Guido? My soul?"

"Ante? We are not playing poker here, Doll. This is big game hunting we're doing. I'm offering you an opportunity to save a guy's life, yet to own him forever. To never let him out of your sight yet plunder and pluck his heart from his chest. I'm offering you revenge on a platter with no culpability in Travis' takedown."

"And how will Travis know that it's me? Because as important as the fact that I own his ass, the more relevant fact is that he knows it's me. How's he gonna know, Guido? What do you propose?"

"Oh, now you want that Travis should propose and marry you?"

"Not exactly," Amy managed after almost swallowing her tonsils. "Though I do recall President Lincoln's tactic of holding his enemies close, even appointing them to his Cabinet while he governed this country through the Great Civil War. TRAVIS' TRAVEL IN TWO is near my Lady Bug Inn, so I can stalk him. I mean I can observe the course of bad actions that will befall him." Wheels began to spin in her head and her heart opened a tweak.

"I see you smiling, Doll. You still got de hots for dat bad-ass...."

Amy flushed so extensively, she felt the heat in her toes. Her fingertips tingled, too.

"Yeah, I thought so." Guido said. "It's important to you dat the bad boy knows you own his ass."

"Yes!" jumped from Amy's lips. Her adamance shooed away her flush. "Please, let me know that plan!" Involuntarily, she found herself rubbing her hands together.

"You ain't never gonna know da plan, Ms. Amy. You'll just have a ringside seat." Guido smiled, beguilingly for a mob boss whose teeth could cut a man's flesh. "As soon as we can wrestle Bartley away from your cohort, we can send him to deliver a message. On a silver platter."

Amy began to smell a rat, but she remained silent. She was in the presence of a Godfather with an army of allegiant soldiers. She felt, however, she'd burst if she didn't ask one small question, so she asked, "What's in this for you, Mr. Guido?"

Guido dropped his serious, dealing-making face. He leaned back his head and laughed as heartily as the best department store Santa ever to allow chubby children to sit in his lap. He laughed as if he hadn't laughed in days. Which he'd avoided, to protect his post-surgery incision after his love-handle fat was surgically sucked.

Yet he popped the final two stitches, one on each side. It was certain the laughter was the best medicine, however, because Guido smiled wider than he had in days.

"My lady of the Lady Bug Inn, I'm so glad you asked. I need to get-away from my girlfriends, mistresses, and/or wives on occasion…"

"You can't expect me to allow trysts on my premises," sputtered Amy. "I hadn't even planned on allowing male guests."

"Hold on, Ms. Amy. Let me finish my idea, please."

Amy shifted her position, as if to untwist her panties.

"While it's true that I swap out ladies often—I ain't a bad man. It comes with the power, you know." Guido winked. "When I settle in with one, I often give in to little requests and demands. Some of them involve plastic surgery. Say, a chin tuck, a brow lift, tummy tuck, or earlobe repair. I want to be able to repose as I heal… I want to reserve my suite permanently at the Lady Bug Inn."

Suddenly Amy felt dizzy. A breeze rose off the lake, transforming into a spirited gust that seemed capable of inciting an asthma attack. Guido's well thought out give-and- take overwhelmed her, in part because she preferred giving orders and being in control. It was a lifetime habit that had held her together through poorer than poor times, and she'd expected her talent for leadership to expand now that she was richer than rich.

"Guido, I'm embarrassed to admit that I have health issues and we must return to the Inn. I've enjoyed our chat and relish your offer. You've made an intricate, multi-layered problem easy for me, and I am in your debt for the thoughts alone. But I've got to sleep on the offer, roll it around in my head, and look at it from all sides. May I have a day or two before I reply?

"Sure, Doll. You ain't used to having peers. You

ain't used to having a godfather who will intercede on your behalf. I don't want to take down your pride. I just want to take down Travis. I have my reasons, and you've got yours. I promise you it'll be a win-win for you and me and a lose-lose for him. Ain't nothing better than the perfect revenge, which is, of course, living well. Let's go home, Lady Bug."

The Porsche roared on the road back to the Lady Bug Inn. Inside the music roared even louder—show tunes for 'The Fantastix' and "Man of La Mancho" as well as the anthems of Queen. "Another One Bites the Dust" blasted when Amy put the convertible top down to glide down Pinnacle Lane.

After pulling into the garage, Amy bounded from the car, ran up the stairs, and raided the frig. She wanted no further interaction with Guido and his full platter of revenge.

Passive revenge, neatly-packaged revenge, not a deed done by her own hand revenge.

She knew she should be elated. His plan was intricate and it would work, but. There was no part for her. She would not experience *the thrill of the kill.*

Amy felt inclined to say, "No dice."

She scarfed the sandwich and sucked the bottle of water dry. She made a quick potty stop, splashing water in her face. Then she ran back to her car. It would be more private for her consults with Hernandez and WoolworthWilma. It would also be more comfortable than a cabana chaise.

'Yes' to Guido would be a difficult decision. But could she backtrack to 'No'? It was clear he intended to take down Travis, who'd gotten too big for his britches. She ought to go along for the ride and get her piece of revenge, too

Amy leapt into the car and slammed the door. She texted Hernandez: IS THIS A GOOD TIME FOR A CHAT VIA PHONE?

YES.

Hernandez answered on the first ring. Amy almost cried. She held back tears by pinching the flesh between her thumb and her forefinger, a control-and-torture measure that a prison guard had taught her in the most direct way. It was a good ploy because it held her close—and because it left no marks.

"I've been given an offer that I can't refuse, Dad."

"Sounds worrisome. Tell me more, Amy. I need all the deets I can get if you want me to dispense advice."

Amy paused. How much could she, should she, inform a parole officer… but Guido had once mentioned that he knew Hernandez…right? She wrinkled her brow…and began. "I believe we share an acquaintance. Mr. Guido Parducci."

"Yes, and," Hernandez hedged.

"He inserted himself into my spa—"

"Inserted? Do you mean the mob boss had plastic surgery? What did he get, a new nose?"

Amy laughed. "Better than that, Dad. He had his love handles removed. Seems he has a new lady friend, and she didn't like what the former wife's cooking had done."

Hernandez chortled. "Sets quite an image before

my eyes, Amy. It does, but why did he check into your plastic surgery recovery spa?"

"His plastic surgeon recommended him. Plus, he once owned the house."

"You've got to be kidding!" Hernandez said. "Your tale is getting more complex, and I'm running out of free time. Can you spit out the final deets, no weasel words or qualifiers?"

"Guido outlined a multi-level plan to take down Travis."

"Again, you've got to be kidding. Do you want to be chummy with a mob boss?"

Hernandez' furious, emphatic tone made Amy blush. "That's a good question, Dad."

"You don't have a good answer, do you, Amy?"

"Well, I do know I want revenge awful bad, badly awful, or something to drive a stake into Travis' heart." Amy curled her hand into a fist and smacked the dashboard.

"Remember what I told you about ruining another person's life, sweetheart."

"I remember, but I won't be doing the deed. I merely get to enjoy what's going to go down. Guido's going to do the hit."

"You don't mean literally, do you?"

"No, figuratively."

"Well, I've got no more advice, and I don't want to know more details. You're driving the bus on this one, Amy. I admit you are my favorite parolee, but I may not be able to bail you out if things go south on this one."

"Thanks for your trust, Dad. I promise I won't let you down."

"Don't promise me that, darling. Promise yourself. I've already forgotten about the call, you hear me?"

Hernandez hung up. Amy just stared at the phone for a full minute, willing him to call back, though she knew he wouldn't. Hernandez was a man who saved his bullets.

Was Guido?

Next, Amy FaceTimed Wilma, where she knew she'd receive a softer, less didactic reception.

Basically, Wilma suggested Guido was a gift from a righteous God and karma. He'd given her a means to achieve the revenge that karma insisted upon for Travis and a first class seat. She should accept his gift and continue to enjoy her lifelong crave: a luxury without limits life.

"Just be sure to get rid of that bad brother, Andy!" was how Wilma ended their call.

Chapter Fifty

REBELUTION

'YES' TO GUIDO was a difficult decision, but Amy couldn't refuse his offer. Nothing scared her more than Guido the Terrible saying, "Something gotta be done" and then not allowing him to get the results he craved. But she felt too intimidated to pose questions. She'd bet on revenge a la Guido. Now she had to let it ride, hope that she hadn't injured her soul with this more-than-ecosystem-altering decision. Could she live without revenge to fuel her plans?

While it bothered her that she was merely a tacit partner in the irreparable rip in Travis' life, she took solace in her new preoccupation: shopping relentlessly online. If she'd made time to think about it, Amy would be required to admit her depression—the needles and pins on which she sat.

She spoke daily to her image in the mirror. "Revenge is mine!" The Cruella DeVille apparition frightened her spirit. She wondered what she'd become. Had her quest for revenge driven her mad?

She'd thought she might go insane while imprisoned. Before that, the trial. She knew she'd ground her teeth during that period because the prison dentist told her so. Perhaps it was time to get her costly dental work done.

But not in South Haven. She wanted to use a different dentist than the inevitable Lions Club member. She'd had it with the busy non-business of that town and the members' constant ploys to use her funds. In truth, the president's demand for dues had offended her. She preferred the days of being the unofficial mascot. Then she'd felt integral. Now, she felt like yesterday's news.

So Amy used the plastic surgery data base and called around, finding a regular dentist for the preliminary work, then an endodontist for the recommended root canals and, finally, a cosmetic dentist to provide a full set of veneers. Cha-ching, cha-ching, cha-ching, but it was all good. Most often, Amy paid cash and received a sizable discount.

Amy liked her face in the mirror better after that. She no longer sneered as she recited her mantra. She smiled and admired her Hollywood teeth.

Smiling was better than seething, because Guido provided no progress reports on his revenge process. His post-surgery wounds healed and he departed, leaving his eau de Guido scent in the owner's suite, which Amy now inhabited. But no hints of his actions.

Since he'd booked online, she had no forwarding address or phone number for him. She wanted to call him ten times a day while she waited for the score. It was unsettling to trust a mobster, but she had no recourse. Though she was rich and could have hired a tail, she declined. Guido was rich, too. Rich in resources to take *her* down. Money translated easily into power, but macho and muscle were equally powerful in his world. *Guido had guys for everything.*

Amy once despised the rich and powerful. It was so much easier to hate them than to hate her poor circumstances. She hated them, she envied them, she hated herself for not being one of them for two-and-a-half dozen years.

It was a tough line to cross that she was one of them, one of the richest in Michigan, now that the auto business had been gutted. No more Chryslers or Pontiacs or Cadillac dynasties. Not even Ford made people rich with its stability.

Amy had hoped to conquer happiness, to conquer it for all time, with her casual outlays of cash. Instead, she felt mighty unhappy. What good was *plenty o' money* without a companion with whom to share it. She began to daydream about Travis. Compassion had laid its hooks in her heart.

When Travis arrived on her doorstep six months later, the ferocity and scope of Guido's karate chop to his character showed. His hair was unkempt and there was no glint in the eye he put to the door's keyhole.

He looked abject, forlorn, hat metaphorically in hand. His knock on the door sounded tentative and weak.

Amy counted to ten before she opened the door. Then, she counted to ten again, cycling through emotions like a hurricane. She wanted to kill him, but as she looked through the peephole for a second time, she could see he already looked dead.

Still, when she opened the door, she screamed as close to his stubbled face as she could get, "Two thousand days! Let me hear you say it. Two thousand days!" She drew back to see her spittle on his face and she bared her new beautiful teeth.

Travis spoke, but his hat or hands or something muffled the words. Amy surmised he wasn't sorry enough yet. He hadn't eaten enough crow. "Two thousand days!" she yelled, grabbing the hat and tossing it into her yard. She had at least that reality, the confession of a worn Stetson thrown to the wind.

"You're high-strung!" Travis shouted.

Perturbed at the loss of his hat? Amy would show him full throttle *perturbed.* Her guts roiled, and she felt rowdy. Amy slammed the door with all the force her long arms could muster.

Thirty seconds passed. Then Travis rapped on the door, more purposeful this time. Amy took a deep breath and opened the door, just a wedge. "I am not high strung, you ape. Take that back!"

Wordlessly, Travis stuck a boot between the door and the jamb. Amy thrust her fist into the space, longing to jam it up his nose. Travis grabbed Amy's fist and forced it open, so that he could grasp her hand and kiss it.

Shock and awe came next when Travis pulled her outside of the house and kissed her lips. Now Amy felt randy and invited him in. A chorus of plastic surgery recoverees, snacking in the kitchen, simultaneously intoned "awww," though Amy might have overheard a "yuck."

Amy flushed with embarrassment and the open capitulation her guests had witnessed. So, she did the only thing she could think of—she trotted him down the hall and into her suite. Behind her she thought she heard the chorus applaud, so she closed and locked the door.

Eager to be in control in her home, Amy led Travis to her bed, the only place she could seat him. It was still unmade, linens rumpled from her nighttime sleep. Her stomach grumbled unaccountably.

A weak-kneed Amy gave in to her bodily impulses. Travis followed her lead, though he looked like he was afraid to smile.

His body did his apologizing for him, or so Travis thought. There was no cigarette afterward, no champagne salute, only Amy's naked glare and finger stab against his hairy chest. Amy wanted 'sorry' to be said. Aloud, a hundred times.

Travis slithered out of bed and began to dress, fast and abject.

The force of Amy's glare turned him right round. She wasn't humbled by sex. She felt emboldened to her own purpose, to exact recompense for two thousand days and the trial that didn't go her way after that. She wanted Travis to bawl and bow down before her.

Plan B came to mind.

"I'm taking you to breakfast, though I wish you had better duds. The Lions Club won't be impressed by your garb. Is the work on TRAVIS TRAVEL INN TWO complete?"

"Not quite." Travis mumbled.

"I can't hear you, Travis. Lift your head and look into the face of the woman who *allowed* you into her bed."

Travis complied.

"Did you enjoy the sex?"

"You know I did, my long-lost love." Travis showed his full set of ultra-shiny teeth.

"Hold the craven compliments, Ape." Amy took a long moment to glare. Travis' smile wilted. She enjoyed watching him crumple from bravado to despair.

"You've reminded me of the reason why I am 'long-lost.' I served 2000 days of *your* prison sentence. You owe me more than sex and a tentative kiss on the hand."

By now, Amy's hands were on her hips as she'd stalked into Travis' personal space. She enjoyed the adrenaline jolt of his withered ego, so close, so close she could reach out and wring his neck. "Let's start your recompense with breakfast. I'll drive."

She began to walk away but tossed a final thought over her shoulder. "Take a shower and try to look better. Don't want your germs to mar the leather interior of my Porsche."

Travis' eyes went from widened to downcast, and he began to walk to the glamorous bathroom. Amy slipped in front of him to fist bump her image in the mirror. "Rebelution!" she shouted and strode down the hall, scooped up the keys, and skipped down the stairs to the underground garage. Her red pony was ready to ride Travis' ass out of town.

CHAPTER FIFTY-ONE

REVENGE IS COMPLETE

TRAVIS SCAMPERED INTO the Porsche, sheepish and contrite. "Your kitchen ladies told me where to find you but hissed as I headed for the stairs." He winced while he reported the facts, then shifted into his well-honed smarm. "Where to? Miss Ellie's?"

"Not exactly." Amy gunned the Porsche out of the garage for full effect of its power—and hers. *Great God, it feels good to be in control. It feels great to be in control. It feels even better that dude doesn't even know what's next.*

Amy controlled the Porsche's speed down the lane. Didn't want to scratch Guido's forcibly gifted Porsche. She looked in the rearview mirror and mouthed "thank you" to the mob boss and then looked at Travis. Dude didn't know the final act.

"I'm embarrassed to admit that I don't have cash on me. You'll have to pay."

"I know. No problem. I have plenty of cash."

"I know," Travis said. "What's the source of your bundles of cash?"

"Ask me no questions, and I'll tell you no lies." Amy turned to Travis and smirked. "You didn't happen to dig into the bundles, did you?"

"No way!" Travis looked shocked. "I don't take what's not mine."

"You took five years of my life away from me, you creep. It would've been ten if I hadn't earned early release." She couldn't halt the finger that shook at his face. "I'd call that taking on a large scale."

"Yes, but you're still young and lovely," Travis tried. "You have your entire life in front of you and you own a plastic surgery respite spa…"

"Don't start! Keep your mouth shut for the rest of the ride. You couldn't find the right compliment if one was whispered in your ear."

Thirty minutes later the Porsche screech to a halt. In front of Travis' bar.

"This isn't Miss Ellie's," Travis cried. "It's my bar."

"Get out of the car." Amy enjoyed being in command.

Soon they stood in front of TRAVIS TRAVEL INN TWO. Amy gestured for Travis to open the door, enjoying the shock in his eyes.

"I don't have the key." Travis sounded apologetic.

"That's all right. I do." Amy now enjoyed the light leaving Travis' face. "I own this bar."

"But…" Travis started to whine, reminding Amy of her dead-beat brother. "I knocked on your door, hoping to request a loan to save my bar."

"Allow me to repeat. I. Own. The. Bar. I saved it. For me." Amy allowed herself to gloat as she spat each word.

Amy ran to the Porsche to toss one final retort. "BTW, the rent is due tomorrow. In cash. See you!"

Her heart flip-flopped in her chest. *The thrill of the metaphoric chill.*

Amy drummed the steering wheel as she put her beast into gear. She honked 'good-by' to the sad sack on the curb, peeled away, and then floored the Porsche.

Travis looked best in the Porsche's rearview mirror, his jaw agape. Amy imagined that his shock echoed the look on her face when the cop had handcuffed her five years ago, arresting her in their grow barn. She'd looked over her shoulder for Travis, but he'd weaseled. Fast. She'd felt like kneecapping him, prior to being dragged out of the barn and shoved into the cop's car.

Amy applauded her finesse and then began her new mantra. *I love and approve of myself, Travis-free.*

While the mantra felt like a victory, it echoed hollow in her head.

Amy thought for a moment, then picked up her phone. She hit one of her saved numbers. "Got a few moments, Dad? I have something to share."

"I'm all ears, favorite parolee," Hernandez said.

"Revenge is sweet."

Acknowledgments

As you may or may not know, writing is a team sport. Here are people to embrace because they helped to bring this story to life, gritty and true, yet it all emerged from my imagination.

- A gaggle of Beta readers, with a special shout-out to Beta 1, my husband
- Jeff Lyons, Pam Sheppard, and Sherry Clitheroe who mid-wifed this book with valuable perspective and input
- Laura Taylor, my long-term editor/mentor/friend
- Writer cheerleaders extraordinaire, Ara Grigorian and Janis Thomas, for their Novel Intensive session that helped me find my revenge story
- Art Plotnik, the masterful Iowa Writer alum, who helped me understand the notion of VOICE, a writing element for which I have been perpetually praised

- Kassie Ritman, my Hoosier writing pal, and Barbara Vortman, who hails for Michigan
- Maddie Margarita and Barbara Howe, a pair of cheerleader shapers of every writer's story
- My folks... they gave me life and their essential gifts of empathy, talent, and wisdom, and wit

Book Club Questions

1. Have you ever felt like a loner in life, either for a short time or forever? How did you gain entry to the *cool group*? Or, did you remain a loner by choice?

2. Select one word to describe Amy. What did you like about her? What did you dislike? What kind of protagonist was she?

3. Amy is a Millennial. Did you like her? Did you relate or did you despise her thinking?

4. Select one word to describe Travis. What did you like about him? What did you dislike? What was his role in the story?

5. Select one word to describe Veronica. What did you like about her? What did you dislike? Was she a good side-kick character?

6. Select a word to describe Amy's parole officer, Juan Carlos Hernandez. Is he believable,

likeable? Was he merely a father figure or a potential romantic partner?

7. Did you adore Woolworth Wilma? Select one word to describe her. Was her past believable? Did she surprise you sometimes?

8. Did you like Amy's revenge? What would you have done if you were Amy?

9. What do you think happens next, after The Jailbird's Jackpot ends?

10. Do you want to re-read The Winner's Circle, to which this book is sort of a sequel? Compare/contrast the two books, which are part of the *Faith, Family, Frenzy!* book series.

11. What would you do if you suddenly won a half-billion-dollar lottery? First... next... and then...

12. I typically write humor and satire. Is The Jailbird's Jackpot a departure? Did you detect humor and satire? What archetype is the plot and into what genre does the book fit?

13. Do you have a favorite character among those who populate the book? Why?

About the Author

PJ Colando was born and raised in the Midwest, yet unabashedly aspired for adventure elsewhere, following her parents' model. She lives in southern California with her family, hobbies, and pets.

PJ writes humor and satire with a literary bent. She is the author of four previous novels and two short story anthologies.

FEEDBACK

Please take a few moments to pen an honest, positive review on book purchases sites, including those online, your local bookstore, and library. A review on GoodReads is prized. Tell your friends, especially if in book clubs because I'd love to hear what readers think of my story, good, bad, or undignified.

A review is the highest compliment a writer can receive. To know a reader has read and relished their endeavor is better-than-great!

Contact

Go to pjcolando.com to

- Learn more about her and her other books
- Locate a bookstore or Zoom book event
- Follow her Boomer blog
- Contact her directly

Made in the USA
Las Vegas, NV
26 October 2020

10351570R00217